Rip Cu

By

Amanda James

First published in 2018 by Bloodhound Books

www.bloodhoundbooks.com

Print ISBN 978-1-912604-42-5

Also By Amanda James

Another Mother

The Calico Cat

Praise For Amanda James

"This is a great read and I would highly recommend it to readers who like a book that turns from a contemporary read into an amazing dark psychological suspense filled read." **Yvonne Bastian – Me And My Books**

"The book was enjoyable, surprising and comprised of layers of storyline that were weaved together to form an enjoyable read." **Susan Corcoran – Booksaremycwtches**

"Another Mother is an intense family drama that will get into your head and under your skin." **Michelle Ryles – The Book Magnet**

"A gripping, slightly chilling, very entertaining read." **Nicki Murphy – Nicki's Book Blog**

"This story will hit you hard. It will mess with your head towards the end and have your heart racing to find out the outcome, very fast paced." **Gemma Myers – Between The Pages Book Club**

"This books has some fascinating characters and I loved the writing style – it is a very good psychological thriller." **Donna Maguire – Donnas Book Blog**

"Readers looking for a page turning, spring time binge read, should add Another Mother to their list of must reads." **Christen Moore – Murder And Moore**

"I never knew where this suspense filled book would take me and I found it to be quite a thrilling read." **Nicola Smith – Short Book And Scribes**

"Once the story develops into a suspense the action built up to the thrilling conclusion, which I for one didn't see coming." **Simon Leonard – Black Books Blog**

To the memory of my mum and dad, both of whom I lost last summer while I was writing this book. Hope you're having fun Barb and Norm, wherever you are.

Chapter One

Anya's hand trembles so much that the eyeliner becomes a charcoal mess under her lashes. She reaches for a box of tissues next to the dressing table mirror, but then lets her hand fall.

What is the point? The men that come to her room barely look at her face. Three men have been in her room today.

Three men have been inside her today.

Anya had tried to shut down her mind – switch off her senses while they shoved, panted, pawed – their stinking breath on her face, slobbering mouths on her skin. It hadn't worked. A silent scream filled her head; a spear of shame pierced her heart.

The fingers holding the eyeliner grip so hard that she thinks the plastic will snap. How has she allowed this to happen? She looks at her reflection again and hardly recognises the pale, thin face, haunted grey eyes and the desperation behind them. Marta always tells her she must look her best. Men pay more for pretty women. If she doesn't try to please them, Jozef will make sure she pays. Marta laughs when she tells her this. Gold teeth in a wide savage mouth assert her status.

'Jozef has big fists and you have a small face, remember that,' Marta said last night. She says this most nights, in fact any time Anya even hints at refusing to do her bidding.

As if she needs reminding.

She thinks about the way Marta's bright blue eyes narrow to ice chips; the way, intoxicated by power, her lips quiver around each word before sending them to Anya's ears. Little drops of poison — lethal to pride, murderers of hope.

Hope is a very dangerous thing to hold on to. People always say that where there is life, there is hope. Anya used to believe it, at least for the first few weeks. Cruelly used, held against her will. She used to think that somehow she would escape, get back home to the life she once knew. But now, more than six months on, Anya knows hope is a luxury she can't afford. She has learned this well. Jozef's fists, days without food, naked and chained in a freezing cellar are all excellent teachers. Anya shakes her head. Survival is better.

Survival is all she has.

In the mirror she watches a ghost of herself brush out her long blonde hair. Anya runs a few strands through her fingers and thinks it has lost its lustre. When she was little, her grandmother used to say that her hair looked like spun gold. Anya's thoughts leap on the memories of those days like starving dogs. There she is now on her grandparents' farm; she draws sustenance from the images of where she spent her school holidays. The days of hiding in the whispering cornfield with a good book. The days of endless blue skies and the flattest verdant landscapes, the days before—

'Anya, you have a gentleman caller in five minutes, be ready!' Marta's voice calls up the stairwell.

Inside her head, the screaming starts.

Chapter Two

I hurry along the rain-soaked street and, as I dodge the puddles in my ridiculously high-heeled shoes and pray that I don't twist my ankle, I wonder if I am doing the right thing.

They say never go back, don't they? The past is never exactly as you remember it, is it? Not when you actively seek it out, give it a poke, hold it up to the light. Under such honest scrutiny it's often flawed, slightly unsavoury, and never measures up to the sparkly warm comforting memories you keep folded in your heart.

I reach the café, but my feet stop four paces from the entrance. Through steamy windows I can see foggy outlines of people sitting at tables, and I hear muted laughter and the clatter of crockery; when the door opens, coffee arabica snakes through the damp air and into my nostrils. I want to go inside but my feet remain unmoving.

Social media is both a blessing and a curse. When I reconnected with Imogen Ransom on Facebook last week it felt like a blessing. Her friend request flooded my memory with laughter-filled summer days that we thought would never end. Nights sharing secrets, hopes, fears, stolen wine and cigarettes under canvas in her back garden. Immi and I had been inseparable. Next-door neighbours and best friends in our teens, until her family had moved to Liverpool, almost a hundred miles away. I stand at the threshold of our reacquaintance, and, at this moment, I wish I was a hundred miles away too.

Today I worry that accepting the friend request feels more like a curse. I worry that once I am through the door and into her life again, an awkward silence will open up like a yawning abyss across the café table. At the bottom of the abyss will be the snapping jaws of 'they say never go back', and I worry that we will have no commonality with which to build a bridge over them. If we do, it won't last. In seconds the foundations will crumble and we'll plunge into those jaws. There's no coming back then, is there?

I worry that, once held to the light, scrutinised and poked, our sunny past will turn overcast, begin to rain, and I'll have no umbrella.

The door opens again and a young, laughing couple step out onto the wet pavement. They look happy, rosy cheeked, refreshed. How bad can it be in there? I swallow my fears and force my feet another two paces forward but, as I step through the door, the biggest worry of all links arms with me. The biggest worry of all is how I will hide from Immi what I know about her father. Even if we discover our past is still bright and sunny and our future a blessing, if allowed to escape, her father's secrets will colour everything black, suck the joy from the day, suffocate us in filth and leave us gasping for air.

Inside I slip off my mac, give it a quick shake and a cascade of raindrops spatter the floor. The chatter and laughter un-mutes and suddenly everything seems too loud, bright and intrusive. The room is packed and smells of wet hair, coffee, the grease of sausage rolls and other people's sweat. A scan of the room – no Imogen. It's not too late to turn and leave, is it?

This was a bad idea. No good can come of it. Turning for the door, my heel sticks in a broken tile and I grab a chair to steady myself. Why the hell did I wear such stupid shoes? To impress Immi, of course. It was ever thus. My hand grasps the door handle and the grey afternoon rushes at me, cool and fresh against my heated cheeks.

'Bryony?'

My heart jumps. No. I didn't hear that. Outside and gone is where I need to be.

'Bryony! Hey, I'm here!'

So near and yet so far. I dredge a cheerful smile from my emergency reserves and turn round, close the door. There she is. Imogen. She's doing the big waving thing she always did as if she's guiding a plane in to land. As if I can't see her about fifteen feet away. Fifteen feet and almost the same in the years have passed between us, yet she looks mostly unchanged. The big navy eyes in a heart-shaped face and long blonde hair styled to frame it. Dark eyebrows, though. They're new.

My feet, more confident than my heart, hurry me over to a corner table at the back of the room. 'Immi! Great to see you!' I say and mean it. We hug. She steps back, takes me in with a sweeping glance.

Hands on hips, she affects a stern expression, though the twinkle of humour in her eyes gives her away. 'Considering you were just about to leave, I find that hard to believe.'

'No, don't be daft. I couldn't see you just now … thought I'd got the wrong place. I'm already late.' My smile is fixed. Only part of that sentence is true.

She nods and grins, but I think she knows it is. 'I'd just popped to the loo.' Imogen flaps a hand at the table. 'Let's sit down then.'

We sit and smile and say that it's so good to see each other at least three times each, compliment each other on how we look, and then a silence grows between us. It's awkward and deep. An abyss. We look across it at each other – stretchy grins on our faces – and I think about my fears again. Never go back. 'Shall we get coffee?' I manage.

'Not before we clear the air.' Immi folds her arms and sighs. 'I worried that things might be awkward after so many years, and they are right now. I reckon you're nervous too, so let's just bloody stop it and be ourselves. No need to impress each other.' She looks round the table at my skyscraper heels and raises a dark, perfectly shaped and waxed brow.

I open my mouth to protest but pull a 'you got me' face instead. Then we're laughing. Genuinely laughing. Not forced or polite in public kind of laughter – but the kind of snot-bubbling explosions we did when we were fourteen. I wipe my eyes, get my breath. 'They were at the back of the wardrobe and thought they might make me look sophisticated. Truth is they hurt like fuck and nearly crippled me. Got the heel stuck in the bloody floor tile.'

Immi's face creases up again. 'I've got a mental picture of you as a copper running after bad guys in them!'

I laugh and take a shoe off, tap the tip of the heel. 'I chuck 'em at the back of their heads. They go down like a sack of spuds.'

The abyss is filled. The next half hour flies by carried on the wings of childhood memories and teenage reminiscences. We are still the great friends we were and I can almost forget about her dad and what he stands for. Block him out. Almost. Then the inevitable happens.

'How's your folks?' Immi asks.

There's just Mum now, and though it's been two years, I can't cast the shadow of what happened to Dad over this sunny conversation. I say, 'Good, thanks, and yours?' Then I clench my jaw. There he is – Kenny Ransom – right between us on the table. Immi's mouth twists to the side and I realise she has tears standing. Fuck.

'Mum died of cancer a year ago. And Dad …'

I imagine she will say that he's devastated, heartbroken. I know he isn't though. His heart could never be broken, because he doesn't have one. What she does say drops my jaw.

'Dad is a bastard. A *real* evil bastard.' Her mouth turns down at the corners as if there's a bitter taste in her mouth. I think she's going to cry but she sticks out her chin, wipes her eyes on the back of her hand. 'The thing is, Bryony, I sent you that friend request for two reasons. Yes, I wanted to see you again, I've thought about you loads over the years. But the real reason is that you're a copper. I know you're after my shit of a father … and …' She swallows hard and looks directly into my eyes. 'And I want to help you get him. Send him down for the rest of his fucking life.'

Chapter Three

Anya has seen the woman before. Well, she thinks she has – the rain on the kitchen window makes everything hazy. She looks more closely. Yes. Dark short hair, a mac, striking features. She walked past twice this morning. That's not unusual, is it? The woman could work nearby, or live on the street. But until yesterday she hadn't seen her before, and now three times. The only pleasure she gets is looking out of the window now and then in-between gentlemen callers. It's her way of reassuring herself that the outside world really is still there, that she's not living in some parallel universe, some purgatory.

Anya realises why she finds the woman's passing by so unusual. The woman glances at the window each time. She glances at the door and the surroundings too. But Anya can tell that she's really scrutinising, but pretending not to – pretending just to glance as a passer-by would. But why? What is she looking for? Hope surfaces in her heart but Anya drowns it. Even if the woman wanted to help, Anya couldn't betray her family back home. Her grandparents, her parents and two younger sisters. They would all be under threat if she so much as hinted at being kept here against her will.

Though she would give anything to see Jozef, Marta and their masters pay for what they have done, the price would be far too high. Marta tells her this almost as often as she tells her that Jozef has big fists. 'Remember that the boss of us is a very powerful man. He has a long reach, Anya, my beauty. A click of his fingers would see the end of your family if you even think of escape.' Marta's lips stretch over gold tombstones, a lascivious light in her eyes. 'And your sister Katya is coming up sixteen, no?'

Marta stomps into the kitchen now and narrows her eyes. 'Gazing out of the window again? You have a caller in ten minutes. Get your hide upstairs and in the shower, and your make-up on. We have a reputation to keep here and you look like a sack of shit!'

Anya nods and scrapes her chair back from the table. As she does, she sees the woman again across the street. She's getting into a car driven by a pretty blonde woman with dark eyebrows. Hasn't she seen her before somewhere too? They drive past and both look at her. Not glance, really look. Anya sighs and hurries upstairs.

A few days have passed, though so much has happened it feels like a month since the first meeting with Immi in the café. I still have to pinch myself that, after so many near misses, soon we might actually beat Kenny Ransom at his own game. Three years he's been criss-crossing our path, but as soon as we get a hold around his neck he wriggles free and off into the undergrowth like a viper. Thanks to Immi we have already located the house where she says a number of Eastern European girls are working as sex slaves and we have a couple of officers surveilling. When I walked past yesterday I could hardly believe such an ordinary house in a respectable area contained so much misery behind its walls. I've seen houses like that in more rundown parts of town though – too many times.

Immi is coming round to mine in a few minutes for dinner, hopefully with a list of names and numbers that might be useful to us. Also the name of a willing witness who says he'll stand up in court and testify against Ransom. Once we've fleshed it all out she's agreed to come down to the station and make a statement. For a daughter to do that to a father, he must be every inch the filth I thought he was.

'Nice apartment!' Immi comes in laden with wine, flowers, chocolate and dessert. 'They must be paying you too much, that's all I can say.'

I laugh and take the flowers, tell her there was no need to bring gifts, wave to the sofa. 'Chance would be a fine thing. I have a mortgage the size of Yorkshire and other debts besides. I do like a nice space to relax though – need it when I get home from the wars.'

Imogen flops on the sofa. 'Not surprised. I couldn't do your job for a million a year.' She points outside to the balcony overlooking the waterfront. 'Mind you, I would love a view like that.'

'It helps.' I pour the wine and we talk about the decor, her day working as a receptionist at the local surgery, and all the time I wonder how to step down from this everyday chit-chat to discuss the betrayal of her father. Not an easy task.

'So you said you went to uni and came out with a criminology degree. Then what, you get this DI number?'

This makes me smile. It was hard enough achieving DI at twenty-eight – some of my colleagues teased me that I must have slept with the boss to get it so quick. 'Not exactly. I had a good few years working my way up the ranks and got the DI two years ago.' I hand her the wine and start chopping onions for the spag bol. My speciality dish … thinking about it, it's my only dish. I do tend to grab food on the run these days. Must try harder to make healthy food instead of eating out, or shoving a meal for one in the microwave.

'Bet your dad's impressed, eh?'

I can't avoid talking about Dad forever but I can't do it tonight. I can't see Immi's expectant little expression crumble, perhaps followed by tears. So I say, 'Oh yes, he was thrilled that I followed in his footsteps. I set out to impress him and that's what I did.'

'Well, I'm glad I didn't follow in my father's footsteps.' Immi's smile fades and she looks into her wine glass. 'That girl's face at the window. I'll never forget her eyes, Bryony. So full of longing and despair. She looked …' Immi gazes out over the river. Through the window the soft glow of the sunset plays across her face but a grimace darkens her features. 'She looked … broken, is the only way I can describe it.'

My hand draws a knife through a red pepper. 'Yes, broken and trapped.'

'And the woman that opened the door to me last week looked like some fairy-tale witch. The one from Hansel and Gretel.'

'Promise me you won't go there again doing your acting bit now we're involved. It's dangerous and if your dad gets wind of you—'

'Give me some credit. I went in disguise, to try and do a bit of snooping, but all I saw was the girl we saw the other day. I saw a glimpse of another girl and a man down the hall, but the witch more or less shut the door on me.'

'Not surprised. I mean why would she want to talk about Jesus when she's running hell in there?' I give her a wry smile and take a drink of wine.

'It was the best I could come up with. And I made a good job of it. The lady across the road asked me in.' Immi gives a throaty chortle.

'Why did you go across the road?'

I receive the raised eyebrow. 'Call yourself a copper? In case people from that house were watching, of course. Had to make it look authentic, didn't I?'

Dinner over, we have to get down to the nitty gritty. I push the serving dishes to one side and make a space on the table. Immi gives me her list of names, dates and telephone numbers and she adopts a businesslike manner. I'm glad she's taken the initiative – it can't be easy for her.

'Okay, so what do you want to know?' she says, head on one side.

'How about you tell me it all again, refresh my memory? You'll be doing this a few times down at the station, so best to get in practice.' My memory is in no need of refreshing, but I think it will help her to go over and over it. Sometimes a detail is easily overlooked the first time.

'Right. As you know I work at the medical centre. I'm friendly with a nurse who runs some of the confidential drop-in clinics and we were chatting one day about the rise in the number of young

Eastern European women that come in with suspected sexually transmitted diseases. There's hardly any conversation. They have very little English and they normally have some man waiting for them. She was worried that some could be sex slaves, but of course they wouldn't admit it, even if they could understand the language.'

'Because they're too scared.'

'Yes. Or they have families that are under threat back home if they refuse to do as they're told.' Immi leans her arms on the table and looks at me. 'So that was fresh in my mind the next week when I ran into an old friend I used to work with, Jan, at a party. Don't ask me how, but we got chatting about it and how awful it was right here on our doorstep. Jan said that a friend of a friend of her husband's had overheard a conversation in a pub with a guy and his mates who had used these poor girls. Mentioned the road the house was on.'

I look down the list. 'That was Greg Holsworthy?'

'Yeah. Greg's ex-army and frightened of nobody. He listens in more, and then has a go at the man. Says he should be ashamed of himself and that he'd go to that street, find the girls and call the police. This guy mouths off at him, warns Greg off, and so do his mates. Later on, when Greg's leaving the pub, they waylay him and smack him around a bit in an alley round the back. Not enough to put him in hospital, but enough to really shake him up. Greg remembers one man had an Eastern European accent. He hissed in his ear that if he so much as sets foot on that street, Mr Ransom would make sure that was the last thing he'd ever do.'

'And because it's an unusual surname alarm bells started ringing?'

'Yes, but not just that. I've heard rumours about Dad over the years. I know he's a wheeler-dealer and he never talked about work much. Just said he's a businessman, might not always play by the rules, but has never done anything really underhand. But over the past few years since we moved back here from Liverpool, he's been investigated by your lot quite a bit. Mum let it slip one day.

She was worried, you see, and Dad had sworn her to secrecy, as he usually did, I found out later. But it was at the time she had just had her cancer diagnosis and she was low, vulnerable.'

Immi sighs and looks at the table. I ask her if she's okay to carry on and she says yes but asks for coffee. I busy myself in the kitchen and she takes up the story again.

'Mum had just peeled the potatoes and she threw down the peeler in the bowl so hard water splashed up the kitchen window. She didn't know I'd come in, and I hurried over to put my arm round her. She broke down then, sobbed and sobbed. Said she was so tired of it all, weary. Said that Dad wasn't all he seemed. He'd led her a merry dance for years, other women, petty crime, drugs – he always said it wouldn't hurt anyone. Mum had believed him because she loved him despite everything. And he was good to us. Always buying presents laughing, joking. The doting dad … when he had time.'

'I remember he was a good laugh when we were kids.'

'Oh, he was. Still is. He's the life and soul all right. Mum told me a few home truths about him that evening though. Told me about you being one of the investigating officers when he was questioned too. That's how I knew you were in the police. Mum was really proud of you. Of how you'd turned out.' Immi smiles, but shakes her head at the plate of biscuits I offer.

I picture her mum, Maggie; such a lovely woman, always smiling. Maggie would never have hurt a fly, but she died and her husband lived. Life stinks sometimes. I sigh and pour water on the cafetière. 'It must have been a shock for her to hear about those poor girls.'

'It was. Mum said that of all the things he's ever been mixed up in, that was the one she couldn't stomach. She overheard him talking to one of his men one night when he thought she was asleep. But she only heard bits, not enough to really be sure what he was doing. She thought he was sleeping with younger girls, not that he was involved in sex slavery. That would have killed her quicker than the cancer. After that, they had separate rooms, hardly spoke to each other and she didn't last more than ten months. Nevertheless, it was so hard to live through.'

I try to imagine what that must have been like. Dad had left us quickly, so it was a shock, but not the prolonged, drawn-out agony it must be watching a loved one fade before your eyes. It wouldn't help Immi to mention that, so I say, 'And so then later, when you heard about what Greg said, you were sure your dad was involved.'

'Yeah. My first thought was to confront him, but I quickly thought again. We had become estranged after what Mum had told me. It made my skin crawl to look at him, but I never betrayed her. She begged me never to tell him that I knew. She had this twisted loyalty, see, that's why she stuck with him all that time. Said he was my dad after all and that he loved me. Yeah, right. He loved me so much that he broke up my relationship.'

This is new. She never mentioned this last time we talked. I put down her coffee and sit opposite. There's an ocean of sadness in her eyes and she swallows hard, sniffs. I put my hand on hers. 'What happened?'

Immi moves her hand from mine, shakes her head. 'Don't be nice to me, I'll be a mess.' She makes her voice stronger. 'I was living with this guy, Leon, for three years when we were in Liverpool. He was a trainee chef and the nicest guy you'd wish to meet. We planned to marry, have kids, the whole thing. I'd had long-term relationships before, but this time I knew I'd found *the one*.'

'Kenny didn't approve of him?'

'Oh, he seemed to when they met. Said Leon was a grafter, a man after his own heart – would own his own restaurant one day. But then just before Christmas, I came home to the flat and he'd gone. All his stuff was gone … everything. It was as if he'd never existed.' Immi's voice trembles and she can't hold my gaze.

'Kenny had warned him off?'

'Yes. I didn't find out for ages. Thought Leon had just legged it. None of his friends knew anything about where he'd gone, nor his family. Because I was heartbroken, I allowed myself to be persuaded to come back here to Sheffield with him and Mum. Dad had a big business opportunity to run, apparently. Though Liverpool had been good to him over the last fifteen years, Sheffield was his home and this deal was too good to turn down. I never got to know more than that. Dad bought me a little new build not too far from his and Mum's ridiculous mansion.'

There's a silence as Immi struggles to keep her composure and I shove half a biscuit into my mouth to dislodge a lump that's forming in my throat.

'Not long after Mum died I had a sympathy card from Leon's sister. She'd heard about Mum from a mutual friend of ours. I phoned and asked her if she'd heard from Leon and she was really evasive, so I pushed her. Laid on the guilt, said I needed to know and that I couldn't cope after Mum's death. She said he'd been forced to leave the country and that's all she would say. It was too risky to say more, but he wasn't considered to be good enough for me. I asked who'd forced him, though I knew in my heart. Then she said she'd said enough and hung up.'

'Bloody hell. Did you say anything to your dad?'

'No. As I said, we'd become estranged. He'd call or come round but I said I didn't want anything to do with him because he hurt Mum somehow in the last few months. I honoured Mum's wishes of not telling him what I knew. I mentioned that they slept in separate rooms, that he was always out working when he should have been home more. He denied any wrongdoing, of course. Said Mum was just finding it hard to sleep because of her illness. I told him I needed space. Then, after I found out about Greg's story, I planned to bring the bastard down.'

I tell her how much I admire her and we drink our coffee in silence for a bit. I marvel at her courage and strength. I'm not sure I could have been like her if I were in her shoes. 'And after that you got friendly with him again, so you could gather evidence?'

'Yep. I decided then that I'd keep a close eye on him. I'd invite him for lunch, dinner, days out. I'd look at his phone after he'd taken a call – you know, past calls etcetera – when he'd gone to the loo before the phone had locked again. I'd look at his messages over his shoulder as I passed by, things like that. Then I'd note it all down. Sometimes took a photo of the messages. I even stayed at his place for a few days; I said I'd really missed him and felt we needed to build some bridges. He was like a dog with two tails, of course. Kenny always liked to control me and his giant ego thrives on praise and gratitude from his minions. The visit was fruitful – I did loads of snooping and listening in on conversations.' Immi taps her nails on a notebook she's placed on the table.

I pick it up and flick through. It's meticulous. Names, dates, times, transcriptions. Her face is full of pride and I tell her she's done really well. And she has. This and the other names she's gathered are useful, some well-known criminals, but it's nowhere near enough yet. Kenny had been really careful when writing the phone messages she shows me photos of too. Always businesslike: *Thanks so much. I will have the product you asked for delivered in a few days.* Immi says it was drugs, because she overheard him later on the phone, but there's no proof. The transcripts are one-sided conversations written down by his daughter. A daughter who holds a grudge. It wouldn't stand up in court. Won't even get to court. To access phone records, we'd need more. My boss was very reluctant to put an officer on watch at the house where the girls are. Immi hinted yesterday that there might be more to tell me, and I hoped for something concrete. 'Is there anything else?'

Immi frowns. 'I told you Greg was prepared to testify against him. He's shitting himself but he says he'll do it.'

The temptation to just pacify her and leave it for my colleagues to handle is strong, but I can't do it. She needs to know the truth. 'That's really brave of him. But until we have solid proof that Kenny can't wriggle out of this time … we don't have enough, love.'

Placing her coffee cup down gently she gives me her hard stare, the kind she used to give me when we were kids and she'd made her mind up to do something. 'I thought you might say that. So I have a cunning plan that will give us what we need. I can't tell you what it is though because you'll say it's entrapment or some twaddle.'

My heart sinks. I sit back and exhale. 'I don't like the sound of this, Immi. You're a registered informant now. Anything you do to jeopardise that—'

'Ooh yes, a CHIS, so exciting!' She frowns. 'Now what's it stand for again? Don't tell me. Um … clever hot intellectual spy. Yes?'

I have to laugh. 'No, it's Covert Human Intelligence Source. I registered you to make sure it would put some distance between us and to protect you from being identified as the source. You can't do anything that would put yourself in danger, or undermine this investigation.' I fold my arms, try to look stern.

Immi mirrors my pose. 'It won't. Trust me.'

Chapter Four

Nathan Walker likes to dream. Dreaming is what gets him through the day. He dreams about moving to somewhere sunny, somewhere where there's a beach. Somewhere where the air is fresh. Clean of the stench of the filth he's mired up to his neck in every waking moment. Somewhere away from Kenny Ransom. In that place he'd set up a little shack on the beach, sell food, drinks, beach stuff. How hard could it be? Nathan wouldn't need much to get by. He isn't bothered about possessions, the high life, he only wants peace. Peace and the knowledge that he isn't hurting anyone. Nathan hurts people on Ransom's behalf daily. Not physically – though he has been forced to strong-arm once or twice – but rather coercing them into doing Ransom's bidding.

He observes his mother watching daytime TV. Slack jawed, expressionless eyes, a slow tap, tap of a nicotine-stained finger on the chair arm. Is she conducting some internal concert or marking the passing of the minutes, hours, days of her miserable existence? Because she is miserable. Since his dad was killed, two years back, she'd become this husk, this automaton … this thing in a chair. Nathan and his younger brothers, Jack and Kevin, keep an eye on her. His sister, Angie, keeps an eye too as much as she can from nearly three hundred miles away in Devon with her husband and two kids. Jack and Kevin still live at home, thank goodness.

Nathan goes into the kitchen to make a cuppa and thinks about Angie. Just two years his junior, they were close growing up. He misses her and is more than a little jealous that she met a nice guy on holiday, married him, and managed to escape. She's the only one who has. Nathan is glad she has, but wishes he could do the same. Perhaps when Mum dies? But she's only fifty-six and has years of life yet. If you can call it a life.

From the kitchen window he sees a sparrow feeding its young on the bird table. That's why he stays. Mum looked after him and now he has to repay in kind. If he left she'd end up in a care home of some sort. Jack and Kevin are good boys, but they're working on their own escape plan, and rightly so. What's the point of all of them being trapped? Jack's got his own website business off the ground and Kevin is a mechanic. Nathan made some wrong choices when he was a teenager, followed in his dad's footsteps because he wasn't academic, had a low opinion of his abilities, but mostly he was lazy back then, if truth be known. If he had his time over again, he would do everything differently.

'Cuppa, Mum?' Nathan puts his mother's mug down on the stained coaster and pats her cold hand. The skin on the back of it feels like chicken skin. Old before her time.

'You're a good lad, Nate. When you gonna get a girl and settle down, eh? You're nearly thirty-one. That job's no good for you. Look what it did to your dad.'

Mum says the same thing every time he comes round. It's as if someone has pressed a 'play' button in her head and out comes the rehearsed script, word perfect. She says it while keeping her eyes focused on the screen, though Nathan wonders if she's actually taking anything in at all.

'Time enough for that, Mum. It will happen, but I'm just a bit busy at the moment.' His mum smiles distractedly and so, his part of the script complete, Nathan leaves her to her TV.

Outside in the car a message waits on his phone. *Mr Haliday is concerned about his delivery. I don't want to have to message you again. KR.*

Nathan sighs and writes back, *I'm on it. Sorry it's late, Mr Ransom.* Swinging the car away from the kerb Nathan feels anything but sorry. He feels humiliation, anger and oppression. One day he'll get out. He has to.

Chapter Five

DCI Mark Bradley looks in no mood for a chat about how to extend surveillance on the house where the girls are being held. I get a cursory glance and then I'm looking at the top of his shiny bald head as he works furiously at some forms piled on his desk. I know from a colleague that he's had a nagging toothache for a week and the dentist is having trouble extracting. Something about the root. He's waiting for an appointment with a dental surgeon and medicated up to the eyeballs. Even when he's okay he's a bit of a spiky character, though he's one of the good guys. Mark really cares about his job and the people he serves.

I clear my throat and try again. 'Sir, I was wondering if we could get a bit more time on the house on Westmorland Street.'

A grunt. 'I looked at what you showed me the other day and sadly there's not enough to go on, as well you know. Not enough to justify the expense of having a couple of plain-clothes sitting there another few days. They've seen comings and goings – young men, older men – seen young women inside passing the windows, but not much else. Certainly not Kenny Ransom. My feeling is just to send a couple of officers round, see how many of the girls are illegal, probably all of them in my experience, and then deport them home. Best all round,' he mutters without looking up from his work.

'Yes, sir,' I say and turn to leave. At the door, I do my Columbo impression. 'It would be a shame to let Ransom go again though … especially as his daughter says she might have something concrete we could use.'

This makes him glance up, a frown furrowing his brow. The sun angling through the window across his face, and the toothache, make him look all of his fifty-two years – and more. He reminds me a bit of James Nesbitt before the hair transplant. 'What kind of concrete?'

'She didn't say.'

Mark's frown gets even deeper. 'Hope there's going to be no fallout from this for you.' He picks up his pen and looks at it. 'You know, with you being old friends and all.'

'Sir?' I raise an eyebrow.

'Nothing that could compromise your position, your job.' He puts the pen down and fixes me with those miss-nothing hazel eyes.

I feign shock. 'Oh no. If there's anything underhand on her part I'll make sure she knows about it, sir.' I leave the room before he has a chance to say anything else.

From the window, Anya sees the blonde-haired woman walking up the street. She was the one who was driving the car the dark-haired woman got into the other day. She has a Bible in her hands and she's trying very hard not to look like she did before. Her hair is mostly hidden under a woolly hat; she has tinted glasses on but no make-up. Though the weather is fine she's wearing a long dark green mac. Anya knows she's the blonde woman she saw before, though, because she has a very good eye for faces. Faces are like TV to her nowadays. She's not allowed to watch TV here but she's allowed magazines. Though the ones she has are out of date and hard to read; her English is far from perfect.

There are at least three other girls in the house but they are confined to their rooms and have different sittings at meal times. They are not allowed to talk to each other. In six months, Liliana is the only girl she's shared a few snatched words with when they passed on the stairs. They were forbidden to interact after that, and they were instructed to look at the floor in future when they met. Even though she'd dearly love to speak to the others, punishment in the damp, cold cellar is too high a price to pay.

Anya's heart goes into overdrive when the woman crosses the road and walks up the path to the house. She looks right at Anya, puts a finger to her lips and shakes her head slightly. Then she points to the window and motions for Anya to open it. Anya shakes her head: no. It would be more than the cellar if she did. The woman mouths 'please' and gestures to the window again. Anya whips her head round and cocks an ear towards the rest of the house. Marta is clattering around upstairs chuntering something to one of the girls, and Jozef is nowhere to be seen or heard. She turns back to the woman and finds her right next to the pane, a pleading look in her big blue eyes. Though Anya's heart aches to open the window, fear locks her hand to her side.

Now the woman presses a sheet of paper to the window. On it, written in big letters, are the words: 'I AM HERE TO HELP YOU!' Then she holds up an envelope in her other hand.

Anya slowly shakes her head. But something in the woman's face makes her open the window and snatch the envelope before she has time to talk herself out of it. She stuffs it down her trousers. The woman gives her a relieved smile and hurries back down the path just as Marta stomps in, all gold teeth and in full yelling mode. 'Aren't you ready yet? You have fifteen minutes to make yourself look like you're worth charging a hundred pounds for. These days it's gonna take you at least an hour!' Marta sneers and cuffs Anya round the head. Anya runs upstairs, but this time her footsteps feel a little bit lighter.

It's almost midnight, the last man has left, and Anya starts her ritual of scrubbing under a scalding shower. Tonight hasn't seemed as bad, because she has managed to almost block out what the men were doing to her by picturing the envelope in her mind's eye. The envelope that might have hope folded inside somehow. She knows that hope is a dangerous concept but she can't help herself. She didn't manage to open it before the first man came because she was late getting ready. But as soon as she gets inside her bedroom, she'll at last be able to see what's inside.

Not wishing to alert Marta by having a light under her door, Anya stands by the window and slips trembling fingers under the flap of the envelope. By the light of the full moon and a street lamp, she reads the first line of the letter and then fear clamps her heart so forcefully that she shoves the paper back inside the envelope. The envelope seems to grow hotter in her hands, as if it contains some lethal poison, and she throws it to the floor before it can seep into the skin of her fingers. Anya takes some deep breaths and allows her rational mind out of the cupboard that fear has locked it in. It's to be expected. Of course she will feel like this after keeping hope buried for so long. Just read the letter and then see. You don't have to act on any of what it might say.

Once more she teases the letter from the envelope and reads:

I am here to help you escape. You and any other poor girl trapped in this house. We know what is happening to you. I have friends that can help and with just a little information from you we'll be able to put the man in charge in prison where he belongs. I know you are afraid perhaps for your family back home, and certainly for yourself. Just a few details from you and it will all be over. You will be free.

Anya stops reading. It has taken her a long time to understand the letter; she has to spell out and whisper each word to help make sense of them. Her heart is thumping and she feels light-headed. The last four words seem to grow and shine, burning themselves into her brain. But can she believe it? And what information can she give? She goes back to the letter.

All I need is the names of the people that keep you in the house. Don't worry if you don't know their last names, just the first will do. Write them down on the back of this letter and then screw it up and throw it out of the window into the yard by the bins. I will be there tomorrow at midday. You should be able to throw it from the bathroom window. I have studied your house and know that you can do this. Make sure it is midday, not earlier or later, as I need to get the letter very quickly before anyone sees me.

You can do it. Good luck. I will be waiting and in a few days you will be out.

Anya shakes her head and screws up the letter. How foolish, to allow hope to beat in her chest. This is too dangerous. What would happen if Jozef walked outside to have a cigarette just as she threw the letter? That would be the end of it. If she was with a client, she'd have to make some excuse to use the toilet, which could be awkward. Some were more cruel than kind. And what would be the point of the woman knowing Josef and Marta's names? They are not the ones in control. It makes little sense to Anya. No. She won't do it. Can't. Dare not.

Anya goes to the bathroom and prepares to flush the paper down the toilet. She steels herself to do it three times but finds that instead she's smoothed it out and placed it under her mattress. Anya sighs and wishes she could make the right decision. In the end she decides that literally sleeping on it might be the best thing to do.

Chapter Six

The full moon shines its light through a crack in my curtains. It's as if it is doing it on purpose – let's keep Bryony awake, make her tired and even grumpier than normal in the morning. I slip out of bed and peer through the crack. There's a silver sheen across the water and the moon's caught in the branches of the tallest tree against the skyline. I open the window, ignoring the chill. It's almost as bright as day and even though the city is not too far away, stars add their light to the moon's one-upmanship, encouraging it to go one better.

I inhale the crisp 2am air, and a washing machine full of thoughts that's been on fast spin in my head for hours now comes to a stop. Calm enters my body with each breath, and I realise how lucky I am. Okay, even though I have a boss who's ready to pull the plug on the case, an old friend who's up to no good to try and solve it – though she assures me she's not – and I have no bloody clue on how to sort out either problem, in the end it doesn't matter. I'm sure the poor broken girl we saw at the window on Westmorland Street would love to have those kinds of problems. I shudder to think what her life is like. A few images come into my head; I shut the window, and go to the kitchen to make a cup of tea to block them out.

The tea drinking exercise hasn't helped too much. Mostly I have been thinking about leaving the police. Was I ever really cut out for it? Did I just join to impress Dad? It's hard to decide, when my earliest memory is sitting on Dad's shoulders with his helmet on, or rather over my face as it was way too big. Yes, he encouraged me, but I've always had a strong sense of justice, of doing the right thing. But what if doing the right thing is actually the wrong thing in the eyes of the law? What if Immi is planning to do something that would compromise my position? Would that actually matter if it led to a conviction of her vile father? If it stopped him hurting any more poor girls?

'Blind eye turning, love.' Dad sometimes used to say that and tap the side of his nose when I questioned something dodgy he'd told me about, or he'd done. It was always dodgy in terms of helping others, when technically he should have reported it. Is there such a thing as a bent copper, but bent in a good way? If so, then perhaps I'm not alone.

In the bedroom again I tug the curtains shut and flop down into my bed. Three hours before I'm up and on the job. I pull a pillow over my face and groan. Then Immi's hopeful face surfaces and I push her away. I *must* sleep. I throw the pillow at the wall and close my eyes. If Immi can get something on Kenny Ransom that involves blind eye turning, then let her. If it was good enough for Dad, it's good enough for me.

Great Uncle Cibor would turn in his grave if he could see Anya cowering from the fight. Did he cower from the Nazis when they rolled into Poland? No. Even though it seemed hopeless, he joined the resistance and fought back whenever he could. He picked off one or two of the bastards from his sniper position on the rooftops of Warsaw. Okay, it was one or two, hardly a game changer – but at least they then had one or two less than they had before. Anya remembers how his eyes would shine with pride when, as an old man, he told her of his antics.

The kitchen clock says 11.45. She has fifteen minutes to decide. Anya bites the skin at the edge of her thumbnail and feels her heart stepping up the pace. Maybe she isn't as brave as Great Uncle Cibor. And besides, his actions wouldn't have involved his whole family's safety if they went wrong. If she failed in her mission … various scenarios present themselves and Anya shuts them down. Nausea squeezes the edges of her stomach.

The clock says 11.55 and she decides that what she's been asked to do is too dangerous and she won't do it. Then Great Uncle

Cibor's voice whispers in her mind that of course it is dangerous. Furthermore, that his family would have been in danger if he'd been caught, but sometimes you have to make a stand. Marta harrumphs from the door. 'If I have to nag you once more this week about getting ready for a gentleman caller, I will tell Jozef to cellar you. You have half an hour.'

Anya nods and hurries upstairs. Marta was quietly spoken just then. When she's not shouting, Anya knows that she means exactly what she says. In the bathroom she brushes her teeth and looks at her face in the mirror. Her eyes are wide, frightened. Can she see a ghost of Great Uncle Cibor behind them? He must have been scared but he didn't give in. Suddenly her hand is pushing open the bathroom window, pulling a ball of paper from her bra, shaking as she prepares to throw. In the yard she sees a shadow by the back gate behind the bins. A woman's shadow. She imagines that the paper is a sniper's rifle; she takes aim, fires.

Anya covers her mouth with her hand to stifle the scream that waits in her throat. She has done it. She has been brave.

But nothing happens.

Nobody comes.

Marta calls her name through the door. Says people are waiting to use the bathroom. Without taking her eyes from the ball of paper by the bin, Anya says she's almost ready, in a voice as normal as she can make it given that every fibre of her being is trembling with the enormity of what she's just done. Then the woman runs into the yard, snatches the paper and runs back out. It happens so fast that Anya isn't sure it happened at all. Perhaps it is all in her head. The empty space on the concrete where the paper used to be tells her otherwise. Gradually she allows her breathing to return to normal and a small triumphant smile to flit across her mouth. Anya thinks that, somewhere, Great Uncle Cibor is smiling too.

Imogen doesn't stop running until she reaches the park. There's nobody following her, she's kept checking carefully, but she wants as far away from that house as possible. It gives her the creeps – all proud, grand and Victorian on the outside, hiding misery, squalor and shame on the inside. Apart from the Victorian bit, the similarity to her father isn't lost on her. The two officers were still outside today, but she knows she must act fast. They won't be here tomorrow, or even by this evening. In her opinion they were a bit useless anyway. When she'd gone in disguise the other day and given the girl the letter they'd hardly noticed. Okay, granted, they couldn't have seen what she did because of the hedge at the end of the path, but they must have seen her walk up it. They certainly didn't bother themselves to get out of the car and ask her anything. Just assumed she was spreading God's Word.

A park bench on the horizon seems a good place to rest and catch her breath, see what the girl has written. The paper has been scrunched so tightly her own writing is barely legible and Imogen thinks the paper has been unwrapped and scrunched more than once. On the back, in what looks like eyeliner, are the names Jozef and Marta. At last there's a name for the Hansel and Gretel witch. Marta. Imogen can't wait for her demise. It's bad enough that men do this to young women, but other women do it too? Makes her skin crawl. A roll of panic in her belly brings with it a barrage of disquiet about her plan. What if it all falls flat? What if her father doesn't take the bait? It will all have been for nothing and she will have let the girl down. The other girls too. He has to fall for it. But first she must make Bryony listen. Make her agree to do what she asks without question.

'I don't know one hundred per cent, but this is our one chance.'

Immi's voice is shaking on the line and I think she might be close to tears. I can't help but snap at her though. 'Oh right. I'll tell that to DCI Bradley, he'll be so pleased.'

'You have to make him listen, but if he won't, you'll have to authorise it. We need at least three of those tough officer types with the battering ram things to break down doors. My dad has never been any good with the threat of violence. Mind you, they might not need to break it down. Those plainclothes officers could go up and knock on the door. The others could be there for reinforcement. One or two need to go round the back in case he tries to leg it.'

My mouth drops open. 'This gets better and better. Sure you don't want to oversee operations? Have you any idea what would happen if I went above my boss's head?' I realise my voice is raised and look through the glass panel in my office to check that nobody heard. All heads are focused on work, but I close the blinds, nevertheless.

'We can't think about that now. We need to get my father arrested and free those women. Don't forget to remain unseen until he's gone. No point in being a red rag to his bull. Make sure you interview Marta and Jozef. Do the divide and rule thing – promise them leniency if they'll testify against my father.'

Who the hell does she think she is? Telling me what to do, and that I shouldn't worry about my job! The fact that I would run the operation exactly as she's outlining is neither here nor there. I take a deep breath and count to ten, interrupt when she's off on another tack.

'Listen here, Immi, I think you've done enough. You need to tell me how you know the names of those in the house, and exactly how you're going to get your father to the house this evening. Furthermore, even if he does show up, we might find that these girls aren't illegal, aren't sex slaves, and—'

'And he's visiting his cousin Matilda for tea and cake?'

I thump my fist on the desk. 'Yes, for all we know!'

Unperturbed, Immi says, 'Well that's impossible because he doesn't have a cousin Matilda.'

Despite everything a smile tugs at the corner of my mouth. I make my mouth straight and say, 'Sorry, but you're really not funny. Imagine what would happen if we go in there all guns blazing and everything is perfectly innocent? He would have our guts on a plate.'

There's a long silence and then Immi says, 'You know as well as I do that things in there are about as far away from innocent as they can get. I can't tell you how I know the names and what I'm going to do, because the less you know the better. You can't be compromised. I realise that your job is important and I want you to keep it. When you get my call, tell the DCI you have to have the manpower right away … say it's a now or never situation.'

I say nothing. My head says no, but my heart says yes. I know that Mark won't act unless he has more information, so that leaves me. Me out on a limb. Me authorising a 'raid' to all intents and purposes with no warrant, no concrete proof. Me without a job. Then I think about those poor girls, Kenny Ransom's self-satisfied grin the last time he walked free from the courtroom, my dad the good bent copper, and before I have time to change my mind I say, 'I'll wait for your call.'

Chapter Seven

'A tip off, Mr Ransom?'

'Yes, would you know anything about that, Nathan?'

'No. No idea.'

'There's not that many people who know about the house on Westmorland. You are one of them.'

Nathan doesn't like the suspicious tone in Ransom's voice. 'Yeah, but I haven't had anything to do with what goes on there … in fact I didn't know about it until you sent me there the other month to collect some money. Jason, the one you normally use, was sick, remember?'

'Yes. You told nobody about that?'

Nathan wishes he had told the police once he clocked those poor girls, but of course he'd kept his mouth shut as usual. 'No, Mr Ransom … could it be a punter?'

'Punters don't know my telephone number, nor my business.'

'Jason?'

'He was here with me at the time of the call.'

'Right. Well, what exactly did he say when he called?'

'Used one of those voice disguisers – sounded all metallic like. He said that Jozef and Marta are ripping me off. They're pocketing some of the earnings. They said that if I ask, they'll say business isn't as good as it was. Say the girls are getting tired, that we need fresh ones.'

'But how does he know all this?'

'Exactly, Sherlock. That's what I'd like to know. He also said that he wants in on it. Says he's always been loyal to me and can run the house better than those two clowns. He'll expect a bit more cash though, he's worth it, you see. I'm to go there at nine tonight. Apparently I'll catch Marta and Jozef red-handed. He knows where they've stashed my money too. He'll call me when I'm there.'

Nathan has the awful idea that Ransom thinks it's him. He doesn't know what to say next. 'I expect you'll just have to go and see?'

'You're loyal too, aren't you, Nathan?' Ransom's voice is menacing.

Nathan's heart sinks. 'Of course, Mr Ransom, but it isn't me.'

'Hmm. Someone I know, though, because they needed to disguise their voice.'

'But that doesn't make sense, because you'll have to know who it is in the end, won't you? You know, if you're going to work with them after you get rid of the two that run it now?'

Ransom pauses. Nathan can almost hear the cogs turning. 'Yes, unless he's hedging his bets. He might think I'll be angry that he's trying to call the shots. Have me running round there waiting for his call. Maybe he thinks that once I calm down after being double-crossed I'd be grateful to him, but angry at the time. Maybe he only knows half a story and is just guessing what Jozef and Marta are up to. Fuck knows! But one thing's for sure, you're coming with me.'

'Me?'

'You.'

'Why?'

'Because I want backup, of course. Jason's coming too.'

Nathan thinks it's because he doesn't believe him, still suspects him and wants him within grabbing distance. But he says, 'Okay, see you at the house in a few hours.'

'Be there, Nathan, or I'll have your balls.'

Nathan listens to the disconnect tone. He feels the same – disconnected from the whole scene. He knows Ransom, knows his unpredictable moods. Nathan is worried that if Ransom's convinced it's him behind it, he might be on the receiving end of his tongue or worse. Jason's fist too. He can hold his own, but it won't be good, whatever happens. Shit. He needs to get out of this somehow. He sinks down on his sofa and closes his eyes, thinks. Eventually he dreams up some semblance of a plan. For his own sake, it has to work.

How many times have I walked past Mark Bradley's office now? Must be at least three. The last time he raised a questioning eyebrow but I just nodded and smiled. Why is he still here at this time? He was supposed to be gone by six tonight. Some university graduation party for his daughter, wasn't it? It would be much easier if he'd gone, because I could justify acting on my instincts – I couldn't possibly disturb DCI Bradley at home you see, and besides, he knew about what was happening, trusts me to act on it implicitly, blah, blah.

The clock on the office wall says 7.30 and I'm running out of time. My heart is keeping time with the second hand. Tick, tick, tick. Shit, this is no good; I have to go and speak to Mark. I knock on his door and he beckons me in through the glass panel. I walk in, though I don't know how I get my leaden legs to move. Nausea rises in my throat. He looks up from his desk, his face expressionless. 'Thought you were going to a party, sir,' I say in a high voice, a too-bright smile on my face.

'Turns out it's tomorrow. I got the date wrong.' He frowns and folds his arms. 'Okay, what's up?'

'Nothing really,' I say quickly and lean my hands on the back of the chair in front of his desk. I need all the support I can get. 'In fact, things might be really good in a few hours. You see, Imogen Ransom just phoned to say that if we turn up at Westmorland Street tonight we'll catch her father there.'

Mark rolls his eyes. 'Not this again. You want me to spend time and money sending a squad round on the say-so of his daughter? How do we know he'll turn up and what time?'

'Imogen said he'll be there around nine, but that she'll contact me as soon as he's gone in, just to be sure.'

'But how does she know?' Mark strokes his hand quickly over his balding head a few times – a gesture I've seen so many times. It usually means that he's unsure but prepared to listen.

'Again, she's unwilling to tell me because she says the less I know, the better it will be.'

He narrows his eyes. 'That's because she's doing something illegal, isn't it?'

'I doubt it, boss.' My voice sounds normal, calm. I need an Oscar.

'I don't like it, Bryony. If this goes tits up we'll be in the shit. You do realise that?'

'I do. But I think it's worth the risk. We won't get a chance like this again.' My gaze holds his for a few seconds. It feels as though his mind is reaching into mine.

Just as I'm about to look away, he says, 'I'll authorise it.' At first I can't quite believe my ears, and then I feel a huge smile split my face. He stands up and jabs a finger at me. 'But if this does cover us in shit, you're the one cleaning it up. Do I make myself clear?'

'Oh, absolutely, sir.' I make my face solemn and scuttle out of there before he can say anything else.

Anya has one more client this evening. He has been here before and he is one of the worst. Old enough to be her grandfather, fat, smelly and disgusting. She can feel the bile rising in her throat at the very thought of him. He's due at nine; twenty minutes. Twenty minutes to prepare her mind … to try and put some defence mechanisms in place. At times like this it's best to imagine that the act is happening to someone else. That her body is someone else's and her mind is free to be anywhere it chooses. Often she's back home in Poland, at the café with friends, or she's at university here, like she was supposed to be.

How could Marta betray her family like that? Pretending she could come here to study and then cruelly send pictures back home of her supposedly studying. Marta was family too. Okay, a distant second cousin of her father's, but family all the same. And the lies. The lies that Anya has to tell her mother every time they speak on the phone. Yes, everything is fine, great in fact. The course is good, I have made friends. No need at all to worry. I will be home to visit soon, probably in the next holidays. Then the next holiday comes and more lies. Sorry, she has a part-time job, things are more expensive than she imagined, so she can't come back just yet. No, please don't send money …

Anya sighs and shakes her head. The preparation isn't working today. Ten more minutes and the client will be here. There's a knock at the door and her heart plummets. He's early. She stands and smooths out her top, tries desperately to shift her mind out of her body. Jozef answers the door and a stocky, smartly dressed man in his fifties sweeps past him followed by another man, a tall, ape-like guy in his twenties. He's been here before to collect money. The first man has too; she has seen him briefly through a crack in a door. He is the boss … the man with all the power.

'Where's Marta?' the boss asks. He has an air of importance, a man to be reckoned with. Anya notices that his silver hair is expertly cut and styled, and a waft of expensive cologne cuts the air when he raises his hand to his chin.

Jozef looks like he's in front of a headmaster. 'She's upstairs I think, Mr Ransom.'

Anya gasps as Mr Ransom's hand flies smartly to Jozef's cheek. 'Then go and fucking get her, you dumbo!'

The ape looks across at Anya, looks her up and down, winks suggestively. Anya looks at the floor and sits back at the table. Jozef runs upstairs, calling Marta with every step. The urgency in his voice soon pulls Marta behind him downstairs. Anya can feel Mr Ransom's steely grey eyes on her, but she daren't look up.

'Mr Ransom. How nice to see you—' Marta begins; her breathy simper sickens Anya.

'Cut the crap. A little bird tells me you've been pulling the wool over my eyes,' Mr Ransom says, and drags a chair from the table she's sitting at over the stone floor. The scraping sets Anya's teeth on edge. He sits down opposite.

'A bird? Wool? I'm not sure what this means, Mr—'

'You've lived in this country thirty years, you stupid bitch. You know exactly what I mean.' Mr Ransom's voice sounds harder on her ears than the scraping noise. 'Jozef's in with you too, so it seems.'

'But I, we …' Marta looks at Jozef '… would never do such a thing.'

Jozef wrings his hands and nods vigorously. 'No, we would never pull the wool.'

The ape sniggers.

'What is it we are supposed to have done, Mr Ransom?' Marta says quietly.

'You are supposed to be keeping some money back for yourselves. Money that these lovely ladies earn for me.' Anya feels a finger under her chin and her face is raised to the scrutiny of his gaze. She swallows when she sees desire take the place of curiosity.

'But we would *never* do this. Not ever!' Marta shrieks. Jozef adds his vehement assent.

Mr Ransom's phone rings and he answers it. 'Oh, well isn't that convenient, Nathan? Your car breaks down just as you're meant to be here!' Anya sees a tic in his cheek start to jump. 'Oh, the breakdown men gave you a report if I'd like to see it? Why, yes, yes I would like to see it. Get a fucking taxi and bring it here right this—' A knock on the door halts his words. Mr Ransom pockets the phone and nods to the ape. 'Answer it.'

Anya hears a man's voice say, 'DS Prosser, CID. Would you be kind enough to answer a few of our questions?'

Mr Ransom scrapes back the chair again and rushes to the back door. A few moments later he's back between two of the tallest policemen Anya has ever seen. They're wearing padded jackets and helmets with visors and Mr Ransom looks very small sandwiched between them. Two men come in behind the ape and flash their ID at Mr Ransom, Marta and Jozef. Before they can say anything, the dark-haired lady with the striking features Anya saw the other day comes in too. She takes out her badge and says, 'DI Masters.' She looks directly at the man between the two policemen and gives him a cold smile. 'Well, if it isn't Mr Kenneth Ransom. What a surprise.'

Chapter Eight

The word on the street has it that Kenny Ransom is under arrest and is likely to go down. Nathan hasn't heard anything directly from Ransom for ten days and, though he desperately wants to know, he won't risk contacting any of Ransom's known associates. Especially not Frank Dawson, his second in command. If the police are rounding Ransom's mates up, he doesn't want his number to be amongst their recent phone records. The word on the street is actually just a whisper in alleyways, pubs and drug-dealing circuits. Nathan believes it, though, because this is the longest he's not heard from Ransom for years. Thank God he wasn't at the house when the police came, because he has no doubt whatsoever that Kenny would take him down with him if he could.

Relief and anxiety have been fighting for dominance in Nathan's head for the last few days. Relief that he might at last be out of Ransom's grasp and free to make a real life for himself, and anxiety at the thought of doing just that. Where had he been working for the last thirteen years since he dropped out of his business studies course? How had he got by? No respectable employer would just take him on without references, would they? How has he paid his rent? Has he paid taxes? And Mum. What will happen to her? The house she lives in is owned by Ransom. If he arranges for it to be sold, what then? On balance, Nathan thinks that anxiety has won.

The view from his top floor flat takes in three of the seven surrounding hills and a wide sweep of the outskirts of the city of Sheffield. Old red brick jostles against new glass and tower block, spires stretch to clouds, and, from this distance and in the silence, everything looks peaceful. Calm. Gazing at the red and yellow streaked sky left behind by the retiring sun, he wishes he'd had the guts to turn his back on the criminal subculture he'd grown up within. His dad had told him to keep away, stay clean, and not to end up like him, but Nathan had seen it as an easy option. Easy money. It's not so easy now, is it? In fact, where his next meal was coming from would fast become a problem. He's got a few savings, but they're for the future. The shack on the beach? Yeah, right.

The doorbell rings. Nathan's heart drums in his chest as he creeps towards the door. He isn't expecting anyone; nobody has left a message on his phone. The fish-eye lens shows a distorted Jason Connor. Nathan thinks it improves his looks. He's alone … hopefully. Nathan takes a deep breath and opens up.

'Alright?' Jason says by way of a greeting and walks straight in.

'Come in, why don't you?' Nathan mutters and has a quick glance up and down the corridor. Jason is alone. Good.

'You heard what's happened to old man Kenny?' Jason's in the living room, picking up an ornament of a dolphin his mum once bought him, looking underneath it, twirling it in his big meaty hands.

Jason wouldn't be calling his boss 'old man Kenny' if he were anywhere near him, unless he wanted to meet his maker early. 'I heard that he was most likely going to be sent down.' Nathan retrieves the dolphin and sets it back down on the mantelshelf.

'Could well be.' Jason lets his bulk flop down into Nathan's best armchair; the springs groan in protest. 'Frank Dawson's running things for him now. You wouldn't know that Ken had gone. Right smooth operator is Frank.'

Nathan sighs inwardly. Something must be wrong if Frank Dawson hadn't seen fit to contact him and explain that he'd be taking over for a while. He sits down on the settee opposite Jason. 'I wondered what was happening. Nobody let me know anything.'

Jason leans forward, elbows on knees, a nasty glint in his eyes. 'Well, that's why I'm here. Frank told me to come over and tell you that Kenny is a bit unhappy with you. In fact, he's starting to think you might have set him up. You might have been the disguised voice on the phone last week. You might have got him there, called plod and got him lifted.'

Nathan's mouth drops open. His mind races. Okay, at the time perhaps Nathan thought Kenny suspected it could have been him on the phone, but not *this* fairy story. 'What? Why the fuck would I do that?'

'He doesn't know.' Jason flops back again and spreads his arms wide. 'But it did look a bit sus', didn't it? You supposed to meet us there at the whore house and then you ring up with some shit about a car breaking down.'

'It did break down! I have the report from the breakdown guy to prove it!' Nathan scrubs his hands through his dark blond hair in frustration and then rubs his cheeks to disguise the heat spreading through them. He never was much good at lying to someone's face.

'Don't shoot the messenger.' Jason holds his hands up in mock surrender.

'*You* were lucky to get off the hook though, weren't you?' Nathan's words are thick with implication and it isn't lost on Jason.

'Me? I was just driving Mr. Ransom. I had nowt do with owt. Coppers brought me in and questioned me, but they had zilch,' he says, glowering. 'Look, Frank says you have to meet him on Monday morning at Ken's place. He wants to talk to you about your future with the firm. Says you have to be there at ten o'clock sharp or don't bother coming.'

'I'll be there. Of course I will.'

'I'll tell him then.' Jason heaves himself to standing and tips an imaginary hat at Nathan. 'See you around?'

'Bank on it.' Nathan follows Jason, then locks and chains the door behind him and leans his forehead against the cool paintwork.

Frank wants to see him about his future? This doesn't sound good. Maybe he's going to have three or four thugs waiting to give him a good hiding. Maybe Kenny wants someone to blame. They obviously haven't found the owner of the voice from the phone call, the person who set up Ransom, have they? So it looks like Nathan is the fall guy. Ransom is clearly furious at being hauled in and perhaps losing his freedom for a while – so someone has to pay.

If he doesn't go on Monday then it's as good as an admission of guilt. If he does, then he could risk a beating, or worse. Could Jason and Frank be in it together? Could Frank be the one that called Kenny? Do they want to punish him to put Kenny off the scent? Nathan's stomach bubbles and nausea rises from it. He needs air. On the balcony he takes in gulps of fresh air sheathed in kebab grease from the takeaway opposite, and petrol fumes from the stationary traffic at the lights below. He retches and runs for the bathroom.

He stares at his shocked expression in the bathroom mirror. His dark green eyes look like two emeralds in snow. The contents of his stomach decide to come up again, and the next time he looks at his reflection he sees colour coming back into his cheeks and he starts to feel more normal, whatever that is. The decision has been made. Whatever happens he will go to meet Frank on Monday and take the breakdown report with him. Frank might rip it up in front of him, but he might believe him. It is an official report, after all. Thank God Kevin managed to tamper with the engine just enough to get it to break down a few miles from Nathan's home. The breakdown guy never questioned it, it seemed legit. Kevin is an excellent mechanic.

Everyone dreads Monday morning, don't they? Today, dread is an understatement. Today, to Nathan, it feels like a death sentence. He's barely eaten since Friday evening after the house call from Jason, and when he managed to grab a little sleep, his dreams were tortured and twisty. Nathan slows his car and prepares to stop at the ridiculously ornate brass gates at the driveway to Ransom's house. Ransom's mansion, the owner often laughingly called it. Okay, it rhymed, kind of, but the childish pleasure Ransom got from uttering those words just made him sound stupid, in Nathan's opinion.

The gates swing silently open so he drives up the long gravel swathe of brown, flanked on either side by lush green lawns. A mock Georgian manor house sits hunched like a self-conscious imposter at the top of an incline, and, at the top of thick white steps, marble pillars reflect the bright morning sunshine. Before Nathan has even switched off the engine the door opens and out steps Jason. My, my, isn't he the flavour of the month?

'Follow me,' Jason says as Nathan gets out of his car, then he turns and leads the way inside.

Nathan eyes the oak panelling and expensive paintings all along the hallway as he follows in Jason's echoing footsteps. He has only ever been inside once since Ransom bought the place a few years back. Business was always done on the step or next to the car. Perhaps he didn't want all and sundry seeing the extent of his wealth. Jason is probably too thick to recognise expensive stuff if it hit him in the eye. He wouldn't know an antique vase from a pint pot. Frank wouldn't be in on anything with him – too dumb. Thick but useful with his fists, that's why he's here. The last of Nathan's thoughts doesn't lighten his mood.

Jason stops outside a door and pushes it open. 'Mr. Dawson is in the drawing room.' He pronounces it 'drawling'. 'Wait here and I'll check he's ready for you.' If the situation wasn't so dire, Nathan would have laughed at Jason's misplaced air of self-importance.

Jason comes back and beckons him in. The room is just as ostentatious as the rest of the place, all oak, marble and gold leaf. In front of a huge floor-to-ceiling window stands Frank Dawson, stocky and resplendent in a designer three-piece suit. The suit fails to hide the paunch and can't compensate for the uncouth belch Dawson greets him with. 'Oops. Excuse me, just ate a shedload of bacon and eggs. Kenny keeps his own hens, you know. Nothing finer than freshly laid eggs.' He smooths his jet-black comb over and, as if in contemplation about the merits of eggs, strokes a pockmarked cheek.

Nathan hasn't seen Dawson for a while and remembers that the hair was thicker and greyer when last they met. Why people try to look younger by dying their hair black is beyond Nathan. It has the opposite effect. Fake tan and dark hair can't disguise the crow's feet pulling at the corners of Dawson's eyes, nor the turkey neck wobbling as he talks.

'So how are you doing, Nathan?' Dawson doesn't wait for a reply, just sweeps his hand at a wing-backed chair next to a grand fireplace. 'Let's sit down, have a little chat.'

Nathan sits and wonders if this is the bit where some henchmen enter stage right and tie him to the seat. 'I'm well, thanks,' he says, perching on the edge of the cushion. 'How are you, Mr. Dawson?'

Dawson flicks the tail of his jacket up and sits. 'Mr. Dawson? Call me Frank. No need to be so formal.'

This isn't what Nathan was expecting at all. Still, he mustn't let his guard down. He decides to tackle what Jason said head on. 'Okay, thanks, Frank. I was a bit worried, to be honest. Jason said that Mr. Ransom thought I was behind him being set up. But my car had a genuine breakdown, you know.' Nathan pulls the report from his pocket and hands it to Dawson.

Dawson nods, scans the report and hands it back. 'Our Jason tends to overdramatise. He has little in the brain department, though to be fair, that is more or less what Kenny thought for a while.' Dawson strokes his scars again, narrows his eyes. 'Well, you would, wouldn't you?'

Nathan takes a moment to realise that this is not a rhetorical question. He spreads his hands wide. 'I guess it didn't look good. But why he suspected me in the first place …' He shrugs.

Dawson relaxes back into his chair. 'As Kenny said, there weren't too many people who knew about that house. He just narrowed it down.'

'But why would I do that, jeopardise everything? I owe everything to Mr. Ransom. My dad worked for him, loyal to the last.' Nathan hopes he's kept the bitterness out of his voice. 'My mum and brothers live in one of his houses for a nominal rent because of Mr. Ransom, and the jobs he sends me are my bread and butter.'

Dawson nods in agreement. 'Hmm.' A pause. A steepling of fingers. 'That's what I told Kenny, and he had to concede I was right. But …' He holds a podgy finger up in the air. 'Mr. Ransom wants you to prove yourself. Once he finds out who was behind it, and he will …' Dawson leans forward and fixes Nathan with his beady black eyes. 'He has a special job for you. No idea when that will be, but you need to be on standby.'

Nathan swallows and watches the older man lean back again, brush imaginary specks of dust from his suit. He wonders if Dawson thinks he's in a gangster movie. Dawson raises an eyebrow indicating that he wants some kind of response. The response in Nathan's head says, no way in hell will he do a 'special' job. Instead he says, 'What kind of special job?'

'No idea.' Frank sounds bored now, dismissive. 'Meanwhile there will be some lucrative deals coming your way. I'm sure you've been a little worried that jobs have been thin on the ground?'

'Er, well, I …'

'Okay, must get on.' Dawson stands and walks to the door, opens it and smiles like a lizard as Nathan walks through it. 'Bye for now, Nathan.'

Nathan musters a smile. 'Thanks, Frank. Goodbye.'

As he drives away, the hulk of a house grows smaller through the rear-view mirror … just like his chances of getting out and starting again.

Chapter Nine

'So you're sure that Marta and Jozef will definitely testify against him?' Imogen twists her hair up into a ponytail and then lets it fall through her fingers. I remember she always did this as a kid when she was feeling unsure or anxious.

'Yep, don't worry,' I say, and lead the way into the Fox and Hounds, a little country pub about ten miles from the city. We had agreed that being seen together by any of Ransom's friends wouldn't be a good idea.

From a table in the corner, Imogen scans the lunchtime clientele, her shoulders hunched, eyes missing no one. 'You sure this place is safe?'

'It's safer than your place or mine.' I place two pints of real ale on the table and hand Imogen a menu. 'Look, just try and relax. We've done what we set out to do and against all odds we look like we're going to get a conviction at the trial next week.'

'I hope so, because all this playing the distraught daughter on my visits over these last twelve months is doing my head in.' Imogen takes a long pull on her pint. She wipes the froth from her top lip with the back of her hand and leans her elbows on the table. 'Do you know he actually asked me who I thought the telephone call was from, the one that led him to the house on Westmorland Street.'

I swallow a mouthful of beer and frown. 'Eh? How would you know that?'

'No idea. I think he's going a bit nuts, you know, now that it looks like he's going down.'

'He's not ashamed about saying what went on in the house then, you know, in front of you?'

'Not at all, because he's still protesting his innocence, you see. He says the phone call said that Marta and Jozef were using one of his houses for prostitution – sex slavery. He had no idea about any of it until he got there.'

'Yes, I know his ridiculous story, but I thought he might have come clean to you given that he might get fifteen years for this.'

'No chance! He thinks he's getting off, so no confession.' Imogen's expression grows pensive and she bites her bottom lip. 'I just hope to God he doesn't.'

'Doesn't what. Get off?' I click my tongue against the roof of my mouth and look at the menu. 'No way.'

'That's what you thought the last few times you got close to him. Why is this time any different?' Imogen picks up a beer mat and starts to shred it.

All the self-assurance and determination I've admired in my old friend over the last year seems to have gone. Why is Immi so worried? 'Hey, come on.' I take the beer mat from her cold fingers and pat Imogen's hand. 'This time it's different because we have so much on him. At last we have the phone company's records and incriminating text messages from him to Jozef and Marta, the next-door neighbour has seen him there on numerous occasions and is willing to testify that he overhead them discussing the girls, he was stupid enough to pay Marta and Jozef by cheque once, and he ran away when we went to the house, had to be dragged back by our officers. Also willing to testify is the wonderful Greg Holsworthy, who you managed to find, who started all this off in the first place.' My wide smile makes no impact. There's no return smile. Not even a little one. It's as if Immi hasn't heard a word.

She sighs and shakes her head. 'But he says the cheque was just a gift to them. He felt sorry for them a few years back when he found them homeless and let them live in his house until they got on their feet.' Imogen sighs again and takes back the beer mat.

What's wrong with her? This defeatist talk is beginning to get on my nerves. Ransom's whole bloody story is a sham. God knows how his defence lawyer keeps a straight face. I muster a calm voice from somewhere. 'But given your father's track record, have you ever heard anything so bloody ridiculous? Besides, those two are going to testify against him to save themselves serving a similar sentence. Haven't you been listening?'

Immi's voice holds a tremor. 'Yes, but he has money for the best lawyers. I just feel there's a chance he'll get away with it …'

I can see that she's close to tears but pretend not to notice. 'Nonsense, he's going down,' I say to the menu. 'Right, I'm having the steak 'n' ale pie and chips. How about you?'

Immi's face breaks into a welcome smile. 'How the hell do you stay so slim given the amount of bad food you eat?'

'I don't eat lots of bad food.' My mind presents ready meals and takeaways and I give her a sheepish grin. 'Okay, you have a point. As for staying slim, must be in my genes.' I wish I had her curvy figure. I've always felt like a guy next to her feminine shape. I grab the menu and hit her on the head with it. 'So what will you have?'

She puts her tongue out. 'The grilled chicken breast and salad. Shame I don't have your genes.'

The pie was delicious and for the last half an hour our conversation has managed to steer clear of Kenny Ransom. Immi has been telling me all about a new doctor, Jonathan, at work and how much she likes him. I've been teasing her about him, suggesting that she likes him in *that* way. She's hotly denies it but her pink cheeks tell me otherwise. Though we've had a nice lunch, I realise I have some work to do when I get home, mention it to Immi, and then she surprises me with a breath-taking change of mood and conversation.

'Why the hell did you ignore me and go to the arrest?'

'Eh?'

'Never mind, "eh?". I told you to stay away from that house when I tipped you off that my father would be there around nine. Said you'd be a red rag to his bull, but you went anyway. Why?'

'I just—'

'Wanted to play the hero, yes. Typical.' Immi turns down the corners of her mouth, her kind blue eyes now chips of ice.

'What's brought this on?' I sit back in my seat, fold my arms.

Her brittle laugh puts my teeth on edge. She points at me. 'Look at your body language. On the defensive because you know I'm right.'

I frown. Perhaps she is, but so what. 'Okay, I did want to be in on it. I've been after him for the past few years and I wanted to let him see that I'd not given up.'

'And you think he'll leave it at that if he's sent down?'

'Can't see as he has a choice.'

'Really? Well I do. He told me the other day that he won't rest until he finds the spiteful shit that stitched him up.' Immi pushes her plate away and mirrors my pose.

'But he thinks it was a guy, right?'

'Yes, he would never suspect a woman …' Immi whispers her last few words: 'Least of all, me.'

'So what are you getting at?'

'I'm getting at the fact that if he told me someone will pay if he goes down, and he's no closer to finding out who the "spiteful shit" was, my guess is it's you who'll pay. He knows who you are, hates the fact that we were neighbours, that we were friends. He sees your joining the force as a betrayal.'

'What? He said that?'

'No not in so many words, but kind of.'

'Come on, Immi. You're just rattled because of everything that's happened. In the end he's still your father.'

I receive a sad smile. Then she tosses her hair and snaps, 'Must be nice to have a knight in shining armour for a dad, eh? What does he think of your big coup?'

Outside the window spring is doing its best to get noticed. Around a paddock of six picnic benches, crocus and daffodils thrust against hedges and camellia buds swollen with new life sway from delicate branches. Bright, cheerful, sunny new life. My dad loved this time of year and so do I. Though now it's tinged with sadness because he's no longer here to see it. Immi is looking at me, a puzzled look on her face. She's waiting for my answer. There's no best time to give it, but I should get it over with. I clear my throat and look back at the daffodils. 'My dad … my dad is no longer with us.'

Her brows form a deeper furrow. 'Eh? What do you mean? He's left the police?'

I pick up my pint glass, drain the froth. I'd kill for another but I'm driving. 'No. I mean he died.'

'Died?' Immi unfolds her arms, ruffles her hair. 'But he can't have. You said he was proud of you when I asked. You never said he was dead.'

'He was proud of me. He died, well was killed, actually, the week after I made DI. I didn't want to tell you at the time you asked. Just didn't seem right.'

I watch her hand take mine across the table but daren't look at her face. 'Oh my God, Bryony. I'm so sorry, love. What happened?'

'He was shot while on duty.' My throat's blocked by what feels like something the size of an orange. I withdraw my hand and take a moment. 'Can we not go over it just now …'

'Of course. So sorry for bringing it up.' Immi pats my hand.

'Don't be daft, you weren't to know.'

'How's your mum?'

'She's getting there. She moved back to Cornwall about a year ago. She's helping my Aunty Jenny run a surf school in Newquay.'

'Shut up, she's not! But that's awesome.'

I look at her wide smile and mine copies it. 'It is awesome, yeah. Mum's fifty-three and fitter than me, I think. Jenny is eight years younger. They make quite a good living and everything is so relaxed down there.'

'Gilly is Cornish, isn't she? I seem to remember that from when we were kids.'

'Yeah, Mum's Cornish. She met Dad when he went there on holiday – he was from here. They fell in love and eventually they married and moved here. She always used to say it was a good job she loved him so much, because she'd be back to her beloved Kernow in a flash if she didn't. Thirty-odd years in Sheffield and she never settled.'

Immi is silent for a minute and then says, 'I wish it was my dad that was dead and not yours. Life isn't fair sometimes, is it?'

The pain in her eyes is almost too much to bear. 'No. No, it isn't, but don't wish him dead. If he did die, you would never forgive yourself.'

'Wanna bet?' she says, standing up and shrugging on her jacket. 'Right, time we were off. I'll see you at the trial next week and let's hope he never sees the light of day ever again.'

As I follow her outside, I notice the slight slump of her shoulders that never used to be there. It's as if she's carrying an invisible weight across them. Hate and resentment weigh more than happiness, obviously. This makes me sad, because the carefree girl I once knew has been forever changed because of the sins of her father. Kenny has to go down next week if there's any justice in this world.

Chapter Ten

Immi looks around the visiting room. It's more like a community centre – bright, breezy, and smells of rehabilitation. There would be no rehabilitation or reformation for her father though. He is far too twisted with hatred, and the desire for revenge oozes from every pore like poison. Across the table her father is talking, talking, talking. For the last ten minutes she has watched his mouth moving, his eyes narrowing and opening wide again, his constant gesticulating, but she's switched off, retired to her safe place, the one where her mother lives, where she lived before all this. When she was younger everything seemed so simple and clear. Every day was an adventure. Since she realised what her father was, her days have been edged by darkness. Tinged with grime … soiled.

'Are you listening to anything I'm saying, Imms?'

Imms. He was the only person who called her that and she had always hated it. Before, she let it go, because it was a term of endearment. Now it makes her want to slap him. 'Must admit my thoughts have wandered.' She leaves the 'sorry' out, because she isn't.

He pulls his neck in, folds his arms across his blue grubby T-shirt. She thinks he looks much older and infinitely less powerful in the shirt and jogging bottoms the prisoners here wear. Just another con. A con that still vainly gels his hair, but in the absence of an expensive barber, fails miserably in achieving the desired effect. Without his top-up tan his skin is grey, like his eyes. Eyes that are now boring into hers, indignation almost palpable. 'Your thoughts have wandered? Charmin'.'

'Yes. Can you repeat what you said? I was up to the bit where you said that a few guys in here know *colleagues* of yours, and will be able to do some business if needed.'

'Yes. Why did you say colleagues as if it was a dirty word?'

'Well, they're hardly likely to be businessmen of the year, are they?'

Her father glances at an officer standing impassively not too far away. He leans forward and lowers his voice. 'Keep your voice down. Why did you say that?'

Immi considers laughing in his face, but lowers her voice. 'Dad, it's no surprise that you're a bad guy. Why do you think you're in here?'

He shoves his hands through his hair, which leaves him looking like he's been standing in a strong wind, and hisses, 'I can't believe this. My own daughter believing the shite they said at trial. And the arresting fucking officer, AKA your best mate, looking on all bloody high and mighty.'

This isn't good. Immi takes a deep breath and tries to keep her composure. Her father has mentioned Bryony before, as a friend of the past, but as far as she knew he didn't know they were friends still. 'It was hard to witness such damning evidence, Dad. And what do you mean, best mate?'

'Don't give me that.' Her father leans back in his chair and links his hands behind his head. The movement reveals dark sweat patches under his arms, wafts a pungent aroma in her direction. She holds her breath. 'Facebook friends, Cousin Jake says.'

Shit, Cousin bloody Jake. She forgot that she accepted a friend request from him ages ago. They never communicated because he's a bit dodgy to say the least, but clearly he's in with Dad. He must have looked down her friends list … did Dad ask him to? 'Facebook friends doesn't mean real friends, does it? I just accepted her request and that was it. Can't even remember when it was now.' Imogen is pleased that her voice sounds calmer than she feels.

'That's as maybe. But I want you to get rid of her from Facebook, nasty little bitch. She put the heavies on Jozef and Marta. They would never have said what they did if she hadn't.'

Imogen puts her hand over her mouth to stop herself from saying something she'd regret. What planet is he *actually* on? She had agreed to see him today just out of curiosity, really. It had been a month since the trial and the first time he'd been allowed visitors. She nearly hadn't come, and was ready to just cut him off, but the way he'd been before – swearing someone would pay for his predicament – had made her change her mind. Imogen needed to make sure she stayed close to him so she could find out his intentions. She had to be realistic though and not just hang on his every word as if he were a poor wronged victim. He'd see through that immediately. She was also intrigued to find out what the hell he would come up with in terms of a story.

'But as I said before, Dad, there was lots of firm evidence against you … and why would two homeless people you saved, took off the street, betray you like that?'

Her dad shakes his head in bewilderment and says through gritted teeth, 'That's not the full story. As I just said, that cow leant on them.'

Imogen holds her breath. Is he about to confess? She leans in and lowers her voice to a whisper. 'But, Dad, you said they were selling prostitutes from that house behind your back at the trial, abusing your good faith. Is that not true?'

Imogen watches recognition dawn behind his eyes – he'd said too much. His gaze flicks to the officer again and back. 'I'm not saying that. But what I am stating is that Masters was out to get me as soon as we moved back here three years since, and she's done it.'

Imogen gives him a wistful smile. 'She always was too clever by half when we were kids. Ran rings round me at school.'

'Yeah, well she's going to be sorry that she crossed me, that's for damned sure.' He speaks so softly that Imogen can only just catch his words. The fire in his eyes speaks volumes though, loud and clear. For the first time in her life she is actually scared of him. Of what he is capable of. She has to act quickly. *Think. Think!*

A deep breath. 'Look, Dad. You say you're innocent and I think I believe you. I mean, I want to believe you. Mum did tell me some stuff just before she died about your business that upset me. I know you aren't legit in some areas … but I know in my heart that you could never do anything so terrible as this—'

'Your mother did what?'

'That's why I fell out with you for a bit … she told me about other women too.' Imogen watches the blood drain from his already grey face. She laces her fingers together on the table to stop them trembling.

'Right. I see … now it all makes sense. No wonder you were so cold to me. How could your mum lie to you like that?' He shakes his head and draws his hand down his face.

'For goodness' sake, Dad, give me some credit. I knew my mum, and she was telling the truth. As I said just now, I think you're telling the truth on *this* one. So what we don't want is for you to go causing trouble or worse for you-know-who. Not if we have a chance of getting you out of here at some point.'

'You mean an appeal?' Hope shines in his eyes and a slow smile curls his lips.

'Don't see why not. You've the money to get the best lawyers and I'll do all I can.'

'You've changed your tune since you came in.'

Imogen allows him a little smile. 'Well, as I said, you aren't Snow White, are you? But in the end you're my dad and I love you. You only ever did any of your dodgy stuff for your family, I can see that. Now there's just me left and I want to help you get out of this hell hole.' Imogen watches her father's eyes fill and hopes she won't be struck by lightning on the way home.

'That's my girl.'

The bell sounds for end of visiting and it can't come a moment too soon for Imogen. A quick hug and she's gone. She's managed the visit without falling apart at the seams in front of him. It isn't until she's safely behind the wheel of her car that she starts to tremble from top to toe, feels the stitches of the doting-daughter cloak unpicking. Caged like this, desperate for revenge, he'd shown his true colours. The veil had slipped on more than one occasion between the persona of

Jack-the-Lad dad, and the *real* Kenny Ransom. Before he'd had a chance to put it back, the nasty, drug-dealing, racketeering, sex-trafficking piece of slime she'd only glimpsed in the past had been revealed in all his terrifying glory. How on earth she'd managed to carry on chatting as if nothing had happened, she would never know.

Imogen closes her eyes and leans her head on the steering wheel. Dear God, she hopes her father listened to her in there about leaving Bryony alone, because if he didn't, she doesn't give much for her chances.

Chapter Eleven

I'm a hero at work. We had a big celebration party down the nick the day after Ransom went down, we had another down the pub that weekend, and there's newfound respect in the eyes of my senior officers whenever we meet in corridors, toilets, canteens … but I feel like it's all a sham. On my part, at least. Because what did I actually do? Okay, I persuaded DCI Bradley to allow me the chance and it paid off. But what if it hadn't? If it hadn't, I would be in a whole heap of shit and, instead of respect, I would be seeing disdain.

These past six weeks since it happened have made me reassess who I am, what I want and where I'm going. Before Ransom was sent down, I'd thought of my dad and decided to be a good bent copper, but is that what I want to be for the rest of my working life? There are thousands of Kenny Ransoms slithering through the stinking dark tunnels of the criminal underworld, leaving misery, depravity and death in their slime trails. As I sit at my desk staring out at the city, twiddling a pencil, coffee steam swirling leaving a round condensation circle on the window, I know they are there. They're out there slithering, tunnelling, gorging … and we will never catch them all. We'll catch some, but more will come. They always do.

Anya's face is never far from my thoughts either. She was one of the poor girls that actually had a passport, came here to stay with her lovely Aunt Marta and hoped to study. She had overstayed, of course, but the pride and determination in her eyes had brought tears to mine and I'd had to look for something in my bag. Because police officers don't cry, do they? Anya said she would be back one day to help others like herself. But first she was going to train as a counsellor back in Poland and go round to schools and villages, spreading the word, telling the young women there to watch for the signs, look for the pitfalls, be aware. Anything to stop others falling into the trap she did.

I take a sip of coffee and draw a smiley face in the condensation. We need more brave people like Anya. More people willing to stand up, fight back, despite the fact that they have suffered the most terrible abuse. A thought flits through my mind. Perhaps I could be a counsellor instead? Do something similar – maybe a teacher – actually feel like I'm making a difference every day, instead of making it once in a blue moon when the Ransoms of this world are put away. With this in mind I decide I'll have a chat to Mark as soon as I can.

'Of all the things I expected you to say today, this wasn't one of them.' DCI Mark Bradley has knitted his bushy black eyebrows so closely together that I think he'll never separate them again. He purses his lips and perches on the edge of his desk.

'Yeah, well, I didn't expect to be saying it … just pondering on stuff lately and—'

'You thought you'd just jack in a brilliant career in the force and go off to be a counsellor, or a teacher.' Mark raises his eyebrows – thankfully they do separate – and holds up a wagging finger. 'And *this* just after you put away one of the worst slimeballs in this area. I'm baffled, Bryony, to be honest, quite baffled.' He spreads his hands wide to show how baffled he is and then turns his back on me, looks out the window.

When he puts it like that it does seem a bit drama-queenish. But it has been on my mind for some time … since Dad really. I sit down on a high-backed swivel chair opposite his desk and fold my hands on my lap. What to say next? The truth might be a good idea. 'Sir,' I say to his stiff back. 'It's not just on a whim. Since my dad was killed, everything seems a bit … pointless, I suppose. I mean, a good man like him just snuffed out in the line of duty. Every day all he ever wanted to do was the right thing. Put away scum like Kenny Ransom, but he was the one that got put away. Permanently.'

Mark whips round, an incredulous expression turning his hazel eyes to hard beads. 'Er, reality check for DI Masters – life isn't fucking fair. How old are you? Twelve?'

Nice. That was a punch in the gut. What the hell is wrong with him? I feel my eyes prickle but there is no way I will let him see I'm upset. 'Not sure what you—'

'Yes, you *are* sure what I'm getting at. You are thirty-one years old, one of the youngest to make DI, and why is that? It's because you're a bloody good copper and have worked your arse off to achieve it. You're a chip off the old block. I knew your dad when we were just starting out here. Steve was one of the best coppers I've ever met, but he wasn't one for high ladder climbing like me and you. He was happy with sergeant, each to our own, but he was just as good as either of us. I would have trusted him with my life. Yes, he was out to get the bad guys, but that's what we all do, day in, day out, isn't it? Sometimes it works, sometimes it doesn't. That's the way it is.'

The not letting him see I'm upset bit hasn't worked. When he started saying nice things about my dad I choked back a sob and now I'm dabbing at my eyes. God, I hate showing weakness in front of superiors. I release a slow breath and say, 'Yes, I know that's the way it is, but it shouldn't be, should it?'

Mark sighs and then in a more sympathetic tone says, 'Well, no. No, it shouldn't, but until the government gives us a blank cheque for more officers'–he counts on his fingers–'more bobbies on the beat, more undercover officers, more surveillance equipment, more money in our pay packets, mo—'

'Yes, I get that.' I sigh too. 'But I do wonder if I'd be best placed to help people if I was a counsellor, a teacher or something.'

'Or something?'

I catch the smile in his voice and look up from my tissue. 'What?'

'You haven't made your mind up to leave at all, have you?'

He has that all-knowing look that I hate. It means he's right and I'm wrong. 'We-ll, I—'

'No, you haven't.' Mark has a big grin on his face now. He comes back from the window and sits behind his desk. 'Look. You have some leave due, why don't you go and visit your mum? A bit of sea air and relaxation will do you the world of good. Take a week to get everything here in order and then bugger off for a fortnight. When you get back everything will look different.'

How can he read me so well? It hasn't crossed my mind before that I'd like to go and see Mum, get by the ocean, but right now I realise that is exactly what I need to do. I smile back. 'Okay, it can't hurt anything, can it?'

Chapter Twelve

It's as though the world has stopped, tipped back in time and flicked me off onto the soft yellow sand of Fistral Beach circa 1997. I am ten years old or thereabouts and my heart is so full of adventure and excitement I can hardly breathe. It's that first-day-of-the-holiday feeling, the anticipation of which has kept me buzzing for the last few days. The fallout from this – packing and repacking, and my endless questioning – 'Is it time to go yet? And can we go in the sea as soon as we get there? Can we have ice cream too?' has driven my poor parents to distraction.

The stage is set. The ocean is front and centre being majestic and shouty, the sky, unfeasibly blue, tries to emphasise its horizon in deeper blue, but the sun smudges it, and the sand, soft as sugar beneath my feet, shifts and slides as I jump for joy at the top of the dunes. I know, of course, that it's not really 1997, and I'm thirty-one, not ten, but I have to try so hard not to whoop as I run down the dune and onto the flat hard sand near the water's edge. I love the feeling of being so tiny next to such a vast expanse of water. It's a great leveller. The ocean feels like a living entity, and for me it captures the true spirit of nature. Until this moment, I had no idea how much I've missed it, longed to be right here. Right now.

Very early on in life my mum instilled in me about how the ocean is our friend if we treat it with the utmost respect. We should never underestimate its powers or take it for granted though, because it takes no prisoners. Mum said that over the years growing up here, she had heard of countless deaths at sea. These were often tourists that didn't heed warnings, or just had no idea about how dangerous the ocean could be. I can't remember a time when I couldn't swim, thanks to her. Surfing came later, but feels as natural to me as riding a bike. Or it did … it must be three years since I've taken a board out. That will be remedied very soon, but for now I'm going in.

My heart thumps and an adrenalin rush speeds my feet the last few metres and I'm in. The Atlantic rollers smash into my belly but I power on, laughing as the cold seeps through my wetsuit and up my chest. Another wave towers above my head and I turn to the beach as it slaps across my back and over my head, leaving a shower of salt kisses on my lips as it rushes to the shore. Perhaps it's missed me. Then I'm swimming. Every stroke takes me further from the shore, from my life in Sheffield, from the stench of criminals, from monsters like Kenny Ransom. My body is cleansed, reborn … purified.

I float on my back, weightless. The sky paints a few herringbones and vapour trails across itself for variety, and a tiny puff of cloud competes against freewheeling seagulls for centre stage. The swell under me lifts, and drops, up and down … my body is purified, but my mind still reaches for answers. I hope I'll find them while I'm here. In a very short while I'll go and surprise Mum and Aunty Jenny. Originally, the plan was to ring and say I was coming down, but something stopped me. The child in me, I suppose. Besides, Mum would inevitably ask about work and I didn't want to tell her all the stuff about Ransom over the phone.

A tickle of excitement in my stomach sets me thinking about what their faces will look like when I pop up out of the blue at the surf school. I might even wait until they come down onto the beach with the pupils and join the queue. Yes, that's what I'll do. I float a bit longer allowing my cares to drift away. Looking round a moment later, I see there's quite a big distance between me and the other swimmers and surfers. The tide's going out and I have relaxed for too long. A reminder about the ocean taking no prisoners pops into my mind and I strike out for shore and a reunion with my mum.

They're late. The clock on the café wall says 12.10 and the Atlantic Waves Surf School normally comes down here at twelve o'clock.

Another coffee isn't a good idea because I'm on a natural high as it is. I don't want to be leaping around Mum and Aunty Jenny like an excited puppy. Defeat nudges my hand towards my phone, but I'm not ready to give in yet. Then I see the familiar green and white VW Camper, sun winking off its wing mirrors, draw to a stop in the car park, and out jumps Mum. Her tawny hair is a few shades lighter because of the spring sunshine, her face tanned. I can't quite see the blue of her eyes from this distance, but I can see her smile. Mum's smile is infectious, warm and … it's like coming home, I guess. An unexpected lump forms in my throat and I swallow the last cold dregs of coffee to shift it. Now to surprise her.

A little knot of novice surfers gathers around Mum and Aunty Jenny on the beach fifteen minutes later. Jenny is waving her arms about directing people here and there like a demented scarecrow while the wind tugs her auburn hair into streamers. The surfers line their boards up and practice their surfing moves on the sand. Mum is going round straightening legs, instructing, encouraging, laughing. They don't see me skirting round a family having a picnic behind a red-and-green-striped windbreak a few metres away.

I creep up behind Mum and say, 'I seem to have forgotten my surfboard. Do you have a spare?'

Mum squeals and turns round, tears of happiness already standing. And now I see the blue of her eyes, the sky fades in comparison. 'Oh my God! Bryony, my baby!' She pulls me to her in a vice-like grip and says into my hair, 'How wonderful to see you! I can't tell you how much I missed you!' Then she's showering me with kisses as the surfers look on, bemused. Aunty Jenny barrels into my side with a few crushing hugs of her own and also says, 'What a surprise!' Then I lose my footing and we topple onto the sand laughing hysterically.

'Okay, okay!' I hold my hands in surrender and help Mum and Aunty Jenny up. 'I think these good people might want to get on with their lesson, ladies.'

Mum, still laughing, pulls a band from her wrist and sweeps her hair into a ponytail. 'Yes, I expect they do.' She looks at the surfers. 'I also expect you might have noticed that I'm…'—she waves a hand at Aunty Jenny—'…we, are over the moon to see this person. Meet my daughter, Bryony, down from the frozen north to surprise us.'

I do a cheesy grin and nod at each face. 'Hello, all. Hope you're having fun with these two crazy people?' Most laugh and say they are. One or two look like they think we're wasting their valuable surf lesson, so I say, 'Anyway. Best let you get on.'

Mum dusts sand from her hands and wags a finger in my face. 'Er, not so fast. Now you're here, you might as well help us out this afternoon.'

I hide a smile. This is what I'd hoped she'd say because otherwise I would have been at a bit of a loose end. 'Really? Aw, Mum, do I have to?'

I receive a pretend slap round the head. 'Yes, you do, young lady. Now go over there and help young Kelly with her balance.'

In the shade of the evening garden, the warmth of the spring sunshine leaves my skin. If it were up to me we would be inside eating around the log burner, but no. No, Mum and Jen, as she now informs me she'd like to be called – Aunty Jenny is too babyish now apparently, especially now I'm thirty-one… nice – want a barbecue. A barbecue in mid-April. It's only 6.45 and it's already getting dark. I zip my jacket up and, through a gap in the tree branches at the end of the lawn, glimpse the last pink fingers of sunset stroking the ocean's horizon.

Mum was so lucky to get this house when she moved back here. I remember when she told me that the description in the estate agent's advert was something along the lines of 'a lovely 1930s characterful property with sea glimpses', and I expected a money pit with a view of the sea the size of a postage stamp. A postage stamp that you could only see by hanging upside down out of the bedroom window. Yes, it had needed work but, because it was built on such a huge hill, the view of the sea was quite lovely, cradled in the V of red rooftops winding down to the seafront. When I was little and we came on holiday we used to stay with Grandma and Granddad, and though they lived closer to the sea, there was no view to speak of. I do miss them both. I miss Grandma's cooking too. Thoughts of her home-made pasties make my tummy rumble.

The sausages are almost done, Mum says. She's said this three times but still jabs at them with a long fork as if she expects them to attack her. Jen is sitting in a deckchair sipping a cocktail, her third to my first, I think, and chatting to her husband on the phone. Uncle Graham has opted to stay home and fend for himself. Uncle Graham isn't daft. Why would he want to be freezing his arse off out here? My cousins, Laurie and Jory, are younger than me and both at uni, so he has the house to himself. I bet he has the log burner going and …

'So you don't want this hot dog then?' Mum's smiling and holding a plate out to me, a charcoal smudge on the bridge of her nose. 'You're away with the fairies this evening.'

I snatch the plate and snort. 'It's you that's away with them, faffing about with the sausages for goodness knows how long.' I take a big bite and wish I hadn't.

Mum gives me a knowing look. 'Be careful, they're hot.'

A gulp of cocktail helps and I sit down next to Jen. She asks about work and I say I have been quite successful lately putting away the bad guys. When Mum joins us with a plate of beef burgers and more sausages and asks about the job, I decide it's time to do a bit of showing off.

'Remember Imogen Ransom?' I take a beef burger and help myself to home-made coleslaw.

Mum nods and speaks through a mouthful of hotdog. 'Yes, of course. How could I forget? We lived next door to them for fifteen years.'

'Well, not so long ago she asked to be Facebook friends. I accepted, of course, but then she asked to meet up. I hesitated about that because of her dad.'

'Not surprised – he's a wrong 'un, that one,' Jen says, pointing a sausage at me. 'Only met him a few times when we came up to see you, but that was enough.'

'You were after him a few years back, weren't you?' Mum asks.

'Yes. But he always wriggled out of trouble. Mr. Teflon – nothing stuck.'

'So what did you say to Imogen?' Jen asks, taking a bite from the sausage.

'I agreed to meet up, because we were best friends as you know.' Mum nods. 'But I hoped to avoid talking about her dad.'

'Not easy,' Jen says.

'No. But the thing is, it was her that brought him up. Said that's why she got in touch with me again – to try and help me convict him!' I watch their shocked faces. And then they both talk at once, asking me what happened. 'Well, believe it or not, I did.'

'What, he's in prison?' Mum asks.

'Yup,' I say, a note of pride in my voice, though I add, 'If it hadn't been for Immi he wouldn't be though. She went above and beyond to put her own dad away. He doesn't know she helped of course.'

'Blimey,' Mum says, dabbing at her mouth with a napkin. 'Poor Maggie must be bedside herself.'

'She was his wife, yeah?' Jen asks. 'Nice woman, seemed a bit downtrodden though by Mr. Nasty.'

I sigh. 'Yes, but Maggie died not too long ago. Cancer.'

'Oh no!' Mum says and her eyes fill. 'She was only my age, perhaps two years older … how bloody awful.' She wipes her eyes but more tears come.

I didn't know Mum would be so upset. 'Sorry, Mum, I didn't realise you were close to her. I wouldn't have told you so bluntly.'

Mum shakes her head. 'No, we weren't that close really. We got on, but we weren't in and out of each other's houses every five minutes … I just feel so sorry that she's dead.'

'Yes, me too. She was always nice to me as a child. He was a real bastard to her, Immi said. That's one of the reasons she wanted him put away. He had other women, throughout the whole marriage apparently.'

'Poor cow,' Jen says and hands Mum another tissue and a glass. 'Hey, come on, Gilly, have a sip of your cocktail – cheer you up.'

Mum takes a sip, gives her sister a grateful smile. 'Thanks, Jen. Why are some men so vile and get to live while others ...' Her voice trails off and neither Jen nor I need to ask what she was going to say next. Immi had said similar recently. Dad was right there with us in all our thoughts.

I say into the silence, 'At least he's lost his liberty and when he's out he'll be ... well, in his early seventies. Serves him right. He's been drug dealing, handling stolen goods, loan sharking, you name it. But the worst thing he did was what we got him on. Sex trafficking young girls – keeping them as sex slaves.'

Jen says a few choice words and Mum's jaw drops. Then she drains her second cocktail in one. 'I hope he rots in there, fucking bastard,' she says quietly.

The vehemence in her words surprises me a bit, but it's a vile thing to be told and also Mum isn't much of a drinker; Jen does enough for both of them. I suggest we go in, get warm, and have a nice cup of coffee. I wish I'd been a bit more tactful instead of blurting it all out like that. Mum knew Maggie quite well and to hear that her old next-door neighbour was dead, and her husband was involved in the worst crimes you can think of, must have been a huge shock.

Broaching the subject of me having a change in career doesn't seem appropriate at the moment. We're gathered round the log burner with hot chocolate, talking about surfing and how brilliant I was helping out today. My work life seems as far away now as the moon outside chasing the scudding clouds across the dark sky. And right now, that's just how I like it.

Chapter Thirteen

If Nathan is going to get another life he needs to find his mum somewhere to live first. Perhaps he can get her a rented flat in Devon near his sister. He would have peace of mind then, and the sea air might do her good. Then if Kenny tried to threaten him with evicting her, or worse if he didn't do his bidding, he'd find that ship had sailed. His brothers will just have to look out for themselves now. They have jobs, so why not? It's time Nathan stopped playing dad and started looking out for himself, before it's too late.

It might already be too late. The jobs he's been getting these past few months since Ransom's been in prison would mean he'd join him immediately, if he was caught, no question. Drug smuggling operations have big financial payoffs – the risks are high – but the misery he's causing to countless addicts by being involved is too much for Nathan to take. He'd been involved in supplying Class B stuff before, which was bad enough, but this is Class A and far too dangerous in every way.

Frank Dawson has been getting all pally recently – saying that Nathan's reliable and well organised. He's even hinted that there might be a promotion in the next few years if he continues to prove himself. Dawson said that with Ransom in jail and himself not getting any younger it will soon fall to people like Nathan to take more of a hand in running things. Dawson has a mind to retire fairly soon to somewhere hot, enjoy the fruits of his labours. Nice for some. Nathan's gone along with it, of course. He has to keep them unsuspecting.

It's rare for him to have an afternoon off, but today is the day. Nathan changes into his running gear and heads out into the spring sunshine. How long has it been since his last run? Too long. After the hours he puts in he's too tired to have time for himself normally, so this afternoon is all the sweeter. Freshly mown grass, nodding daffodils, and an endorphin release as he runs lifts his mood further. With each footfall, his escape feels more possible and, as he powers down a hill, his feet have wings. Then his phone vibrates in his pocket. *Shit. Not now.* He ignores it and clears his mind of possible callers. Five minutes later it vibrates again, so Nathan sits on a bench and swipes the screen. Dawson. Marvellous.

'Nate, my boy.' Dawson has taken to calling him Nate as if they are big buddies. The only people who shorten his name are his immediate family, and Dawson is far from that. 'Can you swing by the Ransom Mansion about four? I have something important for you.'

Nathan would rather stick pins in his eyes. It's nearly three already. 'Okay. I'm out running just now but I'll go back, have a quick shower and—'

'See you at four, Nate.'

Jason opens the door. Does he live here now, or what? He's eating a cream bun and there's a dollop of jam and cream on his nose. Nathan would usually point such an embarrassment out to any normal, decent human being, but he keeps this information to himself as Jason chaperones him down the corridor to the 'drawling' room once more. Dawson's sitting by the fire in a white bathrobe and smoking a cigar. On a stool in front of him, an attractive young woman is massaging his feet, toenail clippings – evidence of a recent pedicure – in a neat pile on a towel.

'Ah, Nate, my lad. Take a seat, Sally has just finished, haven't you, doll?'

Doll? Bloody hell, what century is he in? Nathan takes a seat and keeps his thoughts to himself.

'I have, indeed, Mr. Dawson … unless you'd like the essential oil rub?' Sally keeps her hands stroking his feet, flutters her eyelashes. Nathan wonders if that's code for a bit more than a rub of his feet.

'I'd love to, but me and the boy here have a bit of business. Same time next week.' Dawson grabs his wallet from a side table, leans forward and stuffs a couple of fifty-pound notes down the V of her shirt. Once they are alone Dawson says, 'She's bloody good with feet, that one.' A lascivious wink. 'Good in bed too.'

Nathan does his well-practised fixed smile. The girl must be in her early twenties to Dawson's early sixties. Money talks. 'She was certainly an attractive young lady.'

'Want an evening with her, Nate? You certainly deserve a bonus with all the extra work you've taken on lately.'

Is he for real? She's a human being, not a possession. 'You're alright, Frank. I have a girl, we're thinking of making a go of things.' He hopes his cheeks don't betray him.

'You have? You never mention her.' Dawson knits his bushy brows together.

'It's early days, but—'

'What's her name?'

Shit, what was it? Inspiration comes to him via a book spine on the shelf behind Dawson's head. 'Jane.'

'Jane what?'

For God's sake, don't say Eyre. 'Jones.' Nathan cringes inwardly at his lack of imagination.

'Right.' Dawson unknits his brow and stubs his cigar out. 'Well, there's no reason why you can't spend the night with our Sally. What Jane doesn't know won't hurt her.'

'Thanks, but no thanks, Frank.' Nathan shifts in his seat, looks at the fire. Why the hell has Dawson got it lit on such a nice spring day anyway?

'Nothing like a real fire, eh? This room is freezing at the best of times.' Dawson stands, turns his back to the fire and lifts his robe, then briskly rubs his buttocks. Nathan looks out of the window to avoid the sight of Dawson's genitals wobbling in front of him. 'Anyway, I brought you here so Kenny can call in that special job we were on about a while ago.'

Nathan looks up at Dawson; a sour taste floods his mouth and his heart starts to pound. 'Special job?'

Dawson lowers the back of his robe and sits back down. 'Yeah, you know. We talked about Kenny wanting to track down who the grass was – the one who lured him to that house the day he was arrested.'

'And he's found him?'

'Not exactly … he's decided who's going to pay though.'

Nathan's heart rate starts to gallop. *Shit, what exactly does that mean for me?* 'Oh. Who?'

'The tasty looking DI, Bryony Masters – you remember her from court. Used to be friends with his daughter, still acquainted, apparently. They were neighbours years back – imagine that, your kid's childhood friend banging you up?'

Is he fucking mad? He wants to get revenge on a police officer? Correction – Ransom wants Nathan to get revenge for him. His mind casts about for an anchor, anything to stop his head spinning. 'Um, yeah, that must be tough for Kenny. And I remember her from court? I wasn't in court.'

'Oh no, that's right. Well, I have a photo of her, details of where she lives, where she eats. Loads for you to be going on with. Hang on, I'll send Jason for it.' Dawson speaks into his phone. 'Yes, in the bureau in the dining room. Yes, Jason. Red folder …'

Dawson's droning voice takes on a dreamlike quality as a scream builds in Nathan's head. What the fuck does Ransom expect him to do? The terrifying answer is waiting in the darkest part of his psyche like a murderer in an old Victorian London alleyway. Nathan realises that Dawson has finished speaking and is staring at him. 'Why does Mr. Ransom think that this Masters has anything to do with it?'

'Because she's been after him for a few years. He reckons she got someone to set him up and then arrived at the kill like some, now what were Kenny's words?' Dawson folds his arms over his paunch and looks up to the left. 'Ah yes. Like some conquering emperor.'

Silence settles between them – almost a physical barrier – and Nathan struggles to send his words over it. 'But surely Mr. Ransom doesn't want me to …' No. The words wouldn't come.

'Oh, that's exactly what he does want. To make sure there's no misunderstanding, Nate, Kenny wants you to kill her, yes,' Dawson says, inspecting his fingernails.

Jason comes in with a red file and Nathan wants to pinch himself to make sure he's not in some God-awful nightmare. In a minute, Jason will turn into a kangaroo and hop out of the patio doors, the whole scene will fold in on itself and Nathan will wake up safe and sound in bed.

Dawson takes the file and flicks through, all the while talking, talking. Nathan watches his mouth move but nothing's going in. He catches the word 'appeal'.

'Sorry, what appeal?' he manages.

A sigh from Dawson. 'Please keep up, lad. Kenny's daughter Imogen told him to keep his powder dry. Not to rock the boat out here from inside, because she was sure they'd get an appeal. Try to get the best lawyer in the world to get him out early, all that bullshit yadda, yadda.'

'Bullshit?'

'Yes, course it was.' Dawson looks at him as if he's Jason. 'It was a fairy story to try and keep Kenny from doing anything to her old mate. Everyone knows there's no way in hell he's getting out early.'

'And Mr. Ransom told his daughter that?'

'Dear me, you're not with it today, are you? No, of course not. Kenny's real cut up about her to be honest. He knows she still sees Masters socially from time to time, even though that copper banged him up. He doesn't trust Imogen any further than he can throw her.' Dawson hands him the file.

Nathan takes it and on the first page is a large photo – a head shot. He looks into the eyes of a very attractive woman, late twenties at a guess, then he takes in the hair – dark, short, feathering around her striking features – high cheekbones, square-ish jaw, aquiline nose, full mouth, in this photo slightly pursed, and then his gaze is drawn back to the eyes. The eyes are remarkable. Hazel, almost amber, shot through with green – they draw him in. He turns the page and there are more images of her: walking down the street, in cafés, one in a pub with Imogen. He remembers Imogen from the time she was in the passenger seat of her dad's car last year some time. Attractive, but not in the same way as Bryony. Nathan turns back to the first photo again and then snaps the file shut.

'So that should be enough for you to go on. Kenny's going to speak to you in an hour to get your word that you'll fulfil his wishes.'

Nathan rubs his eyes and once more wishes this was a dream. This can't be happening. Can. Not. He clears his throat. 'What? They listen in on calls inside, you know.'

'He has his own phone.'

'They allow mobiles in prison now?'

'Sometimes I do wonder about you. No, of course not, but Kenny's still a powerful man in there. Commands respect. He can do favours for his friends and they do favours for him. It wasn't hard to smuggle a mobile. One of his friends knew a man who did this work.' Dawson taps the file. 'Supplied these photos. Kenny has a long reach and it will serve you well to remember that.'

The ice in Dawson's voice sets Nathan's stomach churning and in his mind the same thought repeats in various permutations. He is expected to kill someone. Actually kill a person. He could never kill anyone. It isn't in him to kill someone. He is expected to kill DI Bryony Masters. He would never do it. He can't. Has no wish to. Then he hears himself say, 'I can't kill her, Frank. I've never killed anyone in my life—'

'Hmm ... I expected as much.' Dawson's voice is sympathetic, warmer. 'It's not a nice thought, lad, but it has to be done. If you're to be trusted, move up the ladder so to speak, then you'll—'

'No, I can't.' Nathan shakes his head. 'Won't.'

Dawson narrows his eyes and drops all pretence of sympathy. 'You will, Nathan.' He jabs a pudgy finger through the air at

Nathan's face. 'When you've had a chat with Kenny, you will. Now fuck off before I get really angry.'

Nathan looks through the windscreen at a family of ducks on the pond. He's pulled into the park, one he used to come to as a kid with his own family many years ago. They had such fun here. Picnics, bike rides … happy days. The shrieks of kids having fun in the playground come through the open window right now, and he takes deep breaths of the fresh air to try to calm his thoughts. His thoughts refuse to be calmed, though, because his mobile phone sits on his knee like an unexploded bomb. It rings.

'Nathan, how are you?'

Ransom's voice on the line, though expected, chills his marrow. Nathan swallows, clears his throat. 'I'm not too bad, Mr. Ransom. What about you?'

A humourless chuckle. 'As you'd imagine, banged up in here. But let's get to business. Frank's filled you in, I expect, so I'd like to hear what you have to say.'

'The thing is … I've never, you know …'

'Most people haven't, but it has to be done.'

'But it's not in me.'

'It's in all of us if the stakes are high enough.'

'Stakes?'

'Yes. You want to prove yourself to me, don't you? Show me that I can trust you with running things eventually?'

'Er, yes, but I couldn't do what you're asking to get up the ladder.'

'Well, that's very disappointing, Nathan. Very disappointing.' Ransom's tone makes the bile rise in Nathan's throat. 'I might have to change my approach then. If you don't do it I'll shop you, and you'll be in Wakefield with me pretty sharpish. Once you're in here we won't be friends. Do I make myself clear?'

'But—'

'Yes, I have photos of you. Lots of 'em. You handing over Class As, you receiving Class As, you chatting to known drug smugglers … need I go on?'

Realisation punches him between the eyes and his heart plummets. 'So that's why you got me all those new jobs.'

'Bingo. I've always wanted to say that, you know, *bingo*, like they say on those old films.' Ransom laughs.

Nathan can't see the funny side. Ransom is such a sneaky callous bastard, and suddenly he can't keep his temper any longer. 'Well, do your worst. I'm not doing what you ask, Kenny, and that's final.' As he says these words he's already planning to run. Get his mother and run. God knows where – anywhere away from here.

'Ah … you are so predictable. Predictable and gutless, just like your dad.'

'Leave my fucking father out of this! You left him to—'

'So I decided to send your mum on a little holiday until the job's done.'

It takes a few seconds for Nathan to process Ransom's words. A crawling sensation grows in the core of him and spreads to his chest. 'You leave her the FUCK alone!'

'Mind your language and your tone, Nathan, when you're addressing me, or your mum will find that her little holiday becomes very unpleasant. And for your information, she's already gone. Why don't you pop round and see? I'll call you back.'

The disconnect tone fills Nathan's ears and he shoves his fist in his mouth to stifle a scream. Then he guns the engine and flies to his mum's house. The door is unlocked, but then she never bothers to lock it, no matter how many times he and his brothers tell her she must. Nathan's encouraged by the sound of *Pointless* coming from the TV as he hurries along the hallway, but after flinging open the living room door he sees an empty chair in front of it. No. No. NO!

'Mum! MUM,' he yells, and takes the stairs three at a time.

She's not in the bathroom or the bedrooms. She's not in the kitchen or the garden. He's too late. Too late! Instead of thinking up a plan to send her to Devon, he should have just done it there and then. Always thinking, never doing. Damn it! He kicks a stone along the garden path; it thumps into the fence.

Then his phone rings inside on the hall table.

'So I expect you've changed your mind?' Ransom fails to hide a self-satisfied chuckle.

Fury clamps Nathan's hand so hard around the phone he feels the plastic give. 'If you've hurt her—'

'You'll what? Go to the police? Good luck with that one.'

Nathan slumps down in his mum's chair. He's beaten and Ransom knows it. 'Please don't hurt her.'

'Oh, for fuck's sake, what do you take me for? I've known Lou for years, she's sick. I'm holding her to ransom until the job's done. Ransom's ransom. Good, eh?' Ransom sighs when Nathan doesn't respond. 'Please yourself. Anyway, I'll only hurt her if you refuse. Can't keep her on holiday forever, can I?'

Despair rolls out in front of Nathan like a black carpet. 'Okay. You win.'

'I always do. You have a month as it's your first time. And that's me being generous. Dawson has what you need. Don't fail me, Nathan.'

The disconnect tone again. He wishes he could disconnect from this whole fucking nightmare. Nathan puts his head in his hands and tries to think of a way out. He thinks of his mum in some strange place, hopefully somewhere with a TV. He can't bear to picture her locked in a dark room – or worse. An hour later, he has no answers. He's only got one option.

Chapter Fourteen

'Yes. I'm totally serious!' Mum hands me a cup of coffee and pulls her chair up to the wooden table on her patio.

'What, just chuck in my job when it's going so well and move here, work at the surf school?'

'Yep.' Mum fixes me with her piercing blue eyes and says, 'And you can cut the crap with me. I know you're not that happy working there anymore.'

'Eh?' How the hell does she know? Is she a witch?

'Look, I'm your mum. When you were telling me all that stuff about catching that slimeball Ransom you were proud, but later, when I asked you about crime rates and stuff, you were less than enthusiastic. You can't put shit bags away every day of the week, can you? The rest of the time it's one disappointment after the other.' She holds a finger up to my protest. 'Your dad told me what it was like and I doubt it's got a lot better in just a few years.'

Yep. She's a witch. No doubt about that at all. 'You're right. It does get disheartening from time to time. I joined the force to make a difference and I do … but mostly I don't. I get so sick of seeing what disasters people like Ransom leave in their wake. Sometimes I have to have a hot shower to get the stink of work off me when I get in.' I take a sip of coffee. Mum's watching me intently and so I blurt, 'To be honest, I have been thinking about making a change – I just can't decide what would suit me.'

Mum's face breaks into a grin. 'Oh, I am pleased. What ideas have you had so far?'

'Um … teaching or counselling.'

'Excellent! Either of those would be so much better for you. But I can see you teaching! And in the meantime you could teach surfing with me and Jen. If you were on board we could take on more students and be able to pay you.'

'I'm a bit puzzled as to why you're so keen for me to leave. It's a secure job. My pension will be a hard one to leave behind ...' I twist my mouth to the side and give her a look. 'And you used to say how proud you were of me making DI.'

Her hands take mine across the table. 'Of course I'm proud of you, love. But since your dad ... I worry every day that you might end up the same way. You deal with dangerous characters and ... anyway, I don't want to go on. I'm just thrilled that you might at least consider leaving. I saw how happy you were the other day when you were with those youngsters in the surf. I think this is just what you need – for a while at least.'

When she puts it like that it all seems so simple, and perhaps it is. I love being in Newquay and close to the ocean. Love being with Mum too. Will it be enough though? Right now my life is a suitcase bursting at the seams with stuff. If I leave my job it might look a bit empty – socks, toiletry bag and a few good intentions scattered about. Mum looks so eager I have to give her something though. 'Look, I promise I'll give it some thought, okay?'

Two days later I feel like I need another suitcase. I've hardly had time to breathe; what with the surfing, the cooking and shopping – Mum insists we eat properly – and the just being glad to be alive time, I'm exhausted. Exhausted in a good way, though. The despair and frustration that normally threads through me after a hard day at the station is absent.

Cooking, it turns out, is something I enjoy. Yes, Mum taught me the basics years ago before I left for university, but time was short there, and even shorter when I started work. If I'm brutally honest, though, I couldn't be bothered. So it's a bit of a surprise that I'm not half bad at it. My fish pie is going to be legendary, according to Jen and Graham. They had second helpings and this gave me a ridiculous sense of pride. Perhaps I'm actually becoming a proper responsible grown-up at last.

Mum says I've inherited her cooking gene as well as her good looks. I always thought I took after Dad more; I have his jaw – I certainly look a bit masculine. Tall, slim, no real boobs to speak of. I mentioned to Mum that when Immi and I were growing up I was insanely jealous of her curvy figure and blonde hair. Mum says I'm talking nonsense. Mums have to say things like that, though, don't they?

Lasagne is on the menu tonight and I'm wondering whether to add a third clove of garlic to the pan when my phone rings. 'Hi, Immi, how's tricks?' I say, wedging the phone under my cheek while slicing a clove.

'You sound up. Having fun?'

That's an odd response to my question. 'I'm having lots of fun. And guess what I'm doing right this minute.'

'Surfing?'

'Ha, yes, very funny. No. Cooking!'

'You? Cooking? My God, are you feeling okay?'

Though she's trying her best, I know something's wrong. 'I'm feeling really good as it goes, Immi. Anyway, I asked how you are.'

'Oh, you know … same old.'

'No. Tell me.' I turn the gas off, pour a glass of red and wander out onto the patio.

The sun is thinking about setting over the ocean, there's a fresh salt breeze mingling with the scent of early roses on the arbour, and next door's tabby cat runs towards me along the adjoining wall and rubs its head on my arm. I wish Immi could be here right now, see this view, she sounds so down. She's banging on about work and the fact that this new doctor is expecting too much of her, but I get the feeling that's not what's really bothering her.

'Have you nodded off?' she asks.

'Sorry, no, just thinking.' I rub the cat's velvet head and it rewards me with a traction engine purr. 'Is there something else that's upsetting you, other than work?'

After a pause that lasts a bit too long she says, 'Funny you should ask, but Dad's draining me. When I visit, I have to pretend

I'm all cheerful and say I'm hopeful for an appeal and stuff when all I want to do is tell him to rot.'

I had no idea she was still visiting. 'Why? I mean, why visit if you don't want to? And an appeal? There's no way he'd get one.'

'I know that. Look, I'm due for a week off. Can I come and see you for a few days, chat through some stuff?' A moment's hesitation while I think about Mum's response has Immi backtracking. 'Sorry, shouldn't have asked. I know you're spending time with your mum—'

'Don't be daft, of course you can come. I was just wondering if I should ask Mum first, but it will be cool. We'd love to see you!'

'Only if you're sure. I don't want to be a bother.'

'You're always a bother, but I just put up with you for old times' sake.'

She calls me a name and we chatter on for a while longer and make arrangements for her stay. Though she sounds more cheerful at the end of the call than she did at the beginning, a few hours later I can't shake the feeling that the 'stuff' she wants to chat through is not going to be easy listening.

Chapter Fifteen

The gun is wrapped in a cloth inside a bag, inside a box, but Nathan still feels the cool imprint of it, the weight of it in his palm. The weight of what it can do, what he's supposed to do, is heavy in his mind too. For what seems like the millionth time, he wonders if he can actually go through with it, and sits up in bed, a cold sweat on his clammy forehead. The gun waits in the drawer across the room, silent, lethal, terrifying. Last week when Dawson gave it to him he'd said if Nathan wanted to choose another method then that was fine, but he must make sure it was quick and clean. The gun was a sure-fire way; he'd laughed at his 'joke' of achieving the 'target' at a greater distance.

There's a bit of a blip in the plan though. In the last week the target seems to have disappeared. Ransom's sources couldn't find her in the usual haunts and she doesn't seem to be at work either. Nathan is to sit tight until she's been located and then work up a careful plan of action. Ransom had impressed upon him that there would be no fuck-ups, no traces, and certainly no leads back to them. If by some slim chance Nathan was caught he would keep his mouth zipped. If he didn't, his mother wouldn't come home and Nathan's spell in prison would be a short one … and he wouldn't be out early for good behaviour.

In the kitchen he cracks eggs into a pan and sticks bread in a toaster. Why he's doing that he has no idea; his appetite has deserted him since all this began. Autopilot, he guesses. Something to do with his hands, any activity to scrape off the gun's imprint. Inside, all reason seems to have deserted him too. Desertion of appetite, desertion of reason, desertion of family. Nathan's brothers and sister have been chewing his ear off at every given opportunity, blaming him for the kidnap of their mother. And why wouldn't they? It was his fault, after all. They have all conveniently forgotten that he's the one who's kept the Walker family ship afloat, his dirty money that's looked after Mum while they all went off and had a life.

The eggs have the texture of rubber and there's too much butter on the toast, but it's energy, fuel for his body. Nathan's burned a lot of energy over the last few days as he pounded the parks and streets. A new jogging regime designed to tire him out body and mind, exhaust his capacity for worry, anxiety about the coming task he's promised to do. Nothing works though. Even now, his thoughts latch on to what his youngest brother Jack said the other day: 'We've agreed we won't go to the police, not to save your neck, but because we know we'd never see Mum again. How could you let this happen? And what have you agreed to do?'

Nathan's gut had rolled at the look of utter contempt in Jack's eyes. Jack, who'd always looked up to him, respected the fact that he'd taken up the slack after Dad was killed. There was no way he could ever admit to him what he'd agreed to do because if he did, for one, it would become all too real, and for two, his family would never forgive him. Nathan pushes his plate away, wishes he'd not stopped smoking five years ago. Forgiveness? Nathan would never forgive himself anyway. In fact the future is about as bleak as it could get.

The other day he'd realised that he was completely alone now his family had all but abandoned him. The only friends were acquaintances really, criminals like him. Before he'd left college, he'd had real friends, decent people. But as soon as he'd come to work for Kenny he'd dropped them. They wouldn't want to know him once they knew how he made his living. If only he'd acted quicker with Mum, got her out of that house and away. His dream about starting afresh would never have been easy, but now it's impossible. Wallowing in self-pity isn't him, or didn't used to be, but right now his life seems pretty full up with 'if onlys' and not a lot else.

Two hours later he's sitting on a bench at the top of a huge hill in a park he can't even remember the name of. He's run nearly ten miles according to his Fitbit, but still he can't outrun the person he's about to become. The bench has a brass plaque telling the world that Aggie – loving wife, mum and grandma – used to sit here most days and watch the world go by. Anyone who sits here is invited to share her view and let the peace and beauty of their surroundings lift their spirits. Down the hill and across the wide sweep of a valley, Nathan looks at spring strutting her stuff, painting over winter with fresh greens, yellows and white, but inside he's all out of peace. 'Sorry, Aggie,' he mutters and stands to stretch. As he does, his phone falls out of his pocket and picking it up he finds there's a message from Dawson.

Where the fuck are you? Call me.

Nathan realises the phone's somehow been switched to mute with no vibrate and there are three missed calls from Dawson too. Shit, this must be pretty important to call on a Sunday. Dawson normally spends the afternoon having a 'spa treatment' – at least that's what he tells his wife. What if it's news about …? This thought prods his heart rate up the scale. Half of him hopes it isn't *the* news, but the other half of him hopes it is. Best to get it over with. Nathan's feet take him in a tight circle and then he finds he's sitting back on the bench and staring out at Aggie's view. He presses his spine against the brass plaque hoping that some goodness from her will somehow magically transfer to him. But no blinding flash of inspiration or a lightning bolt is on offer, so he scrolls down the contacts and calls Dawson.

'Oh, nice of you to get in touch. I've been trying to reach you for bloody ages!'

'Yes, sorry, Frank. I've been out running and—'

'Never mind all that shite. We've an idea where Masters might be. Inside information tells us she's on annual leave. Where is a guess, but Kenny's girl phoned him to say she's off on a little holiday to Newquay. Surfing of all things. So we thought you'd better get down there and see if her bestie is with her.'

Wait a minute. They want him to go all the way to Cornwall just in case Masters is there? Is this all they have? Nathan's head feels like it's floating above the park. The whole thing is surreal. 'Ri-ght ...'

'What the fuck is that supposed to mean?'

Nathan sighs down the phone. 'It'd just be nice if we had more of a definite—'

'Yes, yes it would. It would be *nice* if Masters phoned us and said, "Hi, you lot, I'm down in Newquay, here's the address – so you can just get Nathan to pop down and kill me".'

Nathan watches his fingers grip the old gnarled arm of the bench. He increases the pressure until he can see the whites of his knuckles under the skin. 'Okay, I was just thinking it was a bit of a long shot, that's all. The daughter and Masters don't spend that much time together, do they?'

'More than Kenny would like. Besides, he's got a hunch and when he gets a hunch he's usually right. He's known Masters since she was a kid, don't forget – the family too. He remembers that her mother was Cornish. She moved here years back when she married a Sheffield man. He was a copper too. Anyway, I have stuff to do. Call me when you get to Cornwall.'

Nathan shoves his phone in his pocket and stands. His legs feel like he's borrowed them from a much older man – they're stiff, reluctant to move. Walking eases the ache, but with each step he's further away from the man he used to be and towards a monster. In a few days he'll be in Cornwall, one of the most beautiful counties in Britain. Once, a good few years ago, he'd been on holiday there with some of his mates on a stag do. Nathan had received a lot of ribbing because he'd been more interested in swimming and walking than propping up the bar. The scenery and wild coastline had left a lasting impression on him, but now, if Bryony Masters is there, he'll remember it for a very different reason.

Chapter Sixteen

Mum was a little surprised when I said I'd invited Immi here the other day, but she said it was fine and that she was looking forward to seeing her again. I'm in the spare room now, making sure it looks welcoming, with a new throw I bought at the market over the old threadbare armchair and a few scatter cushions on the bed. Perhaps flowers? No, that would be going over the top. I smooth the curtains at the window and look out over the garden towards the glimpse of blue through the trees.

It's crazy, but I keep seeing Immi as a teenager in my head. In the image, she looks unsure, vulnerable, but still always more confident than I was back then. It was the boy thing that divided us. Immi had boys falling over themselves to get next to her; I had the opposite. As a woman I can look back and feel sad that we let boys define who we were, how we thought of ourselves, but we weren't alone. Thinking about it, it still goes on to a lesser extent amongst my female friends now. Men, partners, sometimes husbands have an extraordinary dominance in the way women perceive themselves. Maybe that's why I haven't settled to anything long term. I'm a control freak and anyone else having a say in what I wear, what I do, makes me come out in a rash.

The old armchair feels quite comfy with the new throw on it and I settle back and close my eyes. Mum is so sentimental. This armchair used to be in my old room when I was a kid but she can't bear to chuck it. Same goes for the old rabbit with one ear on the chest of drawers. Funny how inanimate objects hold so many memories … little time capsules dotted here and there in our present tying us irrevocably to our past.

Thoughts lazily flit in and out as I think about my past, present and future. Imogen might look vulnerable in my mind's eye because she's lost her mum and her dad … well … we all know about him. Perhaps I'm playing the mother hen, making her room feel welcoming; worrying about how to make her happy while she's here. Looking after people is my job, but on a personal level it's alien to me. As an only child I never had to worry about sharing my toys, competing for affection from parents and, largely because of my control freakery, I haven't had to share my life with anyone either.

There was David, though. I came close with him. Because he was a copper like me we didn't have to explain how we felt after a long day. He was easy going, funny, and we had a great year together … until he started to talk about moving in together; then my defences came up, shut him out. Bam. Part of me wonders if there's something lacking in me, that I build a fortress, because I did regret it, especially when I saw him dating another officer; they got married recently too. My regret wasn't enough for me to try and change it back before it was too late, though. Mum says it's because the right one hasn't come along. I didn't mention that I thought that was a load of baloney.

At the station, Mum parks the car while I hurry along the platform to meet Immi. There's a fizz of excitement in my tummy and I'm reminded of the sleepovers we had as kids. The illicit cigarettes we had in her room at night, blowing smoke out of the window, and then sipping the vodka she'd smuggled up in a little water bottle. We won't have to do that now, especially not the smoking, but the feeling of anticipation of being silly and hanging out is still the same.

The train pulls in and I see her get off straight away – there are only a few other passengers. She's wearing long beige shorts, a green hoodie and flip-flops. A smile curls my lips. I know it's spring, but there *is* a nip in the air. The breeze is intent on whipping her blonde wavy hair across her eyes, but she sees me, grins, and sets off at a jog towards me, dragging her little suitcase bumping behind on unsteady wheels.

'Bryony!' she says, flinging her arms around me. 'I'm so glad to see you and to be here!'

'It's great to have you here,' I say, setting her at arm's length and sweeping my eyes down to her feet, laughing. 'You certainly look the part.'

'Good. I have to hang cool with the surfing duuuudes.' She does the snot-bubbling laugh.

I pull mock disapproval. 'Oh dear, I hope you're not going to say that to Mum and Jen's students.'

We link arms and walk towards the car park. Immi gives a deep sigh. 'I can feel the tension slipping away already, the sea air, the seagulls, the …' Mum gets out of the car and waves. 'Mrs Masters!' She leaves her case with me and hurries over to Mum. I get an unexpected lump in the throat watching them hug, because it's as if we've gone back in time. I sense that Immi must feel the loss of her mum even more keenly today.

Lumps aren't restricted to my throat, it seems. I notice Mum's and Immi's eyes well up as we stand in a circle by the car. 'Imogen Ransom, what a beauty you've grown into,' Mum says, looking Immi up and down.

Though it shouldn't, that comment gets under my skin. Mum often says that kind of thing to me, but I suppose my insecurities run deep. Immi blushes.

'Oh, that's a lovely thing to say, Mrs Masters. Especially as I'm looking a bit dishevelled after my marathon journey.'

'You can stop the Mrs Masters, makes me feel a hundred. Call me Gilly.'

'You are a hundred next birthday, aren't you?' I say, and duck the expected cuff round the ear from Mum.

Immi stands back and looks at us, an unreadable look on her face. Then she says, 'I can't tell you how great it is to be here. I'm so looking forward to seeing your house, Gilly. Bryony has told me how lovely it is.'

Mum starts talking about the house and says you can see glimpses of the sea on a clear day. She'll wax lyrical all day if we let her, so I put Immi's suitcase in the boot and say, 'Right, let's get you back, then you can see it for yourself.'

Immi loves her room and goes bananas about the house. 'Oh my goodness, what a wonderful place to live. How far is it to the beach?'

'About ten minutes' walk to Fistral, the main surfing beach, and about fifteen or so to the others.'

'Is that all? It's bloody paradise,' Immi says wistfully, looking out of her bedroom window. 'What I wouldn't give to live here.'

This is as good an opening as any to let her in on the thoughts I've had bumping about my head for the last few days. I sit in the old armchair and say, 'If it was up to Mum I'd be here permanently.'

Immi spins round and comes to sit next to me on the bed. 'What? So you'd get a job with the Cornwall police?'

'Not exactly. In fact, not at all … I've been thinking of jacking it in, doing something else. In the meantime I would do a bit of teaching at the surf school.'

'Shut up, you haven't!' Immi's eyes are round, and a big smile is spreading across her face.

'I have.'

'But that's fantastic!' She throws her arms up and claps her hands a few times.

'It is?' Again I'm puzzled. Did nobody like the fact that I was a copper and just didn't tell me?

'Yes. It so is. I've been really worried about telling you what my shit of a father has been saying, but now you're quitting and moving he's going to find it harder to carry it through.'

'Er, he said what? And I haven't decided yet.'

'It's a no brainer, Bryony. You have to.' Immi folds her arms, fixes me with a cool stare.

'What has your dad been saying?'

'You know that day in the pub when we were talking – just a week or so before he was sent down?' I nod. 'I said then that I was worried he'd find someone to blame for it, remember? Anyone would do if he couldn't find the one. I was worried he'd come after you … and I was right.' Immi pauses and her bottom lip trembles. Inside, a little worm of fear spirals a chill down my spine. So this is what she was keeping back when we spoke on the phone a few nights ago. 'He mentioned it to me a while ago when I visited. I told him that we'd never get an appeal if he did anything to you.'

I take a moment and then say, 'So that's why you were talking about appeals on the phone the other night. I'm surprised he went along with you. Whatever your father might be, he isn't stupid.'

'Well, he seems to think it's a possibility. I visit as often as I can to discuss various lawyers and stuff. He never seems to be able to decide on the one he wants though.'

'Perhaps he's just going along with you to make sure you keep visiting. Must be killing him being in there.'

'Maybe, but he seems really keen. Anyway, let's get back to you moving here. It's the best news I could have hoped for. If we launch an appeal, once it falls flat, he'll start on about making you pay again, but you'll be long gone. He'd have to be really bloody minded to try find you. And there's no way he'd think of looking for you here in a surf school.'

Immi's face is all smiles and rainbows, but the little worm wriggles again and I hug myself. 'As I said, he's not a stupid man.'

'Nobody would ever imagine you'd chuck in a DI job, forgo a copper's pension and leave everything you'd ever worked for, your hometown, your lovely flat, would they?'

I raise an eyebrow. 'You said you'd love to live here just now.'

'Yes, but I'm a receptionist in a medical centre. It's hardly the same thing. You're respected, admired.' She puts her head on one side, frowns. 'Actually, I never thought to ask, apart from this beautiful area, what the hell has made you think of chucking it in?'

'Simple. I'm sick of trying to catch men like your father and mostly failing.' Then words come out of my mouth that I hadn't known were going to. 'I honestly think that I only went into the force to impress my dad. Initially, anyway. I did enjoy it, I was good at it … but then Dad was killed and it all seemed a bit meaningless. The bad guys had won – and they keep winning, mostly.'

'But you put my father away. You can't expect to do that every day of the week – the world isn't like that, unfortunately.' Immi shrugs.

'Now you sound like my boss … and aren't you supposed to be arguing for me to leave anyway?' I give her a little smile.

She laughs. 'I am. And what you've told me makes it all the more sensible. If my father holds a grudge, others like him might, and somewhere down the line …' She shrugs again.

'So I just up sticks and scurry down here in case a bad man might hurt me … kill me?' I'm teasing now, but only in part. I was never a scaredy-cat.

'No.' Immi narrows her eyes. 'You're twisting it now. I never said he would kill you … but yes, he'd see you hurt. Come on, Bryony. Your heart's not in it anymore. So why not just leave?'

'Be a surf duuuude?'

She laughs. 'Yes, but what job would you do in the long term?'

'I've thought about teaching or counselling.'

'Yes, I can see you as a teacher! Miss Masters, sounds quite the part.'

'Mum said the same.'

'So will you do it then?'

I get up, stare out of the window. Next door's cat is sitting on the patio table looking right up at me as if he's waiting for an answer too. 'Oh, I don't know … I'm leaning more towards saying yes, but I need a bit more time.'

'But I know you'll say yes in the end.' Immi gets off the bed, puts her hand on my shoulder. 'I would if I could. Who knows, I might eventually get a job down here too. Nothing's keeping me in Sheffield after all, is it?'

The catch in her voice makes me swallow hard. She's been through so much over the past few years. First her mother dies and then she makes sure that the remaining parent pays for what he's done. Ensures that he's sent away for a very long time. You don't get through that kind of thing unscathed. Immi is a good person – one of the best. 'Well, if you do decide to do that, whether I'm here or not, it will be a very good move, I'm sure.'

Immi looks at me, a knowing smile on her face. 'Oh you'll be here, Bryony. You'll be here.'

Chapter Seventeen

Another room, another drawer. Nathan shoves the gun to the back of the dresser drawer in his hotel room. Then he thinks better of it and puts it in the safe in the wardrobe. He has to be sure – the maid might snoop while he's out. Unlikely, but he can afford no mistakes. Nathan walks over to the window and looks out over the ocean. It's a grey day and the wind is whipping the waves into stiff crests – an army of water relentlessly assaulting the cliffs ending the beach. Restless, angry, just like him.

Frank couldn't see why he had to book into a hotel. 'It's not a fucking holiday, lad. Just get down there, do the deed and get out.' How stupid is he? Newquay isn't a massive place, but it might take a day or so to find Imogen. There are quite a few beaches in and around and he'll have to go to each one. How else could he find her? She'd not told her father anything about where she'd be staying. A hotel is better than a B&B, more anonymous. There'd be no landlady chatting to him, trying to find out about his life.

Nathan told Frank he needed to do it his own way; more planning meant less chance of him getting caught. Frank had to grudgingly agree with that reasoning.

It's mid-afternoon and there's been no sign of Imogen on any of the beaches so far. He started with Fistral, the main surfing beach, and then wandered all the others in Newquay. Now he's back at Fistral sitting on the beach near the breakers in a wetsuit, pretending to relax, but he's surreptitiously scanning every female surfer that takes to the waves. The photo Frank gave him of Imogen is in his room and he's memorised it well. She isn't here. She doesn't appear to be on any Newquay beach.

Nathan had looked on the Internet and noted down all the beaches. Perhaps Imogen meant just outside Newquay when she told her dad. Mawgan Porth looks to be a popular beach for surfers, but it's about four miles out of town. Should he search there? On the sand to his left a seagull worries at a shell. Perhaps its name is Ransom and the creature inside the shell is called Nathan.

Flopping back on the sand he stares at the gap in the clouds, a glimpse of blue brightened by a lazy sun. It looks set to clear soon. On a cloudy day, his mum always used to say that if you can see a bit of blue sky big enough to make a man a shirt, then it will brighten up eventually. Where is she now? His poor, poor mum. It would kill her if she knew what he was here for. The thump of feet nearby on the packed sand vibrates through him, draws his gaze. A young woman … with red hair in two pigtails. He sighs. Nope. Not Imogen, or Masters for that matter.

Nathan closes his eyes. Shit, all this is so hopeless. He could have easily missed her on any of the beaches. As soon as he'd left one of them, Imogen could have arrived. What would be the point in going to Mawgan Porth? She might appear on this one later. Needles and haystacks. Nathan shoves his hands through his hair and strokes his stubble. He is surprised to find it's more than stubble, but then he supposes it must be a few days since he's shaved. A subconscious attempt at a disguise? There's a false name waiting on his tongue, a hometown too. If he does manage to speak to either woman, she'll ask about his northern accent of course. Bound to.

Nathan sits up and watches the surfers for a bit. Surfing is one thing he's never tried before, but it looks like it could be fun under different circumstances. Perhaps he should hire a board, try it out while he's looking for Imogen. At least he would be less conspicuous. Some of the people out there look so graceful. There are a few obvious experts, cutting through the waves, riding confidently into shore. It looks dead easy, but he can see that it isn't from the efforts of the less seasoned boarders. He imagines he will make a fool of himself until he gets the hang of it and decides that he'll wait until later, once the beach is a bit emptier. It will be easier to try out without the fear of bumping into loads of other surfers too. Remembering that there's a surf hire shop near the car park he sets off to investigate.

There are considerably fewer people on the beach late afternoon as Nathan drags his board to the water's edge. The sky did clear earlier, but now the wind is up and the clouds are huddling together in its wake. He loves the wildness of the scene and fills his lungs with salt air. Nathan considers just taking the plunge, but then he ought to get a feel for the water first shouldn't he, before he takes the board in? One or two surfers are off to the left struggling in a few angry breakers, so he decides to swim away from them to a nice smooth bit of water to his right first. Once he's had a swim he'll come back for the board and tackle the waves.

At first he cuts through the water no problem, and he's glad he's been doing the running lately because he feels about as fit as he's ever been. But after a few minutes he notices that he's much further away from shore than he thinks. The surfers he was watching are tiny now, bobbing up and down on the swell, and he's being dragged ever further out to sea. Panic rises in his belly and his heart thumps in his chest. Nathan knows he needs to get back to shore and fast.

It's as if the water is a solid wall. He's making no headway, no matter how much he tries … he's in some sort of current and he feels like he's about to go under. Nathan focuses his eyes on the shore. Then there's a woman on the beach, he hears her voice before he sees her. She's yelling something at him, pointing to his right. He can't make it out … then her voice carries on the wind.

'SWIM TO YOUR RIGHT. SWIM TO YOUR RIGHT. PARALLEL TO THE BEACH, NOT TOWARDS IT.' She yells this over and over and Nathan does what she says. Almost immediately he finds he can make headway. He takes huge gulps of air and powers along until he feels sand under his feet. He's close to the beach now and drags himself upright, wheezing, spluttering, and shaking. An RNLI lifeguard truck is speeding towards him and he kneels on the beach on all fours, gathering his strength.

A pair of feet come into view as he kneels, spitting bile on the sand, and a woman's voice says, 'Thank God you're all right! I wasn't sure if you could hear me yelling.' His eyes follow up from the feet to the legs and then along her body. And then … and then … he's staring into the face of Bryony Masters.

Chapter Eighteen

The poor guy looks like he's seen a ghost. Must be in shock. No wonder, he could have easily drowned just now. I note the muscular torso, broad shoulders. Someone less fit might well have. He's still looking into my eyes. He's a bit spaced out, but the colour's coming back into his cheeks, which warms his deep green eyes, lends animation to his face. I pat him on his back. 'You okay?'

The guy coughs, looks back at the sand. 'I am, thanks to you. God knows what would have—'

'Hey, mate. Let's have look at you.' A lifeguard is hurrying over to us from the truck. 'Thought we'd have to get the boat out before this young lady did her stuff.' He looks at me with respect. 'Must be a local to know rip currents so well and how to get out of them.'

'I'm not actually, but my mum is. I spent most holidays in my childhood and adolescence here though.'

'What's your name, bud?' he says to the guy and hunkers beside him.

'Jacob.'

'Right, Jacob, sling your arm round me and let's see if we can get you to your feet.'

Jacob does as he's asked and I realise he's over six foot and built like an athlete – a swimmer, funnily enough. He leans against the lifeguard for support for a moment then stands apart from him, breathing in through his nose and out through his mouth. 'I'm fine now, thanks, mate.'

'You might feel fine, but I'd advise you to rest. Sit down over on those rocks for a bit.'

For some unknown reason I say, 'Don't worry, I'll stay with him for a while, just 'til he's feeling himself.'

Jacob looks at me. 'No, honestly. You've done enough …' Then to my surprise he blinks a few times and draws his hand down his face. 'You saved my life.'

The lifeguard slaps him on the shoulder. 'She did, for sure. We were up the other side of the beach with someone who'd hurt his ankle. We saw you eventually, but … chances are …' He shrugs. 'Right, I'll be off then.' He grins at me and says to Jacob, 'Make sure you find out about rips.' Then he jumps in the truck and drives off.

Now it's just me and Jacob I feel a bit awkward. Why did I offer to stay with him? It's as though I'm after some hero crown or something. The smooth rocks halfway back up the beach give me a starting point. 'Let's go and sit on those rocks, eh? I know you said you were fine, but a rest won't hurt. You will have expended a huge amount of energy in that rip.' Jacob looks hesitant and can't hold my gaze. 'Come on, I won't bite. I've got an energy drink in my bag over there too.'

He nods and we walk slowly up the beach. I leave him seated on the rocks and dash over to my bag and board just as Imogen jogs up to me dragging her board behind her. 'Sorry I'm late. I've been chatting to your mum. She's so knowledgeable about the coast round here, isn't she?'

'Well, she ought to be.' I smile and hoist my bag onto my back.

'Where you going? Thought you were going to teach me how to surf?' She looks out to sea and then expectantly up at me.

'The water's a bit grumpy just now. Let's leave it until tomorrow.' I hesitate, wondering how to say what I've done without sounding a big-head. 'That guy over there.' I raise a hand in Jacob's direction. 'He had a brush with death just now, I had to help him.'

Imogen shields her eyes and looks. 'Oh. My. Word. What a honey! And what, you saved him from drowning?' She looks back at me, face shining with excitement.

'Er, yes, I guess.'

'How clever. Did you go in, get your arms round his gorgeous body?'

'Immi, for goodness' sake.'

'But did you?'

'No. He was in a rip current, and if I'd gone in we both might have drowned. People tend to panic when they're in one and if he'd grabbed on to me …'

'He could grab on to me any day.'

I give her a withering look. 'This is serious.'

'And he's seriously fit. Come on, introduce me.' Immi has her board under her arm and is off up the beach before I have time to draw breath.

When I catch up to her she's already rabbiting on and Jacob is doing his best to answer her rapid-fire questions. 'So she's a hero then, really?' she says as I chuck my board down and rummage in my bag for the drink.

'Immi, just leave the poor guy alone. He needs to rest and recharge his energy.' I hand him the bottle which he takes gratefully. Immi and I watch him drink, his head tipped back, throat muscles downing the liquid, and I realise she's almost drooling. I nudge her and she mouths 'what?' at me.

Jacob stops when the bottle's nearly empty and wipes his mouth. 'Sorry, I almost drank it all. I'll get you another from the shop.'

'Don't be daft. Finish it off. You need it more than me.'

'You're not from these parts, are you?' Immi says and perches next to him on the rock.

He smiles at her and she blushes. Dear God.

'Nope. You're not either by the sounds of it.' Jacob smiles at me too. 'Either of you.'

'No, we're from Sheffield. Though she's half Cornish. We're down here on holiday and Bryony'—Immi points at me, as if that's necessary—'might even stay here to help out with her mum and auntie's surf school. Isn't that great?' She treats him to a dazzling smile.

'Er, yes. That's a refreshing way to spend a day's work.' He finishes off the drink and Immi takes it from him, carefully making sure she brushes his fingers with hers.

'Yes, because at the moment her job is—'

'Imogen. Can you please leave my life story alone? Jacob needs to rest and I'm sure he isn't interested—'

'So where are you from, and what do you do?' My jaw drops as she completely shuts me down.

Jacob dusts sand from his hands and says to the ocean, 'I'm from Wakefield and I work in a shop selling electrical goods. I thought I'd pop down here for a few days, learn how to surf.' He does a sheepish grin. 'It's not going well so far.'

'Wakefield, that's amazing, my dad's in …' Immi realises her mistake and corrects herself. 'Umm, business there.' She flushes again and babbles. 'Wakefield isn't far away from us, is it? What a small world. I bet selling electrical goods is interesting too.' She jumps up and points towards the café. 'Would you like to get a coffee with us, Jacob, warm yourself up?'

'No thanks, Imogen. I think I'm just going to go back to my hotel and get some rest if you don't mind.' He takes my hand and looks straight into my eyes. 'Thank you so, so much for saving my life, Bryony. If there's anything I can do for you, just name it.'

'Ooh, now that's an offer,' Immi says and giggles.

I give her daggers and say to him, 'Well, I'd like to make sure you never get in that situation again. Come to the surf school tomorrow. I'll teach you about rip currents and perhaps help you stand up on that board.'

I can feel Immi's eyes on me so I don't look at her. Jacob says, 'No, I honestly couldn't put you to that kind of trouble. You've already done the most anybody could ever do for a fellow human being.'

Immi links her arm through his, leans her head on his shoulder. 'Aw, what a lovely thing to say. Isn't he lovely, Bryony?'

I ignore her question but say, 'You asked what you can do. This is it. Be here at noon tomorrow, okay?'

He twists his mouth to the side, looks at us both for a moment and then nods. 'If you insist. Thank you, I'll be here.'

'Hurray!' Immi yells, doing a little dance and giving him a quick hug. 'See you soon then, Jacob.'

I grab her elbow and steer her up the beach. 'See you soon,' I say as we go past. Out of earshot I say, 'For goodness' sake, Immi, could you have been any more obvious?'

She stops and plants her hands on her hips. 'Obvious or not, my efforts went unnoticed, dear one.'

'Eh?'

'Well, when we were young you used to complain that all the hunky guys went for me.'

'Yeah, well that's because they did,' I say and push my tongue out at her.

'But not with this one. You might have found the most gorgeous man on the planet, rescued him from the sea, no less, and he cannot take his eyes off you.'

Stunned isn't the word. 'Don't be ridiculous. He's just grateful to me for saving him, that's all. He gave you a lovely smile.'

Immi wags her finger side to side in front of my face and affects an American accent. 'Smile or not, it's you he's smitten with, girlfriend.'

I tell her she's talking rubbish and lead the way up the beach. A tiny part of me wonders what I would think about it if she were right. He is pretty gorgeous, that isn't in question, but there's no way anything can come of it. There is far too much on my plate at the moment without chucking Jacob onto it.

Chapter Nineteen

The complimentary fluffy white bathrobe feels like a warm hug – he could do with one of those. Nathan pulls the belt tight around him as he leaves the shower room and pulls a chair up to the floor-to-ceiling window. The beach is empty now and he can barely distinguish the ocean from the sky as night draws in. He pours another whisky and downs it in one. He needs to blot the day from his mind, but Bryony Masters is all he can think about. You couldn't make it up, could you? He comes down here to take her life, and she ends up saving his.

A knock at the door freezes his whole body. Has Ransom somehow found out that Bryony is here, and he's sent a thug to tell him to get on with it? The knock comes again.

'Room service.'

Of course it is. Tension evaporates and he calls himself all sorts of names as he opens the door, takes the tray and bungs the guy a tip. Chicken in white wine sauce with roast potatoes and seasonal vegetables, and strawberry cheesecake and clotted cream for pudding. Nathan's mouth waters at the smell and within ten minutes there's nothing left on either plate. Funny how a near drowning can make you feel so hungry.

Nathan turns the lamps off in the room and sits back at the window. Without the artificial light he can see the beach as a swathe of grey, upon which a charcoal ocean allows its white horses a gentle gallop. As a full moon gradually rises through ragged ink clouds to the west, his mood does too. There's no way he would ever kill Bryony Masters now. If the truth were known, he never could. Honestly? He could never kill anyone in circumstances like this, even though his mum is at risk. Perhaps in war, or to save his own life in self-defence, but not because a guy like Ransom had decided that she was to blame for putting him away.

There must be another way. He'd already considered telling Dawson and Ransom that he couldn't find her, that she wasn't here – they would be none the wiser, would they? In the end she'd go back to Sheffield, though, and then they'd be onto her again, so that would only delay things. It might buy him some time to find his mum though – that's an option. Okay, a long shot, but he needs to think positive. He could get her away, get himself away. Nothing is impossible. Before today that would have been the perfect solution, but how can he leave the woman who'd saved his life at the mercy of another 'Nathan' being forced to do what he couldn't?

There must be a way to let her know she's in danger without giving the game away … but how? Although used to being a loner, mostly, at times like this he really misses having someone to talk things through with. In the past he'd talked to one of his siblings, and there had been Hannah for a while too. Hannah was involved in most of the stuff he was. He'd met her through a friend of Ransom's and they'd started dating. She was lovely, but never had any ambition to break free, break out of the vicious circle they were trapped in. Like him, she'd grown up in it and it was all she knew. He had moved in with her for a year or so, but he was kidding himself that it was enough … that she was enough. He wanted a new life and someone to share it with, someone who had a normal job, a normal life. So he'd left, become a loner. No girlfriend, no friends and, at the moment, no family. It would be so much easier if he could just accept who he had become and get on with it, but a little flame of hope burns deep within him and refuses to be extinguished.

Nathan picks up the whisky bottle and then sets it back on the table. If he is going surfing with Bryony and Imogen tomorrow, he'll need a clear head. The craziness of that thought makes him laugh and he pictures Dawson's and Ransom's expressions if they knew.

No closer to a solution about what to do, Nathan settles down in the comfy bed and is certain that his troubled mind won't allow sleep. But in ten minutes he feels himself drifting. Perhaps his dreams will give him inspiration about how to warn Bryony, how to make this whole bloody mess disappear. He turns his body towards the song of the sea coming in through the open window and surrenders to sleep.

At last he's caught a wave, is standing up! And now he isn't ... he's under the water with half the Atlantic on top of him. Nathan shoves his feet into the sand and powers up and out, the surfboard dragging on the cord at his ankle. Bryony and Imogen are nearby, clapping and cheering.

'You stood up and caught a wave on your first day!' Bryony says, wading towards him. 'I see a great surfing future in front of you, Jacob.'

Though Jacob is his middle name, he has to keep reminding himself to answer to it. 'I don't know about that.' He smiles and shoves his wet hair back from his forehead. 'But I'm pretty pleased I did that after about a thousand attempts!'

'It wasn't that many!' Imogen says, kicking a spray of water at him. 'It took me much longer to master it.'

Bryony turns to her. 'Eh? You've been at it nearly three days and still haven't stood up!'

'That's right, tell the whole bloody beach, why don't you?' She kicks another spray at Bryony and then runs up the beach towards a group of surfers gathered around their boards.

Bryony shields her eyes from the sun and watches her. 'Looks like she's found Mum and my auntie Jen with the surf school. I should be helping out really. Come and meet them though.'

Nathan protests but Bryony just links arms and drags him out of the water. The last thing he wants to do is to get too friendly with the family, because the information he hopes to share with Bryony somehow will make him seem too callous for words. He clears his throat as they get nearer to the surfers. 'Hope your mum doesn't want me to show her how I've mastered the waves this morning.'

'Gilly, this is Jacob, the man your daughter rescued from drowning yesterday,' Imogen crows as they come to a stop.

'No worries about me showing her my mastery then after that introduction,' Nathan mutters to Bryony and she leans into him and laughs.

He shakes hands with her mum and aunt, and her mum says, 'You know when someone saves your life, Jacob, you have to repay them, if not in kind, then as best you can. You are indebted to them for the rest of your life.'

'Mum! For goodness' sake.' Bryony rolls her eyes.

Nathan can see the spark of humour in Gilly's eyes but he knows the essence of her words is true. He aims to honour them to the letter. 'I want to do everything I can to make your daughter happy, Gilly.' He takes her hand and kisses the back of it.

'Ooh!' Imogen says and puts her hand out. 'I'm her oldest friend – do I get a hand kiss too?'

Nathan kisses it and everyone laughs. *So much for not getting to know the family*. 'Now I must be going and leave you to your work.' He nods at the group a little way off, practising their moves on the sand. 'It's been great to meet you all and if you'll just give me your phone number, Bryony, I'll make sure I think of some way to thank you.'

Bryony shakes her head and her wet hair shimmers, flicks round her face. 'No need, honestly. I was happy to do it—'

'Please. I insist. I couldn't bear to think we'll just go our separate ways and I won't be able to ever contact you again.' *Eh? That sounds a bit romantic doesn't it?* Bryony's high colour confirms his thought.

'Here it is, Jacob,' Imogen says, thrusting a damp bit of paper with a number scrawled across it. It also has an address and *Please come to dinner tonight at 7!* written underneath.

Bryony grabs it. 'Imogen! Jacob might not want to come to dinner, he might have other plans.' She looks at Nathan and then away, her colour deepening further.

'Of course he hasn't!' Jen says, snatching the paper and giving it back to Nathan. 'He'd like nothing better, would you, Jacob?'

Nathan opens his mouth to try and make an excuse, but before he can say anything Gilly says, 'He'd love to come! And Bryony makes a legendary fish pie, don't you, love?'

He can't read Bryony because she's looking at the sand, but she does have a ghost of a smile on her face. Maybe he can get her alone somehow this evening, think of a way to broach the problem? Aware that everyone apart from Bryony is still looking at him, waiting for an answer, he says, 'Of course, I'd be delighted. How can I turn down a fish pie of such high standard?'

The wine has loosened everyone's tongue and I can see at the end of the table that Imogen is getting a bit worse for wear. I'll have to watch her very closely. Right now she's telling a joke that she can't remember the punchline of, and everyone's trying to help her out. Everyone being Jacob, Jen, Uncle Graham, Mum, and me. They're having a good time, and so am I, apart from the fact that I'm worried about Immi. She's already told Jacob all about my job, even though I told her to keep it to herself. Some people are funny about coppers. He seemed fine though and asked me a few questions. He totally gets why I want to leave, though of course Imogen's dad never came into it – at least she managed to keep her gob shut about that.

Mum collared me in the kitchen earlier and told me how much she likes Jacob and what a nice couple we would make. For goodness' sake. What's wrong with the women in my life? I told her that Imogen fancies the pants off him, but she, like Immi, said he's not interested in her, only me. I watch my fingers twist the stem of the wine glass round and round on the table. If it's true that he fancies me, his feelings are probably confused because of the fact that I rescued him. If someone saved my life, then I'd look pretty favourably upon the saviour. Probably wouldn't extend to fancying them though. I glance up and catch Jacob's eye. He smiles and takes a sip of wine, his intense green eyes never leaving mine. Oh God. I think they're right. That look says it all.

And my body is not behaving in an appropriate manner. I blush and maintain the eye contact. This is really not a good idea with all the changes I aim to make in my life. I force myself to look away and decide to go out into the garden to cool off.

There's a stiff breeze coming off the Atlantic and I'm glad I picked my favourite hoodie off the peg before I came out. It's lovely, though, standing here, my back to a tree, being buffeted by the salt wind, cosy from the wine and the great evening. The lights round the patio look cosy too. In fact everything is made of cosy. My fish pie went down even better this time too. Maybe I'll try adding a few prawns next—

'Bryony? Blimey, what you doing out here, it's freezing?'

I turn towards Jacob coming round the side of the house and across the lawn. I put a fixed smile on my face. I'm hardly going to tell him the truth, am I? 'Freezing? Call yourself a northerner? Just needed a bit of air and peace and quiet.'

'Yeah, it's noisy in there. Immi is certainly having fun,' Jacob says, laughing.

'Has she remembered the punchline yet?'

'Nope. She's gone on to something else now …'

'Right.' I'm not sure I like the mysterious tone in his voice. 'I'd better go back in and keep an eye on her.' I start to walk past him but he puts a gentle hand on my arm.

'Not just yet. I need to tell you how grateful I am to you. I honestly could have died out there yesterday.' He nods towards the ocean. 'And everyone here has been so wonderful to me. It's a long time since I felt so welcome anywhere.'

Something in his voice makes my heart go out to him. His hand is warm on my arm and I put my hand on his shoulder. 'You've thanked me so many times. So no more, hey? And I'm glad you feel welcome.'

Then his face is close to mine; I can feel his breath on my cheek and he's about to say something when, 'Nah. They can't be out here, it's bloody freezing!' Immi yells and bangs the back door shut.

I step back, laugh nervously. 'We'd better go in if a search party's underway.'

'No, I think she's trying to put your mum and the others off the scent. Immi told me to come out here to you in the first place.'

'She did? What for?' My heart is sinking. I hope she's not said anything ridiculous.

'Well, that's what I meant when I said she's gone on to something else. I went to the loo and she waylaid me as I was coming back. She told me that she knew I fancied you and said you felt the same.'

Never have I been so glad of the cover of darkness. 'I'll bloody kill her when I get hold of her,' I say through gritted teeth.

Jacob folds his arms and puts his head on one side. 'So it's not true then?'

'What, that I fancy you?' I feel like a kid in the schoolyard. What a childish question.

'Yep.' He kisses my cheek and I catch a whiff of alcohol on his breath.

I shake my head. 'Look, we've both had a drink. Let's just go in and we'll talk about this another time.'

'Because it's true on my part. I wish it wasn't, but …' He gives a deep sigh and runs his hands through his hair.

What do I make of that? He likes me but he wishes he didn't. Is he in a relationship? Married? Time to take control. That's what I do best. 'Jacob, you could easily be confused about your feelings because I saved your life. Let's sleep on it and see where we are tomorrow.' I start to walk towards the house. 'Come on, you're right, it is freezing.'

He follows me but stops when we get to the door, turns me to face him. The patio lights show me an earnest face, but is there anxiety in his eyes?

'Please say we can meet up tomorrow. I have something to tell you. I'll call you in the morning, yes?'

The best option is to say no. I know it is. But I hear myself say, 'Yes, okay.' Then I open the door and go inside.

Chapter Twenty

Mawgan Porth is even nicer than the Google images, and Nathan's breath is taken away by the stunning coastline as he drives down the steep hill to the beach. Bryony has agreed to meet him here for coffee, but has declined his offer of a lift as she has 'other stuff' to do later. It's probably just as well, because when he tells her who he is and why he's here, she'll probably just leave anyway. Dawson messaged him earlier to tell him that his 'sources' had found Gilly's address and that he should drive up and see if Imogen and Bryony are there. Nathan was tempted to thank him but say it wouldn't be necessary as he was there for dinner last night, just to hear his reaction.

In the car park, Nathan wonders if there's another way to warn her, but once again he's back to thinking just being honest is the best option. She can't arrest him, can she? At least he doesn't think so; he'd just deny it all ... but then she's a DI and knows the law. He's a criminal on the other side of it. Shit, he has no clue really. What he does know is that he can't kill her and he won't allow anyone else to. Last night in the garden he nearly made a complete idiot of himself. The wine had something to do with it, but nevertheless he still felt the same when he woke this morning. It was more than the fact she'd rescued him too. Much more.

A car swings into the space beside him and he looks through his window. It's her. She looks stunning in a red top, her hair and make-up done. He's not seen her wearing make-up apart from on the photo Dawson gave him, but Nathan thinks she's beautiful with or without. Her eyes crinkle at the corners and her big smile is infectious. As he gets out of the car he vows to keep his feelings to himself. There's absolutely no point – there is no way they would ever work out. How could they?

The warmth they shared last night is replaced by an awkward silence as they walk to the café, and once at a table it becomes excruciating. 'Sure you wouldn't like cake?' he asks, just for something to fill the void.

'No thanks, it's not that long until lunch now,' she says to the table and fiddles with a spoon.

'Oh, well we could have lunch if you'd like?'

'No. As I said, I have stuff to do.'

This is going from bad to worse. Time to bite the bullet. 'Bryony, there's something I have to tell you and you won't like it. But I beg you, please hear me out.'

Her head jerks up – there's already suspicion in those hazel eyes. 'God, this sounds ominous. Okay, I'm listening.'

Nathan's heart is thumping in his chest. 'Promise you'll stay and listen to all of it?'

Her response is quick, impatient. 'Yes, I promise. What is it?'

Nathan takes a huge gulp of coffee and looked out of the window at the ocean. Then he looks back at her. 'Kenny Ransom forced me to come down here. He wants me to find you and … kill you.'

Bryony drops her spoon onto her saucer with a clatter. Her face drains of colour and she grabs the table with both hands. Her eyes widen and bore into his. She sits like a statue, waiting. She opens her mouth but closes it again.

Nathan continues before he loses his nerve. 'I could never do that, of course. I could never kill anyone … but I came. I had no idea what else to do. He has my mother. My mother who has mental health issues. I don't know where she is. I …' His words dry up and he looks at the floor. She is still silent. He looks up, sees anger in her face and something else … can he hope that it's sympathy? 'Say something … please.'

'Say something? It's a wonder I can bloody function after you dropped that shitload on me. What the fuck?' Bryony shakes her head in bewilderment and runs her hands through her hair. 'So let me get this straight. You, what, work for him?' Nathan nods. 'He kidnaps your mother and tells you to come down here to bump me off? So you wheedle your way into my mum's home, pretend to be friends. I fucking rescued you, you bastard!' She jabs a finger through the air at him and a few people turn their heads towards them. 'I should have fucking left you to drown!'

Nathan hangs his head. He was wrong about the sympathy then. 'It might have been best. I can't tell you how sorry I am that—'

'Really? Really, Jacob? If that's your real name.' Bryony drains her cup and slams it back on the saucer. People all around are whispering now. 'How about you try?'

'Shall we walk down to the beach, talk there?'

'Why? Don't you want everyone to know what an absolute cowardly piece of shit you are?'

Nathan covers his face with his hands and sighs. Then he gets up from the table. 'You have every right to be furious, but please, let me explain. We can't talk properly here.'

Bryony jumps up so fast her chair falls over with a bump. The café is silent now. 'Okay. But tell me your real name first.'

He stands too. 'Nathan. Nathan Walker.'

'I prefer Jacob. I prefer the man I thought you were.' There's a catch in her voice and as she marches for the door she bangs her shoulder into him, hard. Opening the door she tosses back, 'Come on then, if you're bloody coming.'

Bryony is already sitting on a bench overlooking the beach by the time he's hurried across the bridge and negotiated traffic on the busy road. Her opener knocks the wind out of him as he joins her. 'What was all that shite about us liking each other last night? Was that just another way to lull me into a false sense of security while you whipped a knife out of your pocket and gutted me?'

'No! Please believe me, that is so far from the truth—'

'Truth!' She whips round to face him. 'You wouldn't know the truth if it ran up this beach and whacked a surfboard round your fucking head, Nathan!'

What a visual image. Despite the gravity of the situation Nathan has to bite the inside of his lip to stop a smile. 'I asked for that.'

'I haven't even started yet.' Bryony dusts sand from the cuff of her jeans, crosses her legs, folds her arms and looks out to sea.

'I think it's best if I just start at the beginning of it all. Tell you everything I know and then we'll see where we are.'

'Might be wise.'

Nathan talks for around twenty minutes with only a raised eyebrow, a huff or stony silence from Bryony. He leaves nothing out, even the fact that Ransom had accused him of being the one who made the phone call that got Bryony round to the house to catch him red-handed. 'Who it was I don't know. Neither does Ransom, but he's sure it's you.' Nathan hesitates. 'Was it?'

'No, it wasn't.' Bryony sighs and looks at him. 'You say that Ransom allowed your family to live in one of his houses? Why would he do that?'

'We've always lived there, for as long as I can remember. My dad worked for him. I just fell into it after I was too stupid or lazy to finish college. My sister got out and my brothers … but when Dad …' To his surprise and annoyance he feels his eyes fill and he looks away up the beach at a woman walking a dog. A boy runs next to them flying a yellow kite high into the blue sky.

'When your dad what?'

Nathan was encouraged by the softer tone to her voice. 'A few years back Dad was involved in a robbery … he was the driver. The police came armed – someone must have warned them, I don't know. Anyway, my poor dad didn't know what was happening. He was unarmed – he'd never carry a weapon. Sat there in the fucking car like a sitting duck. Ransom ordered the others to not go back to the car and they shot their way out. A copper got killed. Dad jumped out of the car when he heard all the commotion and they shot him. Didn't give him a chance to put his hands up. Revenge for their man, I suppose. Ransom wasn't even there of course. Just gave orders from afar, came out of it clean as usual. He blamed my dad for being stupid, said he knew the risks.'

Bryony leans forward and puts her elbows on her knees, her head in her hands. Nathan can hear her muttering, swearing under her breath. Then she sits up, looks at him and dashes moisture from her eye with the back of her hand. 'Your dad was Paul Walker?'

'Yeah … yes, he was,' he says, taken aback. Did she memorise every incident? 'Why? Were you involved in the case?'

She makes a sound in her throat that's a cross between a sob and a cough. 'You could say that. My dad was the copper that got shot.'

'Oh my God … I don't know what to say.' Nathan swallows hard and Bryony's eyes fill again but she flinches from his attempt at comfort, slaps his hand from her shoulder.

'Why the fuck did you keep working for Ransom after what he did to your dad?'

'I felt I had no choice.' He shrugs, looks away from the venom in her eyes. 'Mum was already depressed before Dad was killed. His death tipped her over the edge and if I'd stopped working for Ransom he'd have kicked her out of the house, my brothers too, though they were big enough to stand on their own feet by then. My sister had married and gone.' Nathan shrugs and looks down the beach again. 'I suppose I just thought I needed to be the head of the family. Try to make everything right.'

Bryony clicks her tongue against the roof of her mouth. 'Oh please. You always have a choice, Nathan. You made the wrong one.'

This rankles. 'I don't expect you to understand. I grew up in it, never knew anything else. I do want to get out – have wanted to for ages, but how the hell could I get a job, start again? Imagine my CV.' He laughs humourlessly.

Bryony seems to consider this. 'You have a point there, granted. But I'd want to kill him if I were you, after what he did to your dad. And now I know he was behind my dad's death, I'd like nothing more than to see him join them.'

'Oh, believe me, I'm with you there. When he took my mum I refused to … you know. But he said if I didn't, he'd do something to Mum. I don't doubt for a minute he would, either. But I couldn't do it. Even before you rescued me I'd decided to say I couldn't find you, to try and buy some time, try and find Mum, get her away. But if I succeed, he'd only find someone else to do the job. Once Ransom sets his mind to something, he does it.'

Bryony leans back. She closes her eyes and tilts her face to the sun. 'Yeah, and same goes for me. I set out to nail that bastard and I did it. It tastes all the sweeter now I know he was responsible for my dad. It's all so fucking surreal though. Meeting you in the way I did, then last night, then all this today … it's like I'm in a rip current and can't swim out.' She releases a long slow breath. 'Can't really take it in.'

Nathan looks at her profile: the elegant line of her neck, the swell of her breasts, the rise and fall of her chest as she breathes. Though he'd told himself to keep his feelings inside, he feels them struggling to be free. 'I'm not surprised it won't go in. I knew the story and it still feels surreal.' The last sentence comes out in a rush. 'And last night … last night I meant every word.'

In a second her eyes are open and flashing contempt. 'You're having a laugh. If there ever was anything between us, you can forget all about it now. I mean, really? Really?'

Her words punch him in the gut and he wraps his arms around himself. What did he expect? But at least she acknowledges that there might have been something. Fat lot of good it would do him now though. 'Sorry. Yes, it's a dumb idea.'

'Like most of yours, it seems.' Bryony puts her head back and closes her eyes again.

After a few moments of silence he ventures, 'So what happens now?'

'You go back to your world, I go back to mine.'

At least she didn't say she was going to arrest him. 'Will you leave the force?'

'Probably. I'll go back in a few days, talk to my boss. But I'm almost sure I can't stay there for the next twenty-odd years.' A moment later she asks, 'What will you do?'

'I'll try and find my mum somehow.'

'And where will you look?'

'No clue at the moment.'

'Hmm. I could help you. I have more resources at my fingertips, after all.'

Nathan's heart leaps. 'You'd do that for me?'

'No. I'd be doing it to piss Ransom off. And for your mum, she's a victim in all this.'

'But like I said, Ransom won't leave you alone, no matter what. I can't let you get involved.'

'Can't see as you can stop me. I'm leaving the force and I'll just get Immi to tell her dad that I've gone abroad to live. I doubt he'd be willing to send his thugs across the world trying to track me down. He can't even find me in bloody Newquay.'

'But I told you before, he knows where your mum lives.'

'Yes. But Mum will be briefed too. She'll tell anyone snooping round that I've gone abroad. If he tries anything with her, I swear I'll put him in the ground. You see, Nathan, that's the difference between you and me. I stand up to playground bullies – you give them your pocket money.'

Nathan bites his tongue. She's all bravado and not thinking straight. 'The thing is, if you're moving here, he'll find you when he sends someone snooping to your mum's.'

'For goodness' sake!' Bryony opens her eyes and throws her arms up. 'Then I'll move abroad for a year and then come back when the dust has settled. There's always a solution, *and* a right choice, Nathan. For example, you could help by telling Ransom that you went to deliver some flowers to Mum and pretended she wasn't in, to do some snooping of your own. You could hardly knock on Mum's door and ask where I was out of the blue, could you? So … you'd got chatting to one of Mum's neighbours. She told you that she was upset because I'd gone abroad. See, I thought all this up in seconds. It's not hard.'

Now she's implying that he's thick, but he'll take anything she throws at him, under the circumstances. 'That could work.'

'Course it could. Right, I'm off.' Bryony stands and starts to walk away.

'What? So what are we doing about finding my mum?'

'I'll meet you back in Sheffield in a few days. I'll give you a ring. And don't mention any of this to Immi if you see her. The less anyone else knows the better.'

'I won't. There's no way I'm ever going to be able to repay you for saving my life and trying to save my mum, even if I live to be a hundred.' Nathan tries a smile.

Bryony doesn't smile back. 'If you stay in the game you're in, you won't reach a hundred. You might not even reach fifty.'

Nathan watches her walk away across the road until she's out of sight, and feels his heart sink. Thanks to her, there might be a light at the end of the tunnel for his mum now, but he's certainly messed up any chance of being anything other than a dumb spineless criminal to Bryony. Serves him right. He makes himself a silent promise that he will change, turn his life around, no matter how long it takes or how hard it is. Show her he's more than that. He *will* do it. And though he can never repay her for what she's done for him, he'll do everything in his power to keep her safe from Ransom.

Chapter Twenty-One

It will be hard to leave my flat in a few hours, but leave it I must. I've worked so hard to make it just right, like the rest of my life really, but change is necessary so there's no use in getting sentimental about it. I've booked into a hotel for the foreseeable as Ransom's spies might be still sniffing round here. The river sounds so peaceful as I sit on the balcony and try to relax after the journey up from Cornwall. My head is still full of plans though, so I close my eyes and let them come. I'll arrange to see Nathan Walker tomorrow, and then the day after I'll go see my boss.

Mum's face appears at the forefront of my mind. She was upset when I told her I'd be delaying moving down to Cornwall, but totally understood when I said I wanted to see a bit of the world first. The throwaway comment I'd made to Nathan about moving abroad for a year actually seems the safest option for now. Of course I'd boasted to him that I stand up to bullies, and I do. However, I know when to be cautious too, and this is one of those times.

So Mum is sorted, but Immi is a different kettle of fish. She's like a dog with a bone. She ought to have been a copper. When I'd told her I was cutting my visit to Cornwall a bit short and going home to get things in order, she wanted to know all the ins and outs. I hope she swallowed my story about once having decided to quit my job, I wanted to move on with the next phase of my life. I told her to tell her father that she'd heard I'd gone abroad too, which she liked the sound of, but she still had twenty million questions. Mostly about bloody Nathan Walker. I told her she was barking up the wrong tree and to leave it well alone.

A nip in the late afternoon air drives me inside for a cuppa and, as I make it, I decide not to tell Immi about moving abroad until the last minute, otherwise she'll never stop asking why. God knows what she'd do if she realised that her father was not only trying to hurt me, but have me killed. She'd probably strangle him with her bare hands, Nathan too.

The tea drives the nip away and I put my feet up, flick the TV on. It's an old film. Someone is droning on about how she'd give her life for her man. How she couldn't live without him, no matter how badly he treated her. Dear, oh dear. Thank goodness for feminism. Actually, on second thoughts, some relationships are still like that. I've come across them far too often in my line of work. No man is worth that kind of dedication. A flash surfaces, of Nathan's face close to mine in the garden, so I bury it. How wrong could you be about a person?

Poor Maggie Ransom was wrong for years and years, wasn't she? Dawson's wife too, according to Nathan. Once the dust has settled and I've been off the radar for a while, Ransom will be fixated on something else, someone else, but I'll find a way to make him and his buddies pay. Ransom will find that his easy ride in prison will get a bit harder and Dawson will trip up somehow and, when he does, I'll be waiting. I'll still have contacts in the force who will be only too eager to help me. I owe it to my dad.

I nod off and when I wake the woman on the old film is dressed in a scarlet cloak and packing a pistol. She's had enough of being dumped on and is off to get revenge. Now that's more like it. Yesterday I'd had the idea of shopping Nathan. I'm sure I could dig up loads of incriminating stuff about him if I tried. Or instead, I might even find out where his mother's being held and then get Dawson for it, if not Ransom. Nathan would be implicated in it all by association and he'd go down too. His poor mother would be in the middle of it all, but shit happens.

Then I thought better of it. All that would take time, would involve me staying on in my DI role and getting mired in more filth. The target on my back would get even bigger and I'd be constantly looking over my shoulder. And quite frankly I've had it up to here. I want a fresh start, to do some good in the world, and even have some 'me time', as everyone is fond of saying nowadays. If I'm being very charitable, people like Nathan and his mother are victims to a large extent, pawns in the powerful games of people like Ransom. Having said that, pawns always have a choice, perhaps not great ones, but a choice nevertheless. They have to be strong though, have guts. If they do, they're an asset to any board. Nathan, unfortunately, is not.

The last time he sat here on Aggie's bench he got the news that he was expected to kill someone. Today Nathan is meeting her. The woman who saved his life, the woman who will help him find his mum, the woman who haunts his dreams and every waking moment. Nathan sighs. The woman who wants nothing whatsoever to do with him because she sees him as a weak, spineless piece of … Ah. Here she is striding up the path. Everything about her says confident, intelligent. In control.

'Hi, how are you?' he says as she stops in front of the bench and slips off her jacket, under which she has a green sleeveless top that accentuates her well-defined upper arms and slim waist. As she turns to sit, a side glance reveals long legs in dark jeans, which hug a small but shapely bottom.

'I'm as good as I can be, having left my comfortable flat for a hotel room and planning to leave the country shortly instead of moving to Cornwall as I'd hoped.'

Nathan's mouth drops open as she tells him her plans and the reasons for them. He'd expected a move to a hotel, but not the move abroad. All this was his fault. Well, Ransom's, but he'd gone along with his crazy plot. 'I'm so sorry for my part in this, Bryony.'

'Yes, so am I.' She hasn't looked at him yet, just gazed over the valley, legs crossed at the ankles, hands shoved into the side pockets of her jeans. Then she glances across at him and he tries not to stare into her eyes. 'I was thinking about finding your mother. This might be something you've already looked into, but if not, it could be the easiest way to find her.' Bryony shifts her body to him. 'You say she has mental health issues?' He nods. 'And that she has prescription drugs?'

'Yes.'

'Who normally collects them for her? Does she go out or …?'

'Not recently. She's got more agoraphobic these last six months. I get them or one of my brothers does. She's very keen on taking them. That's one thing she does remind me about – you know, when she's running out. I order them.'

'So how has she been getting them since she's been taken?' Bryony's eyebrows knit together and I feel like I'm being tested. I have already considered this though.

'Well, whoever has her will have got them from elsewhere. It won't be hard. She wasn't due for any until this week anyway.'

'Did you know that some prescription drugs aren't as easy to get as heroin? Not even for the likes of Ransom?'

Nathan found that hard to believe. 'He can get anything. Trust me.'

Bryony shakes her head and stares at the view again. 'Perhaps, but I'm not so sure. And let's suppose that the people holding her want to make sure the surgery don't get worried when one of you lot doesn't turn up as usual to collect this week.'

Nathan wasn't sure where she was going with this. 'There's also the possibility that they have made her go cold turkey … though that would make her more difficult to manage.'

'Yes, and they'd want her quiet, docile and sitting in front of a TV like you told me she does every day. They might just sedate her, or …' She gives him a quick glance and then looks away. 'But let's pursue my idea. I think you could ring the surgery and ask if her tablets have been ordered. Say you weren't sure if one of your brothers had done it already. Then, if they have, ask when they're picking them up. Meanwhile—'

'I wait near the surgery and see who turns up,' Nathan says, his heart lifting. It might come to nothing but it was certainly worth a shot.

'Yep. Chances are you'll know who it is and tail him to where she's been held. Then we can figure out how to proceed from there. You can't be involved. You can still be useful to us if Ransom doesn't suspect you. I can't be seen for obvious reasons, but I have a colleague or two who owe me big time, and whom I'll swear to secrecy. They will turn up and get her out. As I said, not sure exactly how yet, but—'

'But Ransom *will* suspect my involvement. It's my mother they're rescuing.' And she thought *he* was dozy.

'No. The neighbours had heard screaming in the night and alerted the police.'

Nathan nods. That could work. But an uneasy feeling in the pit of his stomach won't go away. 'What if her kidnapper is armed?' He couldn't live with police deaths on his conscience.

'These guys are experienced officers. They won't put themselves at risk until they have surveilled the place and know exactly what to do.'

Nathan's hopes are rising with every moment; but isn't this going to land her in huge trouble if anything goes wrong? If one of the officers were injured, the other would have to come clean to his superiors and that would mean that Bryony would take the fall. He says as much to her, but she shakes her head. 'Nothing will go wrong.' She stands and shrugs on her jacket. 'Okay, go and do your part. We don't know if this will work yet. If it doesn't, I have other ideas.' Bryony nods a curt goodbye and sets off down the path.

Once again he's left watching her walk away, but this time he feels a little less hopeless. She had a good plan, but he has a better one.

Chapter Twenty-Two

So far luck is on their side, and it's about bloody time. Bryony's idea is working. The surgery said that his mum's nephew had ordered the prescription and is coming this afternoon to collect. He said he had to do that because Mrs Walker's sons were all on holiday and he was keeping his eye on her. Funny that, because his mum doesn't have a nephew. Nathan knows that afternoon collections are after three o'clock, so he's parked up in a hire car in case the collector recognises his and is waiting.

Just before four, a car he recognises slows to a stop on the opposite side of the street about twenty yards away. Unbelievable. Of all the people they could have picked. Nathan slumps down in his seat and pulls his baseball hat further down his forehead. He needn't have worried though; Jason Connor gets out of the car picking his nose. He doesn't even bother to look around him, so intent is he on examining what's on the end of his finger … then he wipes it down the back of his jeans. Nice.

While he waits for Jason to come out of the surgery, Nathan tries to contain his excitement. The prospect of rescuing his mum has just got very real – candy from a baby type real. Could his mum be at the Ransom Mansion? Unlikely; Dawson seems to spend more of his time there than at his own place. He wouldn't want a mentally ill woman cluttering up his fantasy of being lord of the bloody manor. If she's at Jason's little terraced house she'll be easier to find than at the multi-roomed mansion, and it would mean there'd just be Jason to contend with too – fingers crossed.

A moment later Jason comes out, gets into his car and tries a three-point turn, which turns into a six point. Dear God. Is he actually any good at anything? Nathan follows him at a distance, and after about five minutes realises that yes, they're going towards Jason's house. He's been there once before to collect some gear when Jason was ill.

Once on Jason's street, Nathan parks a good few doors away and waits for him to park and go in. Then he takes a package out of the glove compartment, unwraps it, and slips it into the quilted lining of his zipped jacket. Swiftly, and keeping to the shadows cast by the tree-lined avenue, he makes his way to Jason's and slips down a ginnel and round the back. From behind the bins in the yard, Nathan sees that a window is open in the kitchen by the back door. He runs to the door and flattens his spine against it. Through the window he hears Jason shout, 'It's only me, Mrs W! Got your drugs, love. Do you want a nice cream bun and a cuppa?'

Nathan hears his mum reply but not what she says; she's obviously in another part of the house.

'Right, duck! Just going to the bog. Be with you in ten!'

Excellent. Things couldn't be going better. The door handle is cool under Nathan's fingers and he gives it a quick press. No. Locked, as you'd expect. He had to try it though given Jason's level of intelligence. Slipping round the front, he peeps through the front room window. Yep. There's Mum watching TV. His heart flips over – she looks no worse for wear, thank God! Two choices present themselves. Get his mum's attention and make her open the front door, or go back to the kitchen and knock, because barging his way in through the front might catch the eye of a neighbour.

What to do? Even if he put his finger to his lips in the shush sign, Mum might call his name out and Jason could hear … it's been at least three minutes since he went to the toilet and he could be on his way back down to make the tea. The back door seems safest. At the back door he pulls the oldest trick in the book. A quick short rap and then duck round the corner of the house. Nathan's heart is thumping hard and an adrenalin rush is preparing for fight or flight. Nothing. Shit. He waits a few seconds then knocks again. Almost immediately Jason opens up and steps down into the yard.

There's a bit of muttering about kids, then he yells, 'Bloody little shits! If I see you round here playing silly buggers I'll skin you al—'

The unforgiving steel barrel of Nathan's gun in the back of his neck silences him, and he allows himself to be meekly guided back into the house. Nathan kicks the door shut behind them. 'Now just be a good lad and kneel down in the corner here and put your hands behind your back.'

Jason stops. 'Nathan?'

Into Jason's ear he whispers, 'Don't turn round. Just do as I say.' Nathan keeps the gun in Jason's neck while he takes some cord from his pocket with his other hand. He drops it as a vicious back elbow to his stomach knocks the breath out of him. As he doubles over, he remembers what it is that Jason is good at.

Then Jason's weight is on top of him, his forearm across Nathan's windpipe, his big iron fist around his wrist trying to wrest the gun from his grasp. Nathan can feel himself floating, but then he hears his mum's voice. 'Hey, leave my lad alone, you big bastard!'

Momentarily the pressure on his windpipe lessens and Nathan brings his knee up into Jason's groin. There's an 'oomph' as Jason grabs his balls and, as he does, Nathan's up and landing him a few choice kicks and punches. Jason curls into a foetal position, covering his head from Nathan's fists, but Nathan's not fooled into letting up. If he does, Jason would be at him again. Though it pains him to do so – he's not a naturally violent man – Nathan pistol whips him. One blow and Jason's out.

Nathan takes in huge gulps of air through a windpipe that feels the size of a straw as he scrabbles for the cord and ties Jason's wrists to his ankles. 'Bloody hell, Nate. What's going on?' His mum leans her weight against the door jamb. 'Jason here has been really nice to me while you've all been on your holidays, then he tries to kill you.' She starts to slump to the floor. 'Oh no … I've gone all of a tremble.'

Nathan catches her before she falls and sits her on a kitchen chair. 'Don't worry, Mum, I'm here now. And that man isn't nice.

If you hadn't come in just then and surprised him I might have been a goner. He took you from your house and I didn't know where you were.' He runs water into a glass and takes her medication from the bag on the table.

'But he said he was a nephew of Margaret thingy, you know. She used to live at number … now where did she live?'

'She lives next door to you, Mum. But he's a liar. Now, take your tablets and we'll get going.' He does the shush sign and points to the prone Jason, then whispers, 'We don't want him coming round and overhearing, but I'm taking you to the seaside.'

The delight in Mum's eyes lights up her face and Nathan's reminded of the old mum he knew as a child. She whispers back, 'The seaside. I can't remember the last time I saw the sea. Our Angie lives by the sea, doesn't she?'

'She does, Mum. Now where's your stuff? We need to go.'

On the way to Devon they stop at some services for dinner and Nathan calls Angie to explain what's happened. He'd talked to her the day before to explain what he'd hoped to do and if he was successful, his plans for their mum to live near her. Angie had been all for it. It's not lost on him that the rest of the family think he's failed their mum, and of course he has to agree with them. There was no point in saying he misguidedly thought he was taking on Dad's role, looking after them all, because going through all that again wouldn't have done any good. This is all about to change though. He's done what he set out to do, and he's never going back to his old life.

Angie had exceeded all expectations. She had found Mum somewhere to live – she couldn't live with Angie because, unlikely as it was, Ransom *could* try to track her there – at the house of someone who used to be a nurse in mental health. Angie's friend's mum Samantha had been widowed a few years ago and was lonely and felt useless since she'd retired. She was only too glad to offer a room to his mum and is looking forward to the company. How perfect is that?

Once Nathan has got himself some kind of work he'll send money to Angie, and his brothers would do the same. Between them all they'll make sure his mum pays her way and wants for nothing. On the road again, his mum gently dozing beside him, he notices her dark hair is now threaded with thicker strands of grey. Is it any wonder? This new chapter in her life will hopefully slow down the ageing process and, with Samantha's expert help, who knows what might happen?

Nathan allows his mind to wander and to actually make plans he knows are no longer dreams. His boats are burned. He'll settle his mum in her new place and then go back up to Sheffield and get some of his stuff. On second thoughts he might have to leave it – there's no doubt he'll be on Ransom's most wanted list once they find Jason hogtied. Never mind. It's only stuff. Stuff that can be bought anywhere. Then he'll be off, cut all ties with his hometown and never look back. There's only one person he'll miss and he knows, at whatever cost, he'll have to see her before he leaves.

Chapter Twenty-Three

Spring has wrapped a blanket of fog around herself this morning and its threads are leaking fat raindrops down the window of my hotel room. More coffee's needed before I ring Nathan, I think. I had expected to hear from him before now. In the hotel café I deliberate about a pecan croissant to go with my coffee, but only for a second or too. Life is too short not to have a bit of what you fancy now and then. My healthy eating regime is underway – sort of – so I can't chastise myself for this, can I?

I draw a high stool up to the counter by the window and look into the fog-drenched courtyard, but the river's hidden. A few daffodils in tubs are doing their best to pretend it's still a lovely spring day, but who are they kidding? Days like these smother any hope of sunshine and green shoots. The coffee's rich, dark and bitter, the croissant sweet and indulgent, both just what I need to galvanise my mood ... my resolve to look to the future with optimism.

I try not to let my mind go back to yesterday when I broke the news to Mark. He was sure after my break away I'd come back refreshed and ready to plunge into police work again. I hinted that Ransom might be gunning for me, but he said if he'd quit the force after idle threats from every toe-rag he'd banged up, he wouldn't have lasted five minutes. I neglected to tell him the threat was real and unlikely to go away if I stayed, because that would have to involve Nathan. Much as I despise him for his part in it, he doesn't deserve that. Under it all I think there's a decent guy wanting to get out. My great hope is that he'll come to his senses once we've got his mum back and try to make an honest living at last.

As I'm about to phone Nathan, my phone rings and it's him. 'About time,' I say as an opener.

'Sorry, been a bit busy. Listen, can I come and see you now at the hotel?'

Is he bloody nuts? 'No. Absolutely not. Imagine if we're seen?'

'Very unlikely. I'm in a hire care and nobody knows where you are, do they?'

'No. But why do you need to see me? Just tell me what you found out when you phoned the surgery.'

'I'd rather do that in person. You see, a lot's happened since then.'

He sounds serious and my heart plummets. God only knows what he's done. 'If you've done anything to bring sodding Ransom to me, I'll swing for you so help me—'

'No. No, of course I haven't! Look, I promise it's good news. Please, I need to see you – there's too much to tell you over the phone.'

Logically I should suspect him … should worry that he's sold me out to Ransom in return for getting his mother back or something. But my gut tells me to believe him. I saved his life, after all; that should count for something. 'Okay, are you in the city now?'

'Yes, I can be there within half an hour unless you're not central.'

'I am. It's the Hilton and I'm in Room 231.'

Twenty minutes later I'm thinking of ringing and telling him I've changed my mind and I won't see him. The whole thing is ridiculous. Then there's a short rap at the door. I look through the peephole and see Nathan. He's on his own, as far as I can see. My training joins hands with natural suspicion and I say, 'Are you alone?'

An affronted look sweeps his face. 'Yes, of course I am.' Then he shakes his head. 'Can't blame you for asking though.'

I pull the door open but leave the chain on. He's got his hands behind his back. 'I have my phone in my hand and my finger on the nine digit. If you're not alone I'm pressing it three times, and to warn you, I have a Taser in my other hand and at the risk of sounding dramatic, I'm trained in defence. What's behind your back?'

Nathan's mouth turns up at one side and the amusement in his eyes is clear to see. 'You're great at spoiling surprises, aren't you?' Slowly his hands come round to the front. In one there's a big bunch of flowers and in the other there's a shiny red gift bag.

A rush of blood floods my face. Damn him. What the hell is he playing at? I step back, take the chain off and wave him into the room. 'Nice of you to think of me, but I'm not accepting gifts from you,' I say in monotone.

Nathan walks through, glancing at my hands, and puts the flowers and the bag on the table by the window. 'You were fibbing about the Taser then?' He raises an eyebrow but I choose not to answer.

He's dressed in a smart navy jacket, light blue shirt and black trousers rather than the usual casual jeans and T-shirt. His stubble is gone and his unruly blond surf-dude hair has been tamed by some product or other. 'So you won't accept my gifts? Well, that's tough, because I accepted your gift to me, and these'—he nods at the table—'are the woefully inadequate things I've brought to try and make a small start at saying thank you. One of the reasons I wanted to see you in person.'

'Gift from me? I didn't give you a gift.' I notice my reflection in the mirror behind him and try to straighten my hair. Must have got blown about when I went out for a quick walk this morning. Then I stop myself. Why do I care what I look like? I have no one to impress.

His green eyes focus on me with such intensity I feel as if he's reading my thoughts. 'You gave me the greatest gift of all. My life.'

This disarms me and I wave him to the sofa next to the bed. 'Well, you really didn't have to.' I perch on the end of the bed and he sits on the sofa, then jumps up again and grabs the bag from the table. 'Here, have this now and then we can talk.'

A sigh escapes me, but I take the bag and inside there's a slim black box. I gasp when I open it. A silver Rolex? 'No. I can't accept it. This is too much – it must have cost thousands … or …' At the back of my mind an uncharitable thought waits.

'It's not stolen, Bryony.' Nathan tries a smile but I can see hurt behind his eyes. I wonder if he actually is a bloody mind reader. 'I sold my car.'

I purse my lips and try to hand it back. 'As I said, I can't take it.'

He folds his arms. 'I can change it if you don't like it.'

'It's not that. It's beautiful …'

'Then please accept it.' The note of desperation in his voice gets to me. Wouldn't I be the same if someone had saved my life? I look at the watch again and then slip it onto my wrist. 'Okay. Thanks, Nathan.'

His face lights up and he gives me a huge smile. 'It looks great on you. Just how I imagined.'

Okay. That's enough of that. 'So what have you to tell me?'

He sits on the sofa. 'Well, I'm happy to tell you that my mum is now safe and living with an ex-mental health nurse in Brixham.'

My jaw feels like it's come unhinged. 'What?'

Nathan laughs. 'That's the reaction I was expecting. Yeah, I found out that the hired muscle that works for Dawson and Ransom had her at his house. I followed him and took Mum. Candy from a baby … mostly. Left him hogtied in his own kitchen. I made sure he could get to his phone though.' He laughs again. 'I expect he had to use his tiny brain to find a way to untie himself, might even have thought of struggling to get a knife from the block after a good while.'

'But the deal was to tell me, I'd get the police round.'

'Hmm. The thing is, I knew I could handle it myself and if others had become involved, Jason might have panicked – I know he had a gun – and, well …' He shrugs.

I'm impressed that he's finally showing some guts, but even so. 'Well, I'm glad she's out safe, but it was really risky. Won't Dawson question your brothers, your sister?'

'Might do. But they'd have to find them too. They've dropped off the radar really, not being criminals. I was the one they always dealt with. My brothers moved out after Mum was taken, and my sister moved years ago. But just in case, I made sure we got our stories straight. If they're questioned they'll say I phoned from an unknown number to explain what had happened. I'm out of the country and Mum was safe and that was all I told them for now. And risky? It would have been riskier for you if anyone had got shot. As I said before, the officers would have dropped you in it, no matter how big the favour they owed you.'

He's giving me that intense look again and I glance away, fiddle with the watch. 'So you risked everything to make sure I was safe?'

'If you like.'

'I'm a big girl, Nathan. I don't need people looking after me.' I know this sounds ungrateful, but would he have done the same if I was a guy?

'I know that. But I saw a way to keep you out of it all and I took it.'

A thought occurs to me. 'This means you're going to be on Ransom's most wanted – this Jason saw you, I assume?'

'Yes, he did. But I've been wanting to get out for ages as I mentioned to you before. This was the perfect opportunity. My mum's safe now so I can leave, make a new life, hopefully.'

'You also said that getting a job without having legit employment history would be almost impossible too, and I had to agree with you.'

'I've considered that. I'll go abroad. France first, I think. I know a smattering of French, loved it at school.' He smiles at me but I don't return it. 'Anyway, I'll do cash in hand stuff ... waiting tables, kitchen work, cleaning. If anyone asks what I did before, I'll say the same kind of work. I won't stay long in one place, keep moving on. Then I'll see how the land lies. I have money left over from the sale of my car and a few savings. I'll be fine.'

'It's a plan, I suppose. You'll have to work all the hours in the world to get a place to live on the money those jobs will pay though.'

It's encouraging to hear that he's trying to break away, but my gut tells me he won't be able to hack it. He is going to be poor. Very.

Nathan raises his hands and lets them fall on the sofa cushions on each side of him. 'Hey, I'm not pretending it will be easy. But I'm determined to change my life. I did have a daft dream of moving somewhere hot, getting a little shack on the beach, making a living that way. That was all it could ever be, a daft dream. *This* might actually work.'

The look of raw determination in his eyes touches me. I believe every word. 'I wish you loads of luck, Nathan. I can't tell you how pleased I am that you want to make a change.'

He grins, and pride colours his cheeks. 'Something else I have to thank you for. Your idea meant that I found my mum and that freed me from Ransom. You saved my life too, obviously. I know I keep going on about it, but I'll never be able to thank—'

I raise my hands. 'Stop. You've thanked me with this watch.' I look at it again and caress the strap. 'But mostly you've thanked me by deciding to leave the stinking pile of shit that is the likes of Ransom behind. You've opted for the right choice at last.'

Nathan nods, leans forward and looks at me as if he's about to say something important. But then he stares at the floor instead. I wait, but the silence is making me feel uncomfortable. There's a tickle of anticipation in my chest. Then he looks up, clears his throat and says, 'You're going abroad too, right?'

I nod. 'Yes, that's the plan.'

'Where?'

'I haven't decided yet. I thought perhaps Spain. I have savings, I'll rent a little place …' I stop. It wouldn't do to say too much. Even though I trust him, he might get caught by Ransom's lot and be made to talk. 'Not sure.'

Nathan nods again. 'Please, Bryony … let's go together. I'll go to Spain if you like, it doesn't have to be France …' He stops, draws his hands down his face, then pushes them through his hair. 'I can see that you think I've gone nuts … perhaps I have. But I can't leave here without saying my bit.'

'Nathan, I don't think this is a good idea—'

'Please. I need you to listen. That night in the garden at your mum's there was a spark between us. I told you that Imogen was right when she guessed how I felt, and I know you felt something for me too.'

I don't like this turn in the conversation. I don't like the way he's making me feel either. The more he looks earnestly into my eyes, the more I feel my heart shift towards him. The way it shifted before I knew he'd been sent to kill me … and now the feelings I buried almost as soon as they surfaced are threatening to break free. This stops now.

'Nathan. There might have been something at the time, but then I found you'd lied to me, that you'd lied about your name, who you were, and you'd been sent to bloody kill me. That kind of information tends to change the way a person feels.'

My words do not have the kind of effect I'd hoped for. 'I knew there was something on your part that night,' he says through an ear-to-ear smile.

'Perhaps you didn't hear the rest of what I said.' I set my mouth into a straight line even though it's trying to copy his smile.

'I did. But I know you're warming towards me. You can see I'm doing the right thing now. Putting all that behind me.' He stands up and walks over to me, but I stand and move back from the bed. The air between us feels charged. My heart is thumping and I can't tear my gaze away from his.

When my back comes up against the wall I tell myself to snap out of it. I look at the floor and put both hands up in a stop gesture. 'This stops now, Nathan. It's just not going to happen.'

He's only a few feet from me and then he closes the gap, lifts my chin with his finger until I'm looking into those intense green eyes – they draw me in. I watch his mouth as it comes down to mine, hear him whisper, 'Please let it happen.' Then he kisses me and though part of me thinks it's completely nuts, I reach up, put my arms around his neck, and kiss him back.

Chapter Twenty-Four

Nathan stretches out in bed enjoying the feel of the cotton sheets against his nakedness, and listens to Bryony humming in the shower. Things like this never happen to him. He never gets a happy ending, never gets the girl. Well, not the one he wants, and he's never wanted a girl as much as he wants Bryony Masters. Just saying her name in his head makes him smile. A worrying little thought tries to rain on his parade. *Early days yet, Nathan. You've not talked about the future at all, have you? No.* They had been far too busy in bed over the past two hours. Thinking about that makes him smile too. He puts an umbrella up against the rain. Bryony wouldn't sleep with him as a one-off. He's sure they have a future … Okay, he's not, but he'll do everything he can to make sure that …

The door is open and she's standing there with just a white fluffy towel wrapped around her. Her hair is damp and she's raking it through with her fingers as she looks at him. That look says she might want to come back to bed. Nathan gives her a slow smile, throws the covers back and pats her side of the bed. 'Fancy a lie down?'

She gives him a smile that lights up her face. 'There's nothing I'd like more. But I have lots to organise. The longer I stay here, the more likely it is I'll be found.' Bryony lets the towel slip and pulls on underwear.

Nathan watches her as the little worrying thought brings its mates round and clears a big space in his head. *She said I, not we.* 'I have lots to organise. The longer I stay here …' *If she wanted to go abroad with you she'd have said 'we', wouldn't she?*

Bryony pulls her top on and flash dries her hair. Then she turns to him. 'What's with the face?'

'The face?'

'You know what I mean. Your face.' She pulls a glum expression to illustrate.

Nathan shrugs. 'Just wondered where that leaves me.'

'Where what does? Stop being so enigmatic, it doesn't suit you.' She laughs and comes to sit next to him on the bed.

'Just now, you said I, not we, when you were talking about leaving, getting stuff organised.'

The smile on her lips fades. 'That's just force of habit. I'm not usually part of a pair – or haven't been for some time. It's not something I'm great at.'

What does that mean? Nathan sits up and he notices her eyes run over his chest; she follows her gaze with her fingers. 'You have a very firm body, Nathan. Do you swim?'

'No. I run.' He moves away slightly, he can't afford to get distracted before he gets answers. 'I'm not used to being part of a pair either, but I thought we were aiming for that.'

Bryony sighs. 'Yes, I'd like to … but I'm not sure plunging headlong into living together abroad is taking things as slowly as I'd like at the beginning of a relationship.'

'It's not ideal, I'll grant you. But I can't see as we have a lot of choice.' He takes her hand and kisses the back of it.

'I … we, do have to get away from here pretty sharpish, but a new country, new life, and a new relationship might put too much stress on us.' She looks into Nathan's eyes and he can tell she's unsure. 'So in the shower I wondered if we should stay in the UK. I thought somewhere remote like the wilds of Cornwall. I remember going to Sennen near Land's End years ago, St Just too, and there's quite a few little hamlets round there that might be just right.'

Nathan's spirits are rising now he's been included in her plans, but staying in England would pose problems. 'Bryony, I have to make a living. Opportunities there will be pretty small compared to abroad.'

'In summer you should find something. The tourist season is pretty much upon us. Though if not, I have substantial savings that could see us both through the next year at the very least. I'll sell my flat too, and that will give us …'

'I can't live off you,' Nathan says quietly.

'And hopefully you won't have to. As I said I'm sure there'll be something.'

Nathan sighs but says nothing. This isn't what he'd hoped for. But he'd never have dreamed that she'd say yes to him in the first place so he'd have to compromise. 'Okay. We'll go for that. It does mean we might be easier to find though.'

Bryony laughs and shoves him back on the pillows. 'Those dozy bastards couldn't find us there. Besides, they won't be looking in the UK. Immi will have told her dad by now that I've gone abroad. You told Dawson that my mum's neighbour said I'd gone abroad, didn't you?' He nods. 'And you told your family to say you phoned them and said you'd taken care of your mum, but you were out of the country too. So if they look anywhere, it won't be here.'

'Ransom doesn't trust Immi though. Dawson said he thought she was disloyal, wanting to save your skin by pretending to sort out an appeal, remember?'

Bryony's eyes take on a faraway look and she flops down on the bed beside him. 'Yes … that needs some thought. Before we leave, we should go see her. Tell her that she should be on her guard.'

'And what if we're seen?'

'I've never been to her house before, because of that reason. So they won't be expecting it now. We'll go late at night … or very early morning.'

'Why not over the phone?'

'They might have her phone bugged. It's been known. She got a new one when we were in Cornwall because of it, but we can't be too careful.'

Nathan thinks that's pushing things too far, but he'll go with it. 'Okay. So when will you be ready, you know, get your affairs in order? I'm good to go now.'

Bryony pulls back the covers and looks him slowly up and down. Under her gaze he feels himself getting hard. She traces a finger down his lower chest and to his groin. 'I can see you're good to go …'

Nathan pulls her on top of him. 'I think we need to discuss this further.'

It's two in the morning the day after I lost my head. I say lost my head, but what actually happened was that my heart overruled it big time. My heart, and one or two other bits of my anatomy. Nathan … well, getting together with him, it's the biggest shock of my life. This is just not like me. I don't do this. Not. Ever. Turns out the new me does. I just hope I don't live to regret it. I worry that it won't last – we won't last. Whatever we have will melt like April snow under the heat of my control freakery. Or just the crazy way we got together might not allow it to thrive. But then if we don't try, we'll never know, will we?

A new hire car is packed with all our stuff out in the hotel car park, the little cottage near St Just is rented, and Nathan and I will be ready to surprise Immi in a while before we drive down south. It will be a hell of a surprise. I hope she won't be too shocked when I arrive at her bedroom door. Nathan assures me he can get us in without hanging on the doorbell, and I haven't asked any obvious questions about that. The whole thing is mad but exciting at the same time. I can't remember the last time I felt so alive. Wish I could tell Mum, but of course I can't. I wouldn't be telling Immi if I could help it.

The bright hope that one day everything will be normal lights my way through the shadowy maze of my immediate future. It's shadowy because there's a chance Ransom's lot could find us. A remote chance, but a chance nonetheless. It wouldn't do to be complacent. Complacent gets you killed. My future is a bit like an old but much-loved Christmas decoration that you thought was lost. When it's rediscovered, it brings joy, warmth and sparkle into your life. Until now, I never thought I'd find it again.

Three in the morning and we're in the car at the end of Immi's street. Nathan said earlier that it feels a bit too cloak and dagger, but we can't be too careful. A few minutes later we're outside her back door and I keep watch as Nathan slips something from his jeans pocket and pokes it in the lock. No lights are on anywhere in the tiny cul-de-sac of new houses and, in the yet-to-be established garden, only a quick fox clocks us as he slinks under the fence. I turn back to Nathan and find that he's already inside and beckoning me to follow.

A little hall table lamp shows us that the inside is clean, fresh and very Immi. The first door off the hall is the living room, and when we get to the kitchen I notice the patio doors aren't covered by the curtains. Immi really needs to get into the habit of closing them each night. Anyone could be nosing round. I hurry over, close them, then flick the light on over the cooker. 'Okay, you put the kettle on and I'll wake her,' I say to Nathan and pull a face. 'I hope she's not too scared.'

He shrugs. 'Well, I did tell you this is all a bit—'

'Cloak and dagger. Yes. Shut your face and make the tea.'

All the doors on the landing are closed. The first is the bathroom, the second the spare room, so the last one must be Immi's. Bloody hell, I hope she's not staying over … perhaps with the new doctor that she's 'really not interested in'. My fingers curl round the handle and I slowly apply pressure and give the door a gentle push. The carpet puts up a little resistance, but then it opens, and I'm in. The light flicks on and I'm looking into the barrel of a gun … oh my God.

Immi shrieks and throws the gun on the bed. 'What the FUCK are you doing? I could have shot you!'

My heart's in my throat preventing speech, so I just lean against the door and gather my wits. She shakes her head, a look of disbelief on her face. She's in pink fairy pyjamas and her hair resembles a bird's nest. A bird's nest stuffed with spaghetti. If the situation weren't so surreal I'd laugh. 'Bloody hell, Immi, I didn't expect that,' I manage after a few seconds.

'*You* didn't expect? What about me?' Immi slumps on the bed and begins to babble. 'I just got up for a wee and then I heard the kettle go on in the kitchen and people talking. Thought I was drunk at first, but then I remembered I'd only had one glass of red. And what kind of burglar puts the kettle on anyway?'

'I'm sorry to scare you, love, but I couldn't think of another way of contacting you—'

'No. Because you've never heard of a phone, have you?'

'The thing is we can't be too careful. I said that before we came back from Cornwall. What I have to tell you is best done face to face.' I fold my arms and nod at the gun. 'And since when did you become bloody Annie Oakley?'

She rolls her eyes. 'Since yesterday when Dawson brought it round. He said that one of his former employees had just gone missing and he has a grudge against my dad. He said it was probably a long shot, "no pun intended", but Dad would be happier if I had some protection.'

The facts that Immi probably has no idea how to shoot, that it's certainly an illegal weapon, and that she'd be in serious trouble if it was found here flash through my mind, but this isn't the time to mention it. Instead I say, 'Ah. Well, there's no need at all to worry about the former employee because he's here with me. He's making the tea actually.'

Now she's really confused and she ruffles the bird's nest even more than her pillows have. 'What the hell are you on about? Who is this former employee?'

'Jacob.'

Her eyes grow round. 'Jacob, Jacob?'

'Yes.'

'The Jacob you rescued. The hot one?'

'Yes. How many Jacobs do we know? Actually he's really called Nathan.'

Immi shakes her head in bewilderment and flops back onto her bed. 'Wake me up when you start making any sense at all.'

I laugh. 'Come downstairs with me and I'll explain.'

Immi has declined a second cup of tea and says she wants brandy for shock. I explain that it's only 4.15am and she replies, 'It doesn't bloody matter what time it is. It's not every day you learn that your father is capable of murder, and that the one he sent to do his dirty work is sitting at the kitchen fucking table, drinking fucking tea!' Nathan and I have explained why we're here and everything that's happened since we saw Immi last. The only thing we've not broached is our intention to make a go of things together. I swallow the last dregs of cold tea and prepare to do just that when she bangs her cup down and heads me off.

'I've a good mind to go into that next prison visit and cut his bollocks off! I mean, I knew he was a vicious, cheating, swindling, scum of the earth – but murderer? I honestly thought he'd not stoop so low. And one of the worst things is that he has no proof it was you that made that phone call in the first place!'

'You said it wasn't you?' Nathan says to me.

'It wasn't her. It was me!' Immi says, sticking out her chin at Nathan.

He raises his eyebrows. 'You?'

'Yes. Me. Him using those poor girls like that was the last straw. And how could you agree to kill someone in cold blood?' Immi jabs him hard in the chest with her finger. 'No matter how tough you've had it, growing up in a life of crime, or my shit of a father kidnapping your mum, there's no excuse.'

Nathan gives her a sad smile. 'I know. I never would have gone through with it even if Bryony hadn't saved me. It's not in me.'

'Yeah, well, you would say that now.'

I get that Immi's in shock and hurting, but she's being unfair. 'Hang on, Immi. Nathan came clean to me. If he was going to kill me, why would he have done that?' Immi just glowers, then looks into her empty cup. 'Try to put yourself in his shoes. If your mum had been kidnapped when she was ill, how do you know that you wouldn't have done the same if you were put in that position?'

Immi is silent for a few more moments then gets up, pulls a bottle of brandy from the cupboard and pours a slug into the cup. Then she stands with her back against the kitchen cupboard, takes a sip and looks at us. 'You might have a point, but I could never have done it.'

'Nor could I,' Nathan says quietly.

'Why are you here exactly?' Immi narrows her eyes. 'It isn't just to tell me this. We could have met somewhere secret like we've done before. Why are you here in the middle of the night?'

'Two reasons.' I sit back and swallow hard. 'One is to make sure that you realise your dad doesn't trust you now. As I said earlier, he told Dawson that he knew you were bluffing about sorting an appeal to make sure he didn't come after me.'

'Well, yeah. That's obvious, given that *he's* sitting there,' she says, looking at Nathan as if he's dirt on her shoe.

'But I think it might be more serious than that. If he suspects you're against him then he might want revenge somehow,' I say, hoping I'm getting through. It can't be easy to hear that your parent might wilfully harm you.

'And as I said earlier, I'm his daughter.'

'Even so …'

'No. I'm the only thing he cares about.' She gives a humourless bark. 'Well, after himself of course. He's always come at the top of his own list.'

'You're right there,' Nathan says.

'And the second reason?' Immi asks. Nathan and I share a look and she sighs. 'You two.' She points at us back and forth. 'You're not sodding *at it*, are you?'

My cheeks colour. 'A nice way of putting it.'

Immi's eyes widen and she ruffles her hair through as if she's trying to wake her brain up. 'My God. You are! You bloody are … even after you found out about him? Shit. You must have it bad!'

What do I say to that? Nathan looks at me and I notice that his face is aflame too. We must look like naughty children who've been caught with their fingers in the cookie jar. 'You were the one was pushing us together when we were in Cornwall,' I remind her, while knowing it's a lame thing to say.

'That was before I knew he was a potential murderer.' Immi clicks her tongue against the roof of her mouth. I can see we're getting nowhere on this tack, so I just tell her that we're off to Cornwall to get away from her father, and where to find us in an emergency. I also tell her not to mention any of it to my mum.

Immi listens without saying anything, but her hand gestures and facial expressions are priceless. When I've finished, she downs the last of her brandy and says, 'I've heard it all now. You're skulking off to the wilds of Cornwall all loved-up with a man who was sent to kill you. Are you bonkers?' She throws her hands up. 'What if he's doing all this to lull you into a false sense of security? What if he's some weirdo that gets off with sleeping with his victim first before he kills them? Not thought of that, have you, eh? No.'

Nathan shakes his head and looks away. I can see that he's trying not to smile. Immi looks so indignant and childlike with her hair stuck up and in those ridiculous pyjamas. I feel a rush of affection for her and wish it all could be different. It can't be though. Her father has seen to that. 'Look, I'm not surprised you're reacting like this. I would be too in your shoes. It will take a while to sink in … but please, please be on your guard, Immi, okay? And …' My throat closes over and I have to fight to keep the tears back. 'And please wish us well. Hopefully we'll all come out the other side and we'll be able to laugh again. Get back to normal.'

Immi's looked away so I nod at Nathan and the door. He stands and we walk down the hallway. 'Look after yourself, Immi,' Nathan says over his shoulder.

Just as we're leaving, we hear the pad of fluffy slippers on the laminate behind us and then I'm enveloped in a huge hug. Immi's face is pressed against mine and I can't tell if the tears on my cheek are hers or mine. She holds me at arm's length. 'You bloody take care, lady. And you.' She wipes her eyes and glares at Nathan. 'You'd better look after her because if you don't, I swear I'll have your balls in a vice.'

Nathan grimaces. 'I promise I will. Bye, Immi.' He opens the door and slips out.

Immi and I hug once more and then I leave too, my heart sinking a bit as I hear the door closing behind me. That's it then. All my old ties are cut. Job, flat, home town, best friend. For now, it's Nathan and me against the world. And right at this moment as we hurry down the sleeping street at the crack of dawn towards an uncertain future, the world feels like it might win.

Chapter Twenty-Five

We have taken the three-hundred-and-seventy-mile journey from Sheffield to Cornwall fairly steadily, stopping for coffee, and then for breakfast. I've been pleasantly surprised about the way we can just slip into talking about trivial stuff and then back into more important issues just as easily. There's been no awkwardness. In fact, everything about being with Nathan feels easy, natural, right. It's a cliché, but it really seems as if we've known each other for ages.

Because we set off before five, the roads are free of traffic queues and it's just coming up to 11.30 as we pass the road sign for St Just. Even though we slept most of the afternoon away the day before, we've been running on adrenalin and looking forward to getting our heads down for a few hours before exploring our new surroundings. I glance at Nathan's handsome profile and his fingers curling round the steering wheel and hope we're not too tired to make love before we fall asleep. I can't get enough of him. Yes, the relationship is very new and that's to be expected, but I've never felt like this before about anyone.

I've tried to analyse my feelings but then given up. My instincts tell me to let it all just happen … see where we end up. This, like many other things that have happened lately, is a new concept to me. In the past I'd want everything categorised, analysed to within an inch of its life and then filed away into the appropriate sections of my head and heart. This new way of thinking is a bit scary, a bit alien, but on the whole, it's liberating.

'Satnav says the cottage is down here.' Nathan looks dubiously down a wiggly track the width of a pencil, squeezed on both sides by a robust Cornish hedge.

'Yeah, this will be it. I looked on Google before we left. It's out of the way, and Cornwall is full of tracks like this. If we meet another car it'll end in a standoff.'

I smile at his less than convinced 'hmm', but he indicates, and on we go.

Luckily we don't meet another car, but have to stop when two pheasants fly into the path ahead. They're unfazed by the car horn and only scuttle off when I get out and shoo them away. Also luckily, the track is no longer than a couple of hundred yards, and round a sharp bend it opens out into a wide gravelled area beyond which stands Trevella Cottage. It's built of local stone, covered in wisteria, drips honeysuckle from a standing arch built to the left of it in a tiny cottage garden and, to its right, there's rolling green countryside as far as the eye can see. Perfect.

'Wow. This is like something out of a fairy story,' Nathan says, switching off the engine.

'It is. And I'm going to use a phrase that I avoid using if at all possible, but this place is "totally awesome".'

'Don't you mean totes?'

'No, Nathan, I do not. If I ever say the word *totes*, you have permission to shoot m—' Nathan's smile dies on his face and I cringe at what I've just said. 'Let's rewind that last sentence and go have a look round.' I twist my hand around the hair at the back of his neck and draw him in for a kiss.

On the threshold of our new home, I heave a sigh of relief. Trevella Cottage is just as perfect as the outside and just as I'd been led to believe from the photos on the website. There had been a nagging doubt at the back of my head on the long drive down, because the description of 'A more quaint, compact, delightful getaway or indeed, more permanent dwelling, in our opinion would be very difficult to find' seemed too good to be true. My apprehension had painted a picture of a Dickensian hovel complete with rats and damp walls, but no, this place was heavenly. Heavenly? Another word I would never use.

Inside, a clean lemon-and-white sitting room and light wood offshoot kitchen are modern yet quaint, and so welcoming. I feel a relieved smile creep over my face; the whole cottage is lovely and quintessentially chocolate box. No doubt Immi would have a ready snort of derision at my expression if she were here. She isn't, thank goodness, and I must stop wondering about whether we've done the right thing. So far it couldn't be better.

Twenty minutes later, as I'm fluffing up the quilt on the double bed in the lovely olive-and-white painted bedroom, I hear Nathan shout that lunch is ready. We'd picked up some fresh bread from the local bakery and a few essentials from the small supermarket. A smile curls my lips. I can't believe how happy I feel right at this moment. Since Dad was killed, happiness has been a stranger. I've only seen glimpses of it from time to time and it never has substance, always leaving, hurrying away before I realise that it was ever here.

It's the little things that matter. They often turn out to be the big things. Right now, the prospect of having lunch in this lovely cottage, making love and then falling asleep in my man's arms swells my heart with joy. I'm not a spiritual person really, but sometimes I think that Dad is watching over me. I send him silent thanks. I'm so grateful for this chance to start again. To make a new life. Tossing a couple of pillows against the brass headboard, I take one last look through the deep sash window over the rolling fields and hurry out to the kitchen.

'We have bread and butter, olives, a selection of cheese and a few slices of that roast gammon.' Nathan pulls a chair out for me at the rough pine farmhouse table and I sit. 'Not sure whether you want beer, wine, water or tea?'

'Wow, this looks delicious. Just water ,thanks, not sure my eyes would stay open if I had alcohol this afternoon.'

'Mine neither. Mind you, we are going to bed after this, aren't we?' Nathan has a naughty twinkle in his eye as he sits down and pops an olive into his mouth.

I watch his mouth as he chews and imagine kissing it … kissing me. 'Not sure,' I tease. I butter some bread, avoid his gaze.

'I wondered if we should have a walk instead, take in our surroundings more. We could pop into the pub down the road …' I stop when I see his crestfallen face. I know exactly what's on his mind. 'You don't fancy it?'

'Yes, but I fancy you more. I thought we were going to, you know …?'

Carrying on the teasing would be too cruel. 'I'm joking, Nate.' Oh, that was a surprise, calling him Nate. I'd not intended to.

His face lights up. 'My family call me Nate. It's great that you did too.'

'Just popped out. I must admit, I like it. I'll call you Nate, but Nathan when I'm angry with you.' I make my lips a thin line and fold my arms.

'Oh. You look angry now,' he says, a hunk of bread hovering near his lips.

'That's because you haven't kissed me for …' I look at the Rolex. 'About twenty minutes, Nathan.'

He laughs. 'Sorry, I need to eat first. Keep my strength up.' He stuffs half the bread in his mouth and gives me a wink.

I love watching him sleep. All the worries and cares of his waking life that he often carries with him like a second skin slip away and he's peaceful, calm, and serene. Maybe I look the same. Sometimes, my worries and cares weigh so heavy across my shoulders I wonder if I'll look old before my time. They aren't the same ones I carried when I was a DI, but they're just as heavy, perhaps more so. No matter how happy I am now and looking forward, until I know for sure that Ransom will leave me alone, I'll be forever looking behind too.

Snuggling down against Nate's warm body I go over again what he's told me about his family, friends and past relationships. As far as past relationships go, like me, he's not had many, not for the same reasons though. I absolutely get why he couldn't fall for someone who was happy staying within the criminal culture – same goes for friends too. Poor Nate. I do think he's been quite lonely for a very long time. Ransom's ilk reach deep inside a person, twist, maim, destroy. When Nate asked about why I'd not settled with anyone I was a bit economical with the truth … blamed the job, the unsociable hours. I don't want him thinking my controlling nature will come between us. And it's funny, but so far I haven't felt controlling at all where he's concerned.

My eyes feel heavy and I close them. Perhaps we'll go for dinner in St Just tonight. Or perhaps go further afield. It's only about fifteen minutes to Sennen and about the same to Penzance. Penzance might be best. We'll be more anonymous there. It would be nice to get to meet the locals, but the more we do, the easier it will be for anyone to find us. Immi is the only one that knows our address, so I shouldn't worry. She'd rather die than tell. Nevertheless … we'll keep ourselves to ourselves, just in case.

Chapter Twenty-Six

Imogen is about to run a bath when she hears the doorbell. It's almost 8pm, not that late, but since Bryony and Nathan had woken her in the early hours two nights before, she'd been a bit jumpy to say the least. At the top of the stairs she can see a tall shadow through the glass panes of the door. Who the hell could it be? She's not expecting anyone. The bell goes again. Making sure her phone is in her pocket, she hurries downstairs and stands to the side of the door. 'Who is it?'

'Frank Dawson. Tried to ring but you didn't answer.'

Imogen's immediately cautious. What they hell does he want? She flicks her phone open and sees two missed calls two hours earlier when she was in the supermarket. 'Right. Well, is it important? I was just about to have a bath and put my feet up. It's been a long day,' she says, opening the door a crack. Dawson's wearing a suit more expensive than her entire wardrobe and stinking of aftershave. His piggy little eyes focus on her legs under her short bathrobe and he smiles. If he has any ideas of that nature he can fuck right off!

'Nothing really important. Silly, to be honest, but I left my favourite pen here last time when I brought you … you know. Can I come in and get it?' The toe of his shiny shoe is already insinuating itself over her threshold.

'Pen? I haven't noticed one. But come in and have a look.' Imogen pulls the robe tight around her and leads the way into the kitchen. She can't remember him going anywhere else last time he was here. Looking at her kitchen with fresh eyes, it isn't any wonder that she's not noticed a pen. It's a tip. A pile of washing waiting to go in the machine on a chair, breakfast dishes on the table, tonight's ready meal cartons on the counter. She really hasn't been herself since Bryony came. Every time she tries to settle to anything, her mind is preoccupied by what she told her. Also she spends a lot of time worrying about her old friend's safety now that she's shacked up with that low life Nathan.

Dawson's lifting her washing, holding it at arm's length. She hurries over and retrieves it; she doesn't want his grubby hands on her underwear, dirty or not. 'I thought I might have dropped it by this chair,' he says, getting down on his knees and looking under the dresser. 'I was sitting on it most of the time, wasn't I? Oh, wait … Later I went over to look at your plants on the windowsill, didn't I? I remembered my old mum used to have a little cactus just like that one.' He gets up and goes to the window. 'Ah yes, here's the pen behind the pot!' He waves it at her in triumph. 'I must have put it down when I picked up the plant.'

To Imogen the pen just looks ordinary. Why he's making a special journey here to get it is a mystery. But now he's got it he can bugger off. 'Oh well, that's good then,' she says, walking back towards the hall. When he doesn't follow, she turns round. 'Was there anything else?'

Dawson's leaning with his back against the sink, tucking the pen in his top pocket. 'Not really, though I am wondering if you're cool with having the gun here. You looked less than enthusiastic when I gave it you.'

What did he expect? Flowers, tears? 'It's a gun. It kills people. I don't like them.'

'But you'd like it less if someone broke in and tried to hurt you and you didn't have it.' He looks at her as if she's five.

'That's hardly likely, Frank.' Immi wonders what he'd say if he knew she'd already had to brandish it at a 'burglar' two nights before. 'But yes, I'll keep it for now, if that's what Dad wants.'

'He does. He's quite worried about you to be honest. This Bryony, she's supposed to have gone abroad, you say?'

This turn of subject unnerves her. 'Yes, that's what she told me.'

'Upped and left the police – just left a good career, went abroad?' Dawson's dark eyes are on hers, cold, calculating.

'Yes. I don't know much beyond that. We weren't really close anymore, Facebook contacts, that's all.'

'Were you? Were you really?' Dawson gives her a thin smile.

'Yes, and if that's all, I'd like to have my bath now.' Imogen walks from the kitchen and waits by the front door. Her heart's thumping, she wants Dawson out. He's beginning to scare her.

He walks down the hall towards her. 'You see, Imogen, I have evidence to suggest that you are more than Facebook contacts. I've some pictures of you with her a few months ago. You seemed to be out for drinks.'

'You have pictures? What the hell for?' Her face is aflame. She folds her arms across her chest, tries to hold her nerve.

'Not denying it then?'

'One drink. Is that a crime?'

'Not sure your dad would be pleased.'

'Oh, for goodness' sake! Can you leave now?'

Dawson holds his hands up. 'Just doing you a favour, that's all. Your dad hates being double-crossed.'

'What? I haven't double-crossed him, whatever that even means.'

'Hmm.' He looks right into her eyes, unblinking. She sets her jaw and looks back. Then he opens the door. 'Anyway, thanks for letting me get my pen, and make sure you lock the door behind me. As I said, there's a bad man on the loose. If he sees you in that robe there'd be no telling what he might try.'

As soon as he's outside, Imogen slams the door and locks it. He's the only bloody bad man on the loose as far as she can see. A shudder runs through her when she thinks of the look in his eye when he spoke his parting shot, and she checks that all the doors and windows are locked. Why was he trying to scare her? Did her dad really suspect that she was against him? The prospect of a bath no longer appeals and she wanders to her room, takes out the gun and makes sure she knows how to load it. When Bryony came round the other night it was empty. There are a few written instructions and it takes a while, but it's ready now if any bad men should come calling.

Used to living alone, Imogen's spooked after Dawson's visit. The house feels too big, too quiet, too … threatening. On impulse she decides to take Jonathan the new doctor up on his offer of a drink. They did have a rough patch, but that's been ironed out now and they've been getting closer lately, but Imogen isn't sure if their work relationship would encroach on a romantic one. It might be awkward, him being a doctor, her being a receptionist. But isn't that putting herself down? Right now she couldn't give a damn because she can't be alone. Not tonight. She calls Jonathan and he's pleased. They agree to meet in an hour, so that's good. No time for her to prevaricate, agonise over what to wear, just shower, change and out.

Heading for the bathroom she feels a bit better, more settled. Nevertheless, before she gets in the shower, she runs to her bedroom, gets the gun, puts it on the windowsill and wedges the linen basket against the door. Better to be safe than sorry.

Chapter Twenty-Seven

Dreams actually do come true. From his seat at the kitchen table, Nathan looks up from his iPad across at Bryony. She's chopping carrots and humming something that sounds like 'You Can't Touch This' and wiggling her bum from side to side in time with the tune. It feels like they've been together years and he honestly doesn't know how he'd live without her. Admitting that even to himself is a hell of a shock. Bryony is everything to him. Two days, that's all it's been. The whole thing is surreal. Surreal and wonderful.

Nathan hasn't broached how he feels in so many words yet because it has been only a matter of days, but he hopes she feels the same. The way she looks at him, the touch of her hand, the little things she says give him hope that she might. Because of his past he's decided to not count any chickens; things like this don't happen to him ... didn't. He needs to take things slowly, gently. If he started all the declaration of love and stuff she might run for the hills. He looks back at the iPad to cover a little smile at the image that thought offers up. Nathan might run for the hills with her – saying anything like that scares the shit out of him. He's never told a woman he loves her before. Apart from his mother, that is.

Bryony looks at him over her shoulder. 'What's funny?'

Nathan frowns.

'You were smiling to yourself.'

She's caught him then. He smiles again. 'Just thinking how nice this is. Sunday morning, you preparing a meal for later before we nip down the local for a pint. Also thinking how good it is that Mum is happy in her new place with Sandra.'

Bryony smiles back at him. 'Yes, it was nice of Angie to call and let you know. And you're right, this is nice.' Then her eyes mist over and she turns back to her chopping. 'My dad would never believe I'm being so domesticated.'

Nathan goes over, puts his arms around her waist and leans his head against her back. 'You miss him loads, don't you?' He feels her nod. 'How would he feel about you leaving the police?'

'Not sure. I've thought about that one for a while. He'd say go with your heart, but I can't help feeling that he'd be a bit disappointed. Mum is all for it though.' She sighs, puts the knife down and turns to him. 'I wish I could tell her about us, that I'm okay, you know?'

'Yes. Well, hopefully we can soon. I hope she doesn't turn against me like Immi did. But I wouldn't blame her if she did. It's to be expected.'

Bryony kisses him. 'If she does she'll come round when she sees how happy I am.'

'You are?'

'You know I am.'

'And is that because I'm the nicest, most wonderful guy in the world?'

'Don't push it.' Bryony releases him and turns back to her chopping.

Nathan goes back to the iPad and says, 'There's a job here in Penzance. A general kitchen help. So dogsbody, I expect.'

'Yep. You'd get paid peanuts too.'

'Gotta start somewhere.'

'Hmm.'

'I might give them a ring tomorrow.'

'If you like, but we could have a few weeks getting to know each other better first? No point in breaking your neck to get a crappy job. I told you, I can keep us going for a while.'

The usual answer, the fact that he doesn't want her keeping him, is on the tip of his tongue, but he decides to swallow it.

No fun in ruining the lovely time they're having by going on about it. 'Well I'm buying the drinks, then.'

'I wouldn't have it any other way.'

The King's Arms in St Just is a lovely old Cornish Inn, complete with wood beams, a friendly atmosphere and a good pint. And it's old, fourteenth century so the landlady said. Nathan loves old places. He wonders how many stories, secrets and lies have been told across the wooden tables over the years, and whispered across the bar. Bryony had been really reluctant to go local, but he's convinced her. The chances of anyone tracing them here are minuscule, and as long as they don't come into town too often he's sure they'll be fine.

Bryony comes back from the loo and pulls a face as she sits down at their table. 'The smell of that Sunday lunch is making me drool. Wish I'd not prepared ours for later now.'

'We can have that tomorrow, if you like,' Nathan says, but at the same time wonders if that was the right response given that she'd spent ages doing it all.

'You don't mind? Oh, that's fantastic, because I'm so hungry.'

'Must be that pint and a half of cider you downed in five seconds flat.' Nathan grins and waits for her to jump on him.

'Hey, it was well over an hour, cheeky!' She chucks a beer mat at him. 'Didn't see you exactly sipping yours either.'

'I'll order the lunch, shall I? And another pint?' Nathan stands and collects their glasses.

'No. A half, or I'll be wobbling over the cliffs if we're going walking after.'

Nathan looks out of the window. 'Not sure we'll go today. There are big black clouds rolling in.'

'So there'll be fewer people on the cliff path then, which is good. I like walking in the rain.'

Nathan isn't so keen and his face must have registered this as he walks to the bar. A guy sitting at the corner of the bar nursing a pint catches his eye and smiles. 'Couldn't help overhearing you chatting there. Make sure you're careful on that path down here in the rain. Some parts can be a bit dangerous if you don't know what you're doing.'

Nathan rolls his eyes. 'Yeah. I'd rather go when the sun's shining to be honest.' The guy nods and sips his drink. 'You local?' Nathan doesn't think so – the man has a tiny trace of a Geordie accent.

'No. I come down here regular though. Love the walks, the scenery.' He looks into his pint, seems distracted.

No further conversation is forthcoming, and after Nathan orders lunch he discovers the guy has gone.

Back at their table something starts bugging him about the man. He can't put his finger on it though. 'What's up? You're quiet,' Bryony says.

'Did you notice me chatting to the guy at the bar?'

'Yeah, forties, dark beard, woolly green hat?'

'Yeah.'

'What about him?'

'I don't know. We just had a quick chat about the cliff path, he said be careful as it's dangerous when it's wet, or bits of it are.'

'Was he local?'

'No.'

'Well, what does he know? I'm better placed than he is to say – we came along cliff paths loads when I was a kid. The one past here too.' Bryony takes a sip of her drink.

'He comes down here all the time walking and stuff.'

'Right. Well if you'd rather not go, it's fine by me.' Nathan can tell that she's made her voice bright and breezy, but she's disgruntled. He's already beginning to read her very well.

'No, we'll go. There was just something about him that I can't put my finger on.' Then it hits him. 'I think I've seen him before … perhaps he's been on telly?'

'I've never seen him. Mind you, I don't watch that much telly.' Bryony slips her hand through his and gives him a peck on the cheek. 'I'll look after you out there on the windswept Cornish paths, my handsome.'

Her broad Cornish accent makes him laugh. Just then the waitress comes out with their food, and all thoughts of the man go out of his head as they tuck into a huge plate of roast beef and Yorkshire pudding. Not long ago Nathan was lonely, hated what he did, could see no way out, but now look at him. A new life in a wonderful part of the world and a wonderful woman to share it with. Could life get any better?

Chapter Twenty-Eight

Two nights in a row. A third would be too much, and besides, it's work tomorrow. It wouldn't do to show up in the same car together, would it? The entire surgery would be full of gossip. Imogen puts four slices of bread in Jonathan's toaster and considers scrambled eggs. Before he went in the shower he said she should have whatever she could find in the fridge, which wasn't much as he needed to do a shop. There were eggs, milk, jam and butter and a few mouldy looking onions. The eggs were in date though, so they might be the best option. He really ought to look after himself better than this; doctors are always banging on about nutrition, aren't they? Mind you, he is really busy.

Imogen sits at the table and digs into her eggs. Jonathan has just shouted through he'll be there in a tick and she decides it feels nice. This domestic thing. It's been a long time since she's shared breakfast with anyone. It's more like lunch, really; they'd had a lazy morning in bed. A pang of guilt surfaces and she swallows it back down with coffee. She only accepted his offer of a drink because she was too scared to stay at home by herself the other night. But they'd really enjoyed each other's company and got on so well. He's completely different outside work. It's as if he slipped off his doctor's persona when he walked through the door of the pub and become more relaxed, funny and … human. It had seemed more natural to stay over when he'd asked than go home, but tonight she'd have to go back.

Jonathan comes in, his dark hair, still wet from the shower, almost black. He has the most amazing blue eyes, almost navy, and Imogen can't help but stare into them. 'Great eggs,' he says through a big mouthful of them.

'Glad you like them. You appear to have not much else in the cupboards or fridge.'

Jonathan looks sheepish. 'I know. I'm so rubbish at shopping, but I'm always rushing around. Every week I tell myself to plan ahead, do a big shop, then I find myself down the chip shop or the Chinese because I haven't done it, yet again.'

'You have an excuse, so I'll let you off. You're a doctor going about saving people's lives. Important stuff like that.' Imogen pushes her plate to one side, and regards him over the rim of her coffee cup.

He takes a swig of coffee and looks at her. 'Tell me if I'm wrong, but do you think there's a problem me being a doctor, you being a receptionist? It's just that you've mentioned it a few times over the past few days and …' His voice tails off.

Imogen realises her cheeks are flushed and Jonathan's looking at them. She considers a white lie, but what's the point. May as well be honest from the off. 'Truthfully? I didn't even think about it at first, but I can hear the tongues wagging already. You know, the "he could do better than her," yadda, yadda.'

'And is that what you think?' He continues with his eggs.

'No, well, maybe.' Imogen shrugs. 'I've been going through a bit of …' She stops, unsure how to tell him about her father, or indeed whether to tell him at all. This might just be a fling with no future, so would there be any point telling him all her backstory?

'Go on.' He finishes his food and gives her his undivided attention.

'What are we doing exactly?' Imogen feels an awkward silence blocking the rest of her words.

'Eating breakfast?'

'You know what I mean.'

'You mean have we just had a nice time these past few days and then going back to our lives – separately?'

Relief moves the silence. 'That's exactly what I meant. I mean, we haven't really discussed it.'

'Apart from when I just said have you got a problem with me been a doctor, etcetera? Why would I say that if it wouldn't be an issue in the future?' Jonathan frowns. 'Unless I'm jumping the gun here, I think it would be nice to keep on seeing each other and see where it goes.'

Imogen smiles. 'That's exactly what I was thinking.' She finishes her coffee and decides to get everything out at once, rather than drip her problems into their relationship bit by bit like acid. 'Okay, I'll tell you what's bothering me. I'm likely to listen to the yadda, yadda voices because my dad is in prison and he is one of the most evil people on the planet. I feel like I've become tainted by him, wonder how much he's influenced who I am and feel sick that wherever I am and whatever I try to do, try to be, he'll ruin it. He's in prison but he's still very powerful …' She stops, tries to read Jonathan's expression, but he's had years of training to hide behind.

'I'm listening,' he says, and reaches across the table for her hand.

'And doctors are clever, aren't they? Have to be really, all that stuff to remember about drugs …' She looks at the table. 'I must be dumb to have not seen what a bastard my father was all those years. What he did to my poor mum. When I did realise, I put a stop to it though, so …' Imogen feels like she's in a counselling session. Not that she's ever had one, but she imagines it must be like this. What the hell must Jonathan think of her?

Jonathan releases her hand and leans back. 'Okay, well it sounds like you've had a shit time lately, and I'm sorry about that and your dad. But to be honest, I don't care about him or anything you see as negative in your past. I care about you in the here and now. And you are one of the nicest people I know, so you can cross the "has he influenced you" thing off the worry list for starters. And what is clever? We're all clever in our different ways. I've known some GPs who are at the top of their game in terms of diagnosis, stuff like that, but have no bedside manner whatsoever. They can't relate to people. And if you can't do that, how can you be a successful GP?' He smiles and pours more coffee.

Imogen wonders if he might be the nicest man she's ever met and tries to keep emotion out of her voice as she says, 'Thanks, Jonathan. You have a knack of putting things into perspective.'

'I'm a GP, we're clever like that.' Imogen laughs and then he says, 'While we're on backgrounds, mine was on a tough council estate. My dad was an alky, Mum worked all the hours she could to make sure me and my brother were fed, clothed and if we ever brought trouble home, we got a belting. She was determined we'd go on to better things and we did. Tom's a barrister.'

This wasn't what Imogen had imagined at all. 'My goodness, it's a good job you had a mum like that … well, apart from the beltings.'

'Yeah, and we only got one or two of those to be honest. We understood where she was coming from and wanted to do our best for her, and for us.'

Imogen nods. 'Are your parents still around?'

'Mum is. Dad drank himself to death about fifteen years ago. She married again and is really happy now.'

She gives him a little smile. 'I'm so glad she's happy … but it seems that we both have had troubled pasts.'

'Yes, but it's the present and future that matters. What we do with each new day and how we respond to others is more important than any skeletons rattling around in our cupboards.'

'What a wise head on relatively young shoulders,' Imogen says, with the accent on relatively.

'Oi, watch it. I'm only five years older than you, miss.' He gets up and looks out of his kitchen window. 'Fancy a walk in the sunshine?'

She says she does and Jonathan clears away the dishes while Imogen's thoughts drift to Bryony. Perhaps she'd been too hard on her over Nathan, because her old friend was always pragmatic, logical, and tough as old boots. If she trusted the guy, then so should Imogen. But love does funny things to a girl's head. Lots of weird chemicals come in and smack common sense around a bit. Bryony might be out of her depth and just can't see it. As Jonathan catches her eye, he blows her a kiss and a wiggly warm feeling spreads in her chest. What was she just thinking about chemicals? It's not love for her though … not yet. But it might be for Bryony. She can't remember ever seeing her look so happy. Still, when she gets home tonight she'll call her, see how she's doing. And, since her chat with Jonathan, she doesn't feel so worried about going home on her own now.

Chapter Twenty-Nine

All I have to do is just admit I was wrong and we can go home. Just a few words and I'd be out of this mizzle and mist, cosy in the cottage, or even in bed with a hot chocolate and my hot man. But I can't do that because I'm me. Stubborn, headstrong, and a bit stupid if I'm honest. We'll just go to the next bit of the headland and then turn back. I hiccup and wonder how much the Doombar has contributed to my mule-headedness. Sometimes alcohol makes my control freakery worse. I wish I'd not decided that it was absent when Nathan was around the other day. It clearly only needs a few pints and a big roast dinner to rear its ugly head. I'll stick to red wine in future.

'At least it's stopped raining now!' I yell to Nathan over my shoulder as I scramble down a steep incline in the path. The loose shale slips under my feet and I have to concentrate on not falling on my arse. The Atlantic to my right is in a really grumpy mood. The breeze and leaden sky has turned it grey and capped its restless swell with white foam. At the moment, because the path winds so close to its surface, it's spraying us with cold salt water every chance it gets as it hurls itself at the jagged rocks leading to the headland.

Nathan's voice comes from a little way off and higher up the path behind me. 'It might have stopped raining, but that mist is getting thicker … it's coming in from the land. How much further do you want to go?'

'Just up to the headland! The path climbs in a bit and then we'll go back on the road. The road's only about five minutes from there.'

'Right. I bloody hope so, because …'

Nathan's voice fades out, but I can hear him talking, though his voice is low and I can't make out what he's saying. I turn into the wind, pushing my wet hair out of my eyes. He's talking to that guy from the pub up the path from me. He's the first person we've seen for a good half hour. Everyone else is more sensible, it seems. I hurry back up the path and say hello.

'Hello, Bryony, I was just saying to Nathan here how the weather's closing in. Might be best to head off home.'

'Yeah, we are in a bit. Only another ten minutes or so …' I stop talking when I catch the look on Nathan's face. He's looking at the man with undisguised contempt; his stance is fight rather than flight, bunched fists, hunched shoulders.

'How did you know our names?' he asks. There's ice in his voice. I had presumed that Nathan had just told the guy our names. Obviously not.

The man isn't perturbed in the slightest by Nathan's manner or tone. He gives us both a slow smile. 'Might have overheard you say them in the pub earlier.'

'That's bullshit and you know it.' Nathan takes a step closer to the man.

A sense of foreboding crawls up my spine. This isn't a good place for a fight. 'What's wrong, Nate?' I put my hand on his arm but he shrugs me off.

'I've just remembered where I've seen him before, Bryony.'

'You've seen me before? Really?' He wipes his wet face with the back of his hand. 'Okay, I must admit you're right, it is bullshit. I knew your names before I came here.' The man takes a couple of steps back and my heart leaps into my throat when he whips a gun from inside his fleece. Nathan steps forward but stops when the man cocks the trigger. 'Get on your knees, both of you.'

My mind is in turmoil, my heart thumping in my chest, but my training kicks in and I pull Nathan down. If we follow orders it might buy us some time. If Nathan flies at him he'll be killed, no question.

'You're one of Ransom's men. I saw you briefly once when I'd come to drop off some shit or other. I never forget a face.' Nathan's voice is a few octaves higher than normal and his shoulder's shaking next to mine. Or is mine shaking next to his?

The man laughs and I realise it's me shaking; in fact my whole body is trembling. My training might have kicked in, but it's not helping now. Thoughts that we're going to die because he's been sent to kill us are on a loop in my head and I don't know what to do. I don't know what to do. I don't know what to do!

'Took your time remembering my face though, eh?' he says to Nathan with a cold chuckle. 'Unlucky.'

Then I think again about buying time – talk. Talk to him! 'But why are you here?' I say in a small voice. Lame but better than nothing.

'Oh, please. You're an intelligent woman. I had hoped to do this with the minimum of fuss in the middle of the night when you were fast asleep. But there was always a chance you'd hear me break in – things might get messy. Then you waltzed into the pub … imagine my surprise. Next you decided to come down here for a walk despite my warnings not to. I reckoned it would be too public. Mist's down now though, nobody about … so I thought might as well get it over with. Couldn't get a clear shot from behind, so thought I'd get right up close.'

I feel Nathan shift and guess he's going to attack, so I put my hand on his wrist. *Not yet.* 'But how did you know where we were?'

'Ransom's daughter.'

'No. I can't believe that.' I swallow my shock and keep a loose grip on Nathan's wrist.

'Oh, don't worry, she didn't grass on you. Dawson took a pen round and left it at hers, except it was one of those recording devices. Very double-oh-seven. Anyway, when he collected it, you were all on there chatting about how it was her that made the call that got her dad banged up – and also your new address …' I squeeze Nathan's wrist twice, hoping he guesses what I'm doing. 'Made my job a piece of—'

We both launch ourselves at his legs and he goes down with a thud on the stony path. Then Nathan's on top of him wrestling for the gun and as I reach up to help him there's a shot that sounds like a cannon roar in the thick air and my heart stands still … until I realise that Nathan's still moving but the man's not. There's a red patch spreading down his arm and across his chest. I strangle a sob, kneel next to Nathan and take his face slaked with mud and blood in both my hands. 'Oh my God, Nate. Are you okay?'

'I … I think so. I turned the gun on him and …' We both look at the man and see that the gun is still in his grasp, but his eyes are closed and he's motionless. Nathan goes to retrieve it and there's a second shot. I scream as he slumps forward onto the path next to the man. The man gives me a sly grin and struggles to sit up, and then there's another scream and a yell from the top of the path. There's a group of walkers and one yells that they're calling the police.

Nathan tries to get up but there's a lot of blood on his chest. I go to help him but he yells at me to run, save myself. I look at the man again and see that he's almost on his feet; he looks much stronger than I give him credit for. Can I take him? He has a flesh wound – I might just be able …

'For God's sake run, Bryony!' Nathan yells and then slumps forward again, blood pooling from under him.

I glance at the man and he's almost in shooter stance, but he's swaying … so I run. I run so fast that I skid on the path and tumble a few feet, but then I'm up and weaving side to side to make sure he can't get a straight shot. I want to look behind but I daren't. I want to go back for Nate, but I can't. My legs and arms are pumping so fast I think I'll fall, pinwheel onto the rocks. It's as though I'm in some surreal fucking nightmare and in a minute a sea monster's going to surface and swallow me whole …

Then a few moments later I hear sirens in the distance. I hear faint shouts and cries, and I stop. Fast. A few pebbles scatter on in front of me down the path and then everything is still. All my senses are tuned for footfalls on the path behind. Nothing.

Nearby a seagull glides silently past in the mist, but all I can hear are the crashing waves and my heart wildly thumping in my ears.

What to do? What to do! Oh God, my poor Nate. I have to see how he is! But if I go back up the hill, I might run into the shooter. Most likely he's gone though, or been caught by the police. But what if he's on the path behind me right now? I look back but can't see any movement through the swirling mist. If I go back to see Nathan I'll have to tell the police who I am. They'd find out I was recently a DI. I'd have to explain why we're here. Who Nathan is … his connection to Ransom. I might make things so much worse for him.

Instinct kicks in. Indecision can be fatal and my feet take over – they carry me to the headland and back onto the road. I can't go back to Trevella Cottage. Not yet. Not until I know what's happened to the shooter. I skirt the borders of St Just and slip into a café. I nurse a coffee, pretend I'm normal, and then when I can bear it no longer run to the ladies', bolt the cubicle door and sob silent tears until they run dry.

Chapter Thirty

If this is a dream it seems to have been going on forever. Bryony should really wake him soon; it doesn't do to sleep so long of an afternoon, because he'll never get to sleep tonight. Is it night already? He tries to open his eyes but his eyelids feel so heavy … so heavy. Nathan thinks he's tried to open them before, but can't be sure if he was awake or dreaming. He can't be sure now, either. Why does he need Bryony to wake him? He should be able to wake up himself, shouldn't he? They were on the cliff path … it was misty. He can't remember getting back to the cottage after their walk, can't remember going to bed – but he is in a bed, he can feel it under his body. Why can't he remember? Was the walk a dream? Was Bryony a dream? Nathan's limbs feel leaden all of a sudden and he's sinking …

An outline of a woman's face fades in and out. His eyes must be open. He can see the woman's face now and a man sitting next to her too. They look to be in their mid-forties, official types and serious. Nathan tries to sit up, but the fire igniting in the depths of his chest makes him cry out.

'Don't try to move, Nathan. You're in hospital and need to rest,' the woman says.

'A hospital? What the hell?' Nathan's surprised that his voice sounds croaky, dry and cracked, as if he's borrowed it from someone much older.

'You were shot in the chest, Nathan,' the man says. 'You lost a lot of blood and have been out of it for some time, sedated to keep you stable, but the doctors say you should make a full recovery. No damage to your major organs. Lucky, really.'

Lucky to be shot? This must be a dream. How could it be anything else? But then a memory of a man with a sly smile, a green woolly hat and dark beard surfaces in the fog of his brain.

'I'm DI Theresa Kelsey and this is DS Robert Mansell,' the woman says. 'We're here to ask a few questions about why Andrew Williams tried to kill you.'

'Andrew who?' Nathan's stomach is churning and his head starts to pound.

'Williams, the man who shot you out on the cliff path,' Mansell says.

'The walkers who alerted us say there was a woman too, but she ran away. What's her name?' Kelsey asks.

Nathan rubs his eyes, tries to think. He can't tell them about Bryony because that would land him right in it up to his neck. Bryony leads to Ransom, Ransom leads to him being a hired killer. That leads him straight to jail, do not pass go. But is Bryony okay? He guesses she must be if they don't know who she is. Something occurs to him. 'This Andrew, has he said why he wanted to kill me? Because I've never heard of him.'

'No. But then you see he died of a heart attack a few minutes after officers arrived at the scene. He had a flesh wound to his shoulder which he would have recovered from no problem. But then he collapsed with massive heart failure.' Kelsey folds her arms and looks hard at Nathan.

'We've run him through our system and he's very much known to Newcastle Police. A real bad lot, Nathan,' Mansell says. 'So why is he down in Cornwall trying to kill you and this mystery woman? Remember her name yet?'

'I don't remember a woman,' Nathan says. He feels seriously sick now and looks around for a bowl. He sees one on the side, clamps his hand over his mouth and points to it, hoping the desperation in his eyes will be enough for one of them to get the message. Kelsey hands it him and he pukes his guts up.

'That'll be the medication,' Mansell says. 'You'll be okay in a minute. Here, have some water.'

They give him a few moments to recover and talk in low voices outside the curtain round his bed. While he has this time, Nathan decides it would be a very bad idea to say anything at all to the detectives. He'll deny all knowledge of why Williams was here, deny all knowledge of Bryony, and say he was just out for a walk and this mad guy jumped him. She must be out of her mind with worry, but she hasn't tried to find him for obvious reasons. God, what a mess.

Nathan sips the water and realises that they won't believe anything he says; he hopes they haven't run a check on him yet. They know his name, but he could have told the doctors or nurses when he was in and out of consciousness, couldn't he? Did he have any ID in his wallet? Driving licence? He thinks he left his wallet at home and just stuffed some money in his jeans before they went to the pub … or did he? The fog in his brain won't clear. He's not sure. Not sure at all. They might go soon, and then he can discharge himself – get away. They won't be allowed to stay long as he's a patient in recovery. The nurse should be along soon to tell them to leave. That's what happens on TV shows anyway.

'Feeling better?' Kelsey says as she comes back round the curtain followed by Mansell. Her voice is full of concern, but her eyes tell him she couldn't give a fuck.

'Not really,' Nathan lies. 'I think I need to rest now.'

'In a minute,' she says. 'So you're saying you didn't know the woman that ran away or anything about Andrew Williams?'

'Yes.'

'Why are you in Cornwall? You're not local with an accent like that.'

This is hopeful. If they'd done checks they'd know where he was from. 'Just a walking holiday.'

'Really?' Mansell says, shaking his head in disbelief.

'Yes, really.'

'We know that's a big fat lie, Nathan. In fact we know lots about you,' Kelsey says, and whips out a notebook from her jacket pocket. Nathan's heart teeters on the brink and then plummets into his belly. 'See, we ran checks on you too. Found your driving licence in your wallet with your name, address etcetera. Didn't take us long to discover who you are.'

'I …' Nathan begins and then stops. No point in giving them anything to pounce on. They're ready for him, alert. He's no match for them in his state.

She reads from her notebook. 'You're thirty-two and live in Sheffield. You're a petty criminal with one or two cautions and community service but no jail time'—Kelsey's grey eyes regard him coolly over her black thick-rimmed specs—'yet. In the past your name has been linked with some of the bigger fish in the filthy little pond up there. Frank Dawson, for one, and Kenny Ransom. Nothing concrete, but people talk, don't they? We know that your dad most definitely worked for Ransom for some time … till he got killed, of course. Most unfortunate.'

'It would go better for you if you just told us what you know, lad.' Mansell tries a smile. Dear God, does he think Nathan is just going to fall for that? Good cop, bad cop? Pathetic.

'I've told you, I don't know anything.'

Kelsey sighs. 'Would it surprise you to know that Williams has been involved with Ransom in the past? He's a nasty thug – well, they both are, or were in Williams's case. Williams has done time for GBH. Ransom, as I'm sure you're aware, is currently serving time. But that doesn't stop these bad lads from doing bad things from behind bars. There's always people like Williams eager to take on jobs,' Kelsey says and stuffs the notebook back in her pocket. 'We have our ear to the ground, Nathan, have narks, or, as we're supposed to say nowadays, intel. As I said, people talk, and the word is that you and Ransom have had a falling out.'

'As I said, I don't know what you're talking about.'

'Oh, I think you do,' Mansell says, giving Nathan the hard stare. Nathan's tempted to ask him if he's forgotten that he's supposed to be playing good cop. 'I also think that if you don't suddenly remember everything and tell us, you might end up behind bars too. I'm sure Mr Ransom will be only too pleased to find some dirt on you. He won't be pleased that Williams failed, and I wouldn't be surprised if he doesn't sort another Williams out to complete what he couldn't … just as soon as he learns of all this.'

Nathan looks from one to the other, clicks his tongue against the roof of his mouth and shakes his head, but he knows they're right. 'I need to rest now. You can't question me like this without a lawyer anyway.'

'That's a shame. We thought you'd like to help us with our enquiries,' Kelsey says. 'Most innocent people would like to know why they've been shot at and answer any questions that would lead to the perpetrator's punishment.'

Nathan snorts down his nose. 'You said this Williams was dead. Hard to see how he could be punished.'

'But Ransom can be,' Mansell says. 'He's in for fifteen years. If we can pin this on him, he's never seeing the light of day.'

What does he say to that? How could they find proof that Williams was on Ransom's payroll? And what about his own safety if he helped them? He'd be forever looking over his shoulder.

Not before time, a nurse opens the curtains at the foot of the bed and looks at her watch. 'Okay, I'm going to have to ask you to leave now. This patient needs peace and quiet.' She looks pointedly at Kelsey and Mansell.

Nathan sees the look that passes between them. They thought he was going to cave … and he might have if they'd kept on. No. He needs time to rest, to think …

'Right, we'll be back very soon. Once you're strong enough, I suggest you appoint a solicitor so we can have a proper chat,' Kelsey says and Mansell just nods. Then they leave and the nurse checks his dressing, his drip, gives him water and painkillers and leaves too.

Relaxing back against the pillows Nathan tries to formulate a plan, but his eyes feel heavy again and he's weak, so weak. As he drifts, all he can think of is Bryony running down the cliff path away from him. He hopes she's safe and out of danger. What he wouldn't give to see her face, kiss her lips. With her name on his, he falls into a deep sleep.

Chapter Thirty-One

St Michael's Mount is a stark black silhouette against the soft amber glow of sunset. The retiring sun is an artist, colouring the clouds lavender and the sea purple. The beauty of the view takes my breath and brings more tears, just when I thought there were no more left to fall.

From my window in the guest house in Marazion, I watch a couple walk by on the street hand in hand; they're laughing, pointing at things. It looks like they don't have a care in the world. They have ordinary lives, normal hopes and fears, unafraid to saunter on through the sunset, orange light warming their faces. They don't look behind. They have no need. I turn away and walk into the bathroom.

Behind my eyes, fear skulks, rimmed by smudged eyeliner and mascara. My face is white … my mouth a pale line. I hardly recognise the woman in the mirror. It's as if my strength and confidence have been sucked from me and left behind on the cliff path twisting in the mist. I watch my hand flick the shower on, press my spine against the cool wall tiles and slide down to the floor. I hug myself, shoving my cold hands under my armpits, and allow the hot water to soak into my skin, watch the mud and sand trickle from my legs and down the plughole. Though I try to relax and think, I'm aware of my heartbeat. And with each thump, it whispers, *Nathan. Nathan. Nathan.*

If he's dead I promise I will avenge him. I don't care what happens to me, or how long it takes. I'll avenge my dad too. Yes, Ransom's in prison, but I want to make sure he never gets out. I want him to die in there. Suffer in there. My dad's face comes into my mind – kind, warm, smiling that smile he saved just for me. Unbelievably I'm crying again. Sobbing loudly, keening like an injured animal.

Then I curl my hand into a fist and strike the floor. This is defeatist. I will not crumble. I cannot. I need to find out where Nathan is, what happened to him. I need to find out what happened to the shooter too, and last, but certainly not least, I need to get in touch with Immi. She has to be warned that her shit of a father knows she betrayed him. I have left three voice messages telling her to get back urgently, but she hasn't so far. Maybe she's called while I've been wallowing in self-pity in the shower. *Get your sorry arse up and out, get dressed and show some fucking guts, Bryony.*

Imogen hasn't phoned back. I ring again but get the messaging service. Damn it. What if he's got to her already? No good thinking like that. Right, I need to think clearly. The digital bedside clock says 9.30pm, it's Sunday. Mark Bradley might be at home if he's not working late at the station. He tries not to work Sundays if he can help it though – perk of his job. He's the only one I can think of who could help. But how can I ask for information without alerting him? Mark's like a dog with a bone and would demand to know why I'm asking such odd questions. I finish the sandwich I got earlier from the Spar across the road and decide I have no choice.

'Bryony? I hope you're ringing to say you've made a terrible mistake leaving us and wonder if I can help you get back on the job.'

Mark's deep chuckle down the line is like a warm hug. It isn't until this moment that I realise how much I've missed him. I take a swig of tea and make my voice calm. ''Fraid not, boss. And sorry to bother you at home, but I do have a huge favour to ask.'

A deep sigh comes down the line this time. 'Go on.'

'Well, I'm down in St Just, Cornwall, at the moment. I'm not going abroad for a few weeks. And, well … an odd thing happened this afternoon. I heard that a guy shot another guy on the cliff path. They struggled for the gun and then fire was returned. They were both injured and I'd like to know who they were and what happened. The police came, but seeing as I'm no longer a copper I couldn't ask, you see.'

'Ri-ght. So why do you need to know so badly that you ring me at home on a Sunday? And don't tell me it's just because you're curious.'

'Okay, I won't tell you that.'

'Bryony ...'

'Look, I can't tell you, boss. All I can say is it is of the utmost importance to me. I promise that I'm not doing anything illegal or unlawful, I just have to know.'

There's a few moments' silence and I cross my fingers. Then I hear him exhale long and loud. 'If it was anyone else, the answer would be no. But I'll get back to you tomorrow—'

'Oh, thanks, Mark! I can't tell you how grateful—'

'There will be no more favours after this, are we clear?' Mark's tone is serious, firm.

'No. Of course not. I promise, boss.'

'Okay. Goodnight, Bryony.'

The silence following the end of the call is all consuming. I feel so much more alone than I did before I spoke to Mark ... disconnected from everything I ever knew. Perhaps I'll go out to the Spar again, get a bottle of wine. I need something after the day I've had. I'm tempted to phone Nathan. I haven't so far because I'm worried that the police have his phone. No. No, I'll leave it until I hear from Mark.

Out in the street night has fallen and there's only a man walking a dog ahead. I look behind. Nobody. I zip my hooded jacket up and pull the hood over my head. My mouth's dry and there's a flutter in my chest. What if the shooter has somehow followed me? What if he slipped on the bus I took earlier, when I wasn't looking, came down here to Marazion with me? What if he hung around, saw me go in the B&B, and now he's going to waylay me, finish what he started?

Though it's been a murky day it's a clear night, cold too. The moon's trailing a sprinkling of stars but the street lights are few and far between. The Spar looks welcoming at the end of the street and I quicken my pace. I grab a bottle from the shelf and hand over the cash. My hand is shaking as I do and my heart is thumping in my chest. God, what a state I'm in. As I turn to leave, a man comes in wearing dark woolly hat. My heart leaps into my throat. He has a beard too, but half the male population do nowadays. It isn't him. Of course it isn't.

Outside I lean against the shop window until I feel calmer; I talk to myself, force rationality from its hiding place back into the forefront of my mind. I've been a copper for many years. I would have seen the shooter get on the bus, would have seen him follow me. I'm just letting everything get to me, freak me out. Not surprising, considering what happened this afternoon. Not surprising at all.

Back in my room I pour a drink and look at my phone. Nothing from Immi, so I message her again. Then I scroll to Nate's number. My finger hovers over the call button, but once again I restrain myself. I'll wait to hear from Mark, then I'll decide. I pour another drink and check that the door to the room is locked properly. Again. The sooner I hear from Mark, the better.

Chapter Thirty-Two

With the taste of Jonathan's goodnight kiss on her lips, Imogen closes the front door and locks it. Before she goes to bed she needs to check all the windows and doors, though she has to admit she's a lot calmer than she was a few nights ago when she'd gone to meet Jonathan for a drink. He'd asked her to stay over again, which was nice because it means he's keen, but it's Monday tomorrow and she needs to make sure she's organised.

Ironing looms large on her immediate horizon, but she'll stick the TV on and watch *Poldark* while she does it. The holiday at Bryony's mum's has made a big impression on her. Cornwall is so beautiful, and watching the series will give her a much-needed fix. She had been serious when she'd told Bryony that she'd love to move there one day. If things work out with Jonathan that might complicate things, but there are surgeries down there too, after all. Plugging in the iron, she allows her mind to picture a bright future full of sea, windswept beaches, country walks and fresh air. Then the reality of work nudges all that aside and she picks up her first creased garment from the basket.

She and Doctor Jonathan Blake agreed earlier that they'd keep their relationship under wraps from the rest of the staff at the surgery, just for a while. Even though Imogen's worries had been put to rest by their little chat, neither wanted gossip to get in the way of how they felt. It was nobody's business but theirs anyway. It was quite nice having a secret. A delicious, exciting secret that made her happier than she had been for a long time – since her dad had put Leon off, sent him packing. Thoughts of her dad make her stomach twist, her heart sad. Immi turns up the TV to drown out her thoughts.

The ironing is done, and the programme almost too, when her landline rings from the arm of the sofa. Probably Jonathan to say she'd left her mobile there; well, she hopes she has, otherwise she's no clue where she left it. It will be nice to have the chance to say goodnight again. Imogen hurries over, butterflies in her chest. For goodness' sake. What is she, fifteen? The butterflies disappear when she thumbs the screen. Nope. It's an unknown number.

'Hello?'

'Imms, love. How's tricks?'

Imogen sinks down on the sofa. He's the last person she wants to speak to right now. 'Dad,' she says, her voice flatter than the ironing board she's been standing at for the past hour. 'I'm fine, how are you?'

'Bloody hell, don't sound too enthusiastic. Thought you'd be pleased that I phoned. I haven't seen you for a good while. When are you coming to visit next?' His tone has become belligerent, goading.

'I don't know. I've been pretty busy lately …'

'Right. So not heard from that bitch Masters, then?'

Imogen wants to put the phone down. Wants to tell him that she knows all about the fact that he sent Nathan down to Cornwall to kill Bryony. She wants to tell him that she never wants to see him again. That he's dead to her. But she can't, of course. He's suspicious of her enough as it is – knows that she pretended to want an appeal to stop him going after Bryony. A fat lot of good that idea was.

'No, Dad. I told you, we don't see each other now. We had a drink once and that was it. And I also told you she's gone abroad. Don't you remember?'

'Of course I bloody remember. But I'm finding out that you don't always tell the truth, do you, love?'

What does he mean by that? 'Not with you.'

'No. And that's the problem … you're not with me. In fact you're very much against me, aren't you?'

The ice in his voice brings goosebumps up all along her arms. 'Dad? What's wrong?'

'The fact that I can't trust my own flesh and blood. My little … little g—' A sob breaks up his words. 'My little girl that I worship and adore … could …'

'I-I haven't done anything, Dad.' Immi hopes her voice sounds normal, but she catches sight of her reflection in the mirror above the fireplace, ashen face, and wide, fearful eyes.

'Oh, you have – too much. Everything I have ever done has been for you. I wanted to make you happy, make sure you'd never have to worry about the future, and then …' He gives a heavy sigh. 'But it wasn't enough, clearly.'

Goosebumps travel from her arms to the rest of her body. There's no way she's admitting anything. Her instincts tell her to keep up the pretence and her words come out in a rush. 'Dad, I don't understand. What am I supposed to have done?'

'Goodbye, Imogen.' He's sobbing openly now. 'A father's love … can only be tested so far … and you've tested mine to the limit.'

Imogen's lost for words, but he's ended the call anyway. She chucks the phone on the sofa and hugs herself. It's as if he knows it was her that grassed on him, got him arrested … but how could he possibly? A spatter of rain on the window makes her heart jump and she's right back to being terrified again like she was the other night. Imogen rushes to the patio doors, draws the curtain against the deluge and makes sure the doors are locked. Then she checks all the windows upstairs and down.

The rain is lashing against the window in her bedroom as she gets under the duvet and thinks she just heard a distant rumble of thunder. Great. Dad's call has really spooked her. If he knows somehow, though he'd have to be a bloody psychic to know – nobody knows apart from Bryony and now Nathan – he might send Dawson round to scare her. He scared her the other night, but then why would he have given her a gun to protect herself from a bad man … who was actually Nathan, obviously? None of it made sense. Was Nathan still working for her father somehow? Had Nathan told him that Imogen was the one that made the phone call? That didn't make sense either, because he was with

Bryony now – he'd had umpteen chances to harm her, so why hadn't he?

She's coming up from the bottom of the ocean. It's dark but getting lighter … there's a rush in her ears and then her eyes snap open. Imogen gulps air and realises she's in bed. How the hell she fell asleep at all is beyond her, the state she was in. The bedside clock displays a digital green 3.10am and thunder growls a little way off. It must have passed over head just now, waking her. She takes a sip of water from the glass on the bedside table and settles back down. The alarm will be yelling at 6.30 and she was awake until past one. She'll feel like death if she doesn't get back to … Was that a creak on the stairs?

Imogen sits up in bed, holds her breath, heart racing. Nothing. Still she sits listening, until rain pelts the window so hard it sounds like handfuls of gravel being hurled by a giant's hand. Startled, her own hand shoots to her mouth to stifle a scream. *For God's sake calm down, Imogen.* Annoyed with herself, she slips out of bed determined to check round the house, just to be sure … and there it is again – a creak on the top stair. Unmistakable. Bryony wouldn't do the same thing to her again, would she? No. No, of course she bloody wouldn't.

Imogen slips her dressing gown on and retrieves the gun from her drawer. She stuffs her pillows in the bed to create a sleeping form and pulls the duvet up. The two last words her father said play over in her mind. 'Goodbye, Imogen.' He never says goodbye. He would say bye, see you, cheers, love … but not goodbye. Goodbye is final.

Flattened against the wall behind the door, Imogen waits. The gun is cold and heavy in her hand and she places her other hand under the barrel, her finger ready to cock it if need be. And it seems it will be: the door handle gives a little squeak as it's depressed by someone outside on the landing. *There's someone outside on the landing. There's someone outside on the landing. There's someone outside on the landing.* Oh, dear God, she has to keep calm, breathe in through the nose, out through the mouth. She has the element of surprise, not him. He thinks he has, because she's in bed asleep, but he's sadly fucking mistaken. That's right, let the fury flow. Better than fear. Much. How dare they try to hurt her?

The door slowly opens and a hulk of a man creeps in. Oh shit, he looks so powerful, even in the scant light from the street lamp shining through a chink in her curtains. He sneaks over to the bed. He's got something in his hands. Imogen can't make it out … he's leaning over the bed. Her heart hammering in her chest, she tells herself that it's now or never and flicks on the light. The man spins round, his hands coming up to shield his eyes, and she sees a plastic-sheathed wire dangling from them. The bastard was going to garrotte her in her sleep!

'Don't fucking move or I'll drop you!' Imogen is relieved to hear how strong she sounds.

The hulk loses the wire and puts his hands up in surrender, his eyes round, his mouth opening and closing like a landed cod. 'Hey, hey … I … Look, don't do anything daft. I know you're not used to guns.'

'Do you? How?'

'Um …'

'Because Dawson told you? Or that pathetic waste of DNA otherwise known as Kenny Ransom?'

'Um …'

'Yeah, thought so. And you don't have to be used to guns to pull the trigger.'

'Look, love. I didn't want to do this – it's not what I do. I'll just go now and—' He takes a step towards her.

'Stay right where you are!' Imogen raises the nose of the gun level with his head.

'Okay, don't wave that thing about!'

They stare at each other for a few moments and Imogen swallows hard. What the hell should she do now? To phone the police she'd have to force him downstairs and there would be plenty of opportunity for things to go wrong in that scenario. Why the fuck had she left her mobile at Jonathan's? There's no other option though.

'Right … I'm going to call the police—'

'No!' Hulk clasps his meaty hands together in prayer. 'Please don't do that. I'll get sent down and—'

'You should have thought about that before you came here to kill me, shouldn't you, you fuckwit?' Anger is back and it feels empowering. Good.

'I didn't want to … it was …'

'Yes, why don't you tell me who it was, and why they want me dead? And what's your name?'

'My name?'

'Yes, I can't keep calling you fuckwit, can I?'

'Er … Harry.' His face flushes.

'No it isn't. If you don't tell me your real name I'll shoot you in the foot and then look at your ID.'

He unclasps his hands and holds them up again. 'Okay, it's Jason.'

Imogen remembers that the man holding Nathan's mother was a Jason, and a 'dumb ass ape' according to him. Hmm. Yes, this guy fits the bill. 'Okay, Jason, tell me everything. If I think you're spinning me a line I'll shoot you in both feet. I'm Kenny Ransom's daughter, as of course you know, and I'm just as tough as he is, so be careful.'

Jason nods, rubs his hands over his face a few times and begins. 'It's … it's all to do with your dad. Well, and Mr Dawson. He left a recording device here—'

'A what? What kind of a device?'

'It was a pen. It picked up you having a chat with your dad's enemies and you admitted to grassing your dad up …' He lifts his arms and lets them fall back to his sides with a slap.

If the wall wasn't supporting Imogen's back she would have collapsed. Fucking hell! That's why Dawson was so keen on collecting the pen. So her dad knows everything … now his call makes absolute sense. He also knows where Bryony and Nathan are. No. No. NO! Anger, her friend for the last few minutes, trickles away and instead sorrow floods her heart. Her dad sent a thug to kill her. To *actually* kill her. Yes, she'd betrayed him, but he is her father. Her flesh and … Jason takes a step forward.

'Stay where you are,' she says in a small voice. It's as if the awful realisation of what her father has tried to do has drained her of all strength. The gun shakes in her hand and her legs are trembling.

'Look. If you just let me go I promise I won't come back. I'll tell them that you weren't here. You weren't here last night, so—'

'My God. You came here last night?'

'Um …'

'Determined, then.' Imogen cringes as a tear slips from the corner of her eye and rolls down her cheek.

'So they'll believe me—'

'My … my father phoned me here earlier. So he knows I'm here. Then I expect he phoned you and told you to come.'

Jason takes two steps forward and raises his hands. 'I just want to be let go. I promise I'll never come back …'

Imogen shakes her head. 'Stay there … you're too close.'

He smiles as if he's her bestie. 'Look, Imogen, I can see you're upset. I would be if my dad had … you know. But that gun's shaking and it might go off. How about if I just go out now and that will be it. Yeah?'

Imogen shakes her head. 'No.' She has to find strength from somewhere. He's too close now. A few more steps and …

'You don't want to shoot me, do you?'

'No, but I will if I have to.' There's a click as she cocks the weapon and Jason's face drains of colour.

'Right. Move away from the door because I'm going through it.' He lowers his arms and then runs at her. Not at the door … *at her*.

Imogen steadies the gun and pulls the trigger.

Chapter Thirty-Three

Considering that my head was all over the place last night I was out like a light as soon as I closed my eyes. Perhaps half a bottle of red wine helped, but today I do feel a bit more like myself. I look more like myself too. The lady that runs this guest house, Pat, helped to take my mind off everything at breakfast. She told me the history of the Mount and asked if I'd be going over to take a look. Much as I'd love to, I need to be absolutely sure that my phone has a signal in case Mark calls. Cornwall is dodgy for signal at the best of times, so I don't want to be stuck out on an island really.

It's coming up to midday and I'm gazing out of the window at St Michael's Mount again when I hear my phone ring. I had a real panic earlier when the charger I borrowed from Pat didn't work, but I managed to get another from a phone shop in Penzance. Now I can't find the sodding mobile! Bathroom? Yes, thank God.

'Mark?' I say, trying to keep the tremor out of my voice.

'Hello, Bryony. Well, I found out part of your answer. There was a man involved in an incident yesterday. His name was Andrew Williams.'

'Past tense? So …'

'Yep, he's dead. He had a gunshot wound to his right shoulder, but just a scratch really. When officers got to him he fell to his knees and died. A massive heart attack apparently. Only forty-five. Life in the fast lane must have got him in the end.'

Relief and guilt fight for dominance. Relief that he won't be coming after me, guilt because I'm relieved that a man's dead. 'Right. What did you mean about life in the fast lane, Mark?'

'He was a known criminal, Newcastle mostly, but he has been known to operate in Yorkshire from time to time. Ransom was an acquaintance, he's been linked to him, but as usual we could never pin him down until you nailed him, of course.'

Guilt abates a little. Then I ask the question that's been on my tongue for almost twenty-four hours. 'What about the other man?'

'That's what I meant about only having part of your answer. There was no news of another man.'

His reply kicks me in the gut. What? But that's impossible. There would be no way Nathan could have walked away from that. He must be having medical care somewhere. Mark sighs and I realise I have to say something. 'Are you sure? I heard that the other man was quite badly injured.'

'I'm positive. The reports are only of Williams. If there had been someone else involved I would have found it.'

My brain won't produce another explanation ... what Mark's saying is illogical. I shove my hand through my hair, stand up, begin to pace the room. Mark's waiting for a reply but I don't have one.

'So if that's it, I need to get back to work, Bryony.'

'Yes. Thanks so much once again, Mark. You've been very helpful.'

'Take care, Bryony.'

'You t—' I begin, but he's ended the call. Great. He's pissed off because I won't tell him why I asked about Williams and 'the other man', and I would be too if I were him.

My pacing increases and there's a ball of energy in my stomach needing release. I feel like a caged animal and need to get outside, go for a walk. *Think.* Outside I find the beach, kick off my shoes and pick up a brisk pace. *Think.* Nathan must have got away somehow before the police came. An image presents itself of him face down on the path again, a crimson pool spreading from under his chest. No. No way. Could they have taken him to hospital and he somehow discharged himself? Did he have any criminal connections down here? It's possible. Could they be hiding him? I stop walking and look at the horizon. No. No, of course not, because even if it were true that he'd discharged himself, there would still have been a police report about him being involved with the Williams shooting. If there had been a report, Mark would have found it.

The idea that I need to do something fast grabs hold and won't let go. There's no need to be here now, is there? I should take a bus, go back to the rented cottage, get my clothes, my car. I can't stay there though because as soon as Ransom finds out about Williams he'll send someone else. Then I'll track Nathan down and find out exactly what the hell's going on. I'll ring the main hospitals in the area. If there's no joy, I'll call him. I have to. This not knowing is killing me.

In my car outside Trevella Cottage I push away thoughts of arriving here just a few days ago with Nate. We were so full of excitement and optimism. Now things couldn't be more different. The cottage is locked up and the key back with the owner. She was surprised that I'd terminated the agreement, but as she had her rent in advance, she didn't look too worried. My case and Nathan's holdall are in the back. I hope to God I'll be able to give it to him very soon. The two main hospitals said they couldn't tell me anything as I wasn't a relative. I could have said I was next of kin, but they might have had his mum listed. Then they asked for his address and date of birth. I can't believe we hadn't talked about when our birthdays are. The address … no idea either. I had to end the call. Now I'm so desperate, I'm going to pull one last trick.

'Yes, Detective Inspector Bryony Masters, here. Can you tell me which ward Nathan Walker is on please?'

'When did he come in?'

'Um … Sunday.'

'Which department?'

'A&E I think.'

'Can I take the address and date of birth?'

'Sorry, don't have those.'

'Right … okay, just a moment. Can't see anyone with that name. I'm afraid you'd have to come in, show your ID for me to look any further.'

I end the call and make another to the other hospital – same response. It's not as if I expected anything else really because of hospital security, though it's just one more setback. Chances are he's not at either hospital though. There would have been something on the screen, surely. Just one thing left then. Nathan's number. Suddenly I'm hot, can't get enough oxygen, so I wind the window down and take in a gulp of country air. Honeysuckle is sweet on the breeze and I take a few deep breaths to calm my jittery nerves.

Here goes. I press call and lift the phone to my ear. It connects to an annoying beep: 'I'm sorry, the number you have dialled has been disconnected.' Eh? But that's ridiculous. I hang up and try again. Same. Damn it! What's going on? I'm about to put the phone away when I'm startled by it ringing in my hand. Nathan? No – unknown number.

'B-Bryony … it's me.'

'Immi?' I can hardly make her out. There's a buzz of traffic in the background and she's sobbing. Heartbreaking, racking sobs.

'I'm in a phone box … I haven't got long. Ch-change is running out. I'm heading to Spain. I'll call you when I'm settled … I shot someone last night, Bryony.' My hand grips the phone harder and I'm biting my lip to stop myself crying out. 'Shot his ear half off. Blood went up my wall … across my mirror. He was one of Dad's – Jason – the one that had Nathan's mum. Dad sent … he … he sent him to k-kill me.'

'Oh my God. Immi, I—'

'He's not dead. He ran off. But I can't stay now. I'm not safe. Be careful, you and Nathan. Love to you.'

'Immi? Immi, are you okay?' Disconnect drones in my ear and I throw the phone on the passenger seat, leaning my head on the steering wheel. Oh God. Poor, poor Immi. Nathan had described Jason: dumb hired muscle. How could a father actually consider killing his child, no matter what she'd done? I thought he might want to punish her … but this?

I look through the windscreen at the cottage but just see chaos. I see chaos and misery and loss. Nathan is gone. He's either in hiding with someone from his past, or the police have him somewhere … but where? Why? It's obvious I won't find out any time soon, so it's pointless looking. If he wants to contact me he will. He has my number … or did. What if the worst has happened? There was a lot of blood. I shut that thought down. Fast. My stomach churns and I know I have to get away. I don't know where, but I have to go. Now. I turn the key in the ignition and drive.

Chapter Thirty-Four

For three days I have been in a hotel in Dover. Three days of indecision and anxiety. Every day I tell myself that if Nathan hasn't got in touch I'll buy a ticket and go on the ferry crossing to Calais. From there I'll just drive. I've often fancied the south of France, but under the circumstances I couldn't give a shit where I end up. I'm currently in a backstreet café with a cup of cold coffee in front of me. It tastes like marmite and wood shavings, but again, I don't give a shit. In fact, as each day passes I'm finding it harder to give a shit about anything apart from Nate, and that isn't where I want to be.

The clock on the grease-coated café wall says it's 10.15am, and all of a sudden I make a decision – and this one's final. If he's not phoned by this afternoon I'm leaving tomorrow. There is absolutely no point whatsoever hanging about here any longer. I can't find out if he's alive or dead. Last night I was so desperate I nearly phoned Mark again, but he wouldn't have helped me … and I don't really blame him. And how could he help anyway? In order for him to phone the morgues I'd have to give him Nathan's name and then we would be back to square one.

Kenny Ransom has so much to answer for and if he were here right now I swear I'd kill him. I imagine my hands around his throat squeezing the life out of him, but then I shake my head. That would make me just as bad as him. With any luck, one day he'll push his luck a bit too much, and some other delightful prisoner will take that job off my hands. I wonder how Immi is and where she is. I wish I could speak to her, try and help somehow. She must be going through hell. Once she's settled she'll get in touch. I hope. My mobile rings in my bag and I grab it, frantically thumbing the screen. Please God let it be him. No. It's Immi.

'Hello, Bryony Masters?'

I'm tempted to end the call. Why is a strange man ringing from Immi's phone? Curiosity won't let me though. 'Yes?'

'Dr Jonathan Blake here. You don't know me, but I'm a good friend of Imogen Ransom.'

'Ah, right. Yes, you work together don't you?'

'We do … but, well, we're also in a relationship … or we were. That's why I'm phoning. She's disappeared off the face of the planet since Monday and, well, I'm going through her phone trying to find anyone who knows where she is.'

Poor Immi. Finally finds a man and her dad ruins it again. 'She left her phone behind?'

'Not on purpose. It was under the passenger seat of my car. She must have dropped it when she was at mine last weekend. I only found it when I rang her before I drove to work.'

So that's why she never answered when I was frantically trying to warn her about her dad. Now what to do? I can't tell him I've heard from her and what's happened, because if she'd wanted him to know she would have called, wouldn't she?

'Bryony, are you still there?'

'Yes … it's just a bit of a shock to hear she left without saying anything to anyone. What about work?'

'She just didn't turn up on Monday. I've been round to her house a few times, but she's not there. Car's gone too.'

My heart goes out to him. He's obviously in a state, but I can't betray Immi. 'Oh dear. That's worrying. Have you tried the police?'

'Yes, but they've drawn a blank so far. Will you call me if you hear anything?'

'Yes, of course. What's your number?'

I end the call and leave the greasy spoon, hurry back to the hotel to pack. I know I told myself I'd wait until this afternoon, but I've had just about as much as I can take. If I'm lucky I could get a ferry ticket for late afternoon. It will cost me, but once again, I don't give a shit. The sooner I get away from all this chaos and misery the better. As soon as I set foot over the threshold of my room I hear a text beep through. Probably Jonathan texting his number. I check anyway. Unknown. When I read the first line, my legs give way and I slump onto the bed.

Bryony, I'm sorry it's taken me a while to get in touch. I bet you've been worried. I'm okay, lost a bit of blood, but they patched me up and I'm out of hospital now. The thing is the whole situation brought me up with a bit of a start. Even though the man that shot me died of a heart attack I won't be safe … we won't be safe as long as we're together.

My heart comes up into my throat and I can't bear to read the rest. I look at the well-worn beige carpet and the stain on the sink; try to think of nothing while I gather my wits. When I think I'm ready, I look back at the screen.

We might not be safe if we're apart, but we'll stand a better chance. I will miss you of course … it hurts me to write this, but I'm ending it. It's best we go our separate ways. Let's face it, we were never going to work with our history. I do care about you, you saved my life … but not enough to get myself killed. I'm a selfish bastard at heart. Take care, Bryony. Best wishes, Nathan.

Best wishes? Best fucking wishes? No kisses? No love? This isn't Nathan. This isn't my Nate. Before I can think, I call the number and it's answered immediately. 'Nathan, is that you?'

'Yes.'

'What the hell are you thinking? I know you don't mean any of that.'

'I do. I'm sorry … I'm going to hang up now because no matter how long we talk we'll never work out a solution.'

I can tell he's on the brink of tears. 'But Nate … Please, you can't!' I hate the whiney tone of my voice but I can't help it.

'I'm blocking your number. Goodbye, Bryony. Be happy.'

No. No. No! I'm on my knees rocking to and fro, the phone pressed against my heart. How could he do this? How? After everything he said about never being able to repay me for saving him from that rip current. That he'd spend his life trying to do right by me? All that was a heap of bullshit? Was it? Was it really? I wipe my tears and my nose on my sleeve. He has to talk to me, has to listen. Pride is something I have always been big on, but now I don't care. I dial the number again and it rings once and goes to voicemail. I ring again and it does the same. He's blocked me. He really has.

Four hours later I'm watching the white cliffs grow smaller from the deck of the ferry as the wind whips my hair into my eyes. It's far too long … really must get it trimmed, it's making my eyes water. How could I be so wrong about a person? How could I let myself become so fond of him? Never again. That's me and men finished. My heart won't take it. I turn my face towards France and my hair streams out behind. Now I only care about me. I'll rent a *gîte* or something, chill out for a while, treat myself to some me time, whatever the fuck that is. Then when my head is clear I'll think about the future … figure out a way to come home. Right now, I'm not sure I'll ever be ready.

Chapter Thirty-Five

Inverness used to be just a place on the map to Nathan. Now he looks out of the cottage window at the stunning Scottish countryside and it begins to sink in that he lives there. Well, about five miles away over the bridge in a little place called North Kessock, right on the banks of the Beauly Firth. Under normal circumstances he would be over the moon to live amongst such beauty, but his circumstances are far from normal. The last six months have been tough. Really tough. A new name, new history, new job. Those things took a little getting used to, to say the least, but compared to the pain of losing Bryony … thinking about it, nothing could compare to that.

That last phone call they'd had sometimes wakes him up at night. The things he said, wrote, the cold way he brushed her off. His voice had almost betrayed him, but he thinks he held it together until he ended the call. She must hate him. The way she'd pleaded with him. He'd hate him if he was her. Bryony had saved him from that rip current, saved his life and he had repaid her by breaking her heart. He supposed he had; she might not have felt the same way about him as he had about her. Nathan hoped that she hadn't really, because it would have been easier on her.

Mist is rolling in from the damp fields over the Firth. November is grim in the city, but here it has a lighter feel, even though it's dark for much of the time. Nathan wonders where Bryony is. He guesses she won't be in Cornwall, with Ransom still hell-bent on finding her. He knows he hasn't given up – he has a few colourful contacts on the inside and out too. Nathan wishes he didn't have to speak with them, but part of his new life is dependent on it.

Nathan makes a cheese sandwich and coffee, takes it over to the window and stares out over the Firth. Weekends are the worst. He's been invited out plenty of times by his work colleagues, but so far he's preferred his own company. He's worried about letting something slip about his past too. Still, he'll have to get used to it eventually. Sometimes he wonders if he made the right decision, to forgo everything he ever knew including Bryony, but overall he knows he did.

During those days he spent in hospital it became obvious to him what he should do. Kelsey and Mansell agreed with his plan; they'd organise a new ID, get him away from Sheffield, get him a CV – something he'd never have otherwise – and a chance to make a new life. A real life. In return, he would inform on Dawson and Ransom and one or two others he knew of. Tell them every dirty deal they ever did, try to find out anything they were still up to, until they had enough to put Dawson away, and maybe pin something else on Ransom. This made him happy. Whatever it took to make that bastard pay for what he'd done. Nathan would see his father avenged. Having a CV made him happy too, and a legitimate work history was something he thought would never be his, but the main reason he did any of it was to keep Bryony safe.

If only she knew what he'd given up to protect her. Family, his identity … her. But then it was only what he owed her for saving his life. As long as he was with her she'd never be safe. As long as Ransom lived, she'd never be safe. Ransom hated both of them, but Nathan guessed he'd be top of the list because of the way he'd turned on him, gone over to the other side – the straight and narrow. And that he'd got into bed, quite literally, with a copper. Or an ex-copper. He'd swooped in and taken his mother from under Jason's nose too. That must have really made Ransom furious. Bryony would be second on the hate list now, because he'd found out that it was Imogen who had made the call that got him banged up and not her. Ransom still wanted her hurt though … he had become even more bitter and twisted since his only child vanished.

Nathan chuckled when he thought of what Imogen had done to Jason. The dumb ass. The one-eared dumb ass now. By all accounts, Ransom was beside himself with rage at the way his own flesh and blood had betrayed him and then disappeared off the planet. What did he expect? Did he think she'd wait around for her maniac father to organise another assassination attempt?

Nathan puts the last of his sandwich in his mouth and thinks about his own family. His contact in the police had said they'd arrange for him to see his mum some time soon, but it would have to be under their terms. It was a bit like witness protection, but he wouldn't be at trials. He was a glorified informer. There was a completely new backstory for his mum, too, and for his sister and brothers. He'd sent money to Sandra, the lovely lady looking after his mum, regular as clockwork, and said that he was working abroad, probably never coming to live back in the UK, stuff like that. Soon Nathan wouldn't know what was a lie and what was the truth anymore … who he was. Try as he might, he can't get used to thinking of himself as Adam Jackson. He answers to it daily at work, but sometimes it takes a while to realise he's being spoken to.

The job is one of the aspects of his new life that he absolutely loves. He's a driver for Highland View Tours. Sometimes he'll drive a minibus, other times a coach, and take tourists, mainly American and Japanese – though lately there've been quite a few Chinese sightseers too – to the places of interest. Whisky distilleries, dolphin centres and boat trips, Loch Ness and other lochs, castles, battlefields, and lots more. Every day is different and that's how he likes it.

At first he'd been a bit worried that this job would be too exposed, that he might be recognised, but the chances are pretty slim. How many Sheffield criminals would be up in this neck of the woods taking a tour? Besides, he's had a lighter colour put through his now shoulder length hair and grown a beard. And in his spare time he walks a lot and his skin has become tanned. One of the tourists said he looked like a Viking the other day. Not even his mother would recognise him. That thought wipes the smile off his face and he goes to answer his phone ringing somewhere upstairs.

It's David, his contact in the police. 'Hi, David, how are you?'

'Very good, Adam. In fact, bloody fantastic!'

'Oh. Has something happened?'

'Yes, we've arrested Dawson. We have the bastard on at least three big ones. His little toe-rag Jason, too. He's squealing like a stuck pig, on both Dawson and Ransom. Can't wait to do a deal to get himself less jail time.'

Nathan lowers himself onto his bed. He suddenly feels unsteady. 'Jeez.'

'And Dawson's put the finger on Charlie Kreswell for the same reason. He's as big a fish as Ransom. Bigger in fact.'

'Kreswell? Bloody hell. He and Ransom are big enemies.' Nathan remembers that Ransom once had three of Charlie's casinos closed down, did some shady deal and got them raided for drugs and fraud. He was in competition with him at the time. Kreswell lost a packet and did jail time. He never knew it was Ransom for sure, he had no proof, but he suspected.

'Are they? Well, Ransom had better hope that Charlie doesn't get sent to Wakefield then.'

'Yeah.' Nathan laughs. 'If he does, there'll be a big showdown.' But even as he says this an idea is forming in a dark part of his mind.

'I just wanted you to know how much your help has contributed to this arrest and I'll keep you up to speed. But as far as I can see, your job is done.'

After they end the call Nathan wanders around the cottage doing chores before he has to go out to the local supermarket to do his weekend shop. The idea he had at the end of the phone call is like an itch that demands scratching. He didn't say anything to David, of course, but Dawson had mentioned to Nathan that Kreswell's brother, Rob, was in Wakefield a while back. Rob hadn't his brother's aptitude for business but was handy with his fists.

He was a bit of a loose cannon by all accounts and in for GBH. Rob would not be best pleased to find that Ransom's number two was responsible for getting his brother arrested. Since Charlie had already been inside, the next jail time would be far longer. And Rob certainly wouldn't be pleased if he knew beyond doubt that Ransom was responsible for getting him in there the first time.

Nathan shoves these thoughts to the back of his mind and walks out to his car. He still can't get used to the country air and the way everything looks clean, green, picture postcard. No litter, grime or crime. He isn't naive enough to think there wouldn't be all that in the big cities not too far away, but up here in the hills by the water, it seems like a different country … a different world, far away from everything he's ever known. Now he's done his job, given the police what they wanted, he could just live his life out here, pretend that the old world didn't exist. That it had just been some sordid little dream he'd once had – a nightmare. It hadn't happened. Nathan Walker hadn't happened. He'd always been Adam Jackson: a down to earth, honest man, off to do his shopping of a misty Saturday afternoon.

Inside the car Nathan closes his eyes. But he can't pretend, can he? He's not the clean, upstanding, unblemished Adam at all. The nightmare was real, and the ones that had put him in it are still lurking in the wardrobe and under the bed, ready to pounce as soon as the lights go out. There's one last thing he can do as Nathan. Bryony deserves it, and so do countless others not yet plunged into the nightmare. Young lads sucked into Ransom's world, trapped in a life of crime, filth and despair. But should he do it? Maybe he should just stay well out of it. Move on. Move up. An image of Bryony laughing on the beach comes to him, her hair wet from the sea, sunlight on her skin. She's so real he can almost touch her. Nathan opens his eyes, starts the engine and drives down the tiny track towards Inverness.

Chapter Thirty-Six

I have to admit to myself that I'm becoming used to French life. Or life in a small village in the Loire Valley, at least. How did I ever manage without fresh bread from the local bakery and the choice of so many delicious cheeses? My waistline is actually expanding for the first time in my life; I have curves and it suits me. Well, I think it does, judging from the appreciative glances I get from the men in the village. Which reminds me, I need to decide whether to accept Valentin's invitation to dinner at the weekend or not. He's such a nice man and attractive, and though I have made a few friends here, I do crave more social interaction. I've always been outgoing, not really happy with my own company for huge lengths of time. But a man? I said never again.

It's still only 7.30 but I know the bakery will be open as I set off from my *gîte* into the tiny lane winding through the ancient village. On my mental to-do list are: buy a baguette, a pain au chocolate, and maybe one of those apple and cream choux things dusted with icing sugar and coffee. Shall I have a takeaway coffee or get a table? Then to the little shop for milk and fresh veg. I smile when I think of my Monday morning to-do lists not that long ago when I drove to work at the station – how different could the two be?

The only person I've mentioned my old job to is Valentin and he couldn't believe it. He said he couldn't imagine such a relaxed, calm individual being a police officer. I wasn't the same person back then though. Besides, I think Valentin has a skewed view of what it is to be in the police from American cop shows. His view of the world is very narrow anyway, I remind myself. He's only ever lived in this village, owns two *gîtes*, one of them being mine, and has a small pottery business that does really well in the tourist season but not so well outside it.

At the bakery, Chantelle, the owner's daughter I've become quite friendly with, greets me in flawless English. I have tried to speak French with her, and although it's improving, I think she gets impatient and finds it much easier to have a natter in my mother tongue. She does sometimes get things muddled though, which can be funny.

'Coffee, Bryony? Here, sit.' Chantelle wipes a table and pulls out a chair. That's the decision whether to take away or not taken care of. 'Now, I want to know all the gossip about you and Valentin.'

'There's no gossip.' I laugh and fiddle with my napkin.

'Well, there should be.' Chantelle winks and says she'll be right back with a pastry and coffee.

While I wait, I look through the window and wave as Monsieur Laval the grocer walks past lugging a sack of something on his back. He points at the sack, rolls his eyes and puffs on. I almost feel like a local now, even though it's only been eight months. Almost. When I allow it house room, there's a tug in my heart pulling me towards the English Channel and home. I miss my mum, Aunty Jen, Immi – though at the moment she's still in Spain – and one other, though I wish I didn't. No idea where he is and I shouldn't give a shit, but I do. I told myself that I didn't for a while, but what's the use in lying to myself?

Chantelle returns and puts a plate – with an enormous choux and chocolate creation on it – down in front of me along with the coffee. She's got a coffee of her own and quickly pulls up a chair, her dark curls bouncing, her chocolate eyes alight with eager anticipation. 'So are you going to dinner?'

'I expect I will eat dinner later … it's only breakfast time, Chantelle,' I tease and take a sip of coffee.

'Oh stop it. You know what I mean. I don't get you. If Valentin had asked me I would have said yes, yes, yes!' Chantelle emphasises each 'yes' with a slap of her hand on the table. From behind the counter, her mother raises her eyebrows but says nothing.

'I'll tell him you like him next time I see him.' I smile and take a bite of my pastry.

Chantelle's eyes grow round and she puts her hand on mine. 'No. You mustn't do that! His poor dead wife was one of my friends and it wouldn't do to let him know I've always had a'—she twists her mouth to the side and struggles for a word—'hard dot for him.'

At this I nearly choke on the pastry. 'You mean soft spot.'

'Oh yes! Anyway, are you going to see him?'

'I don't know …' I wipe the icing sugar from my mouth with the napkin and consider her question. 'I don't think I will. I just want to finish my online counselling course, enjoy the rest of my time here in your lovely village, and then go home and see my family.' *When I've done a bit of investigation to see if Ransom's still looking for me, of course.* 'I used to have a very stressful job, but I left it all behind and being here is just what I needed.'

'To re-find your battery?'

'Yes. That's it exactly.' I don't correct her as I think it fits.

'But I'm sure that Valentin would be able to do much more for your battery, if you know what I mean?' She gives a lascivious wink.

I give her a withering look and sip my coffee. Of course I have missed physical contact, but not enough to take all the complications that would go with that. 'Seriously, Chantelle. I'm sure Valentin wouldn't think badly of you if you were to ask him for dinner.'

A shake of her curls. 'No. I couldn't. Apart from the fact that he's known me forever, I bet he thinks I'm a rubbish wife or something, because why would Albert leave me, go off to Paris with a woman nearly twice my age?'

'You told me she was a rich widow. Doesn't that speak for itself?' I say, attacking the pastry from the other side now.

'*Oui*, but … oh, I don't know.' Chantelle shrugs and does a thousand-mile stare over my shoulder at the wall.

I think I do. I think she's lost so much confidence after her husband left that she's decided to build a wall around herself, protect herself by being the jolly happy-go-lucky confidant … when all the time she's really someone else. My counselling course has helped me arrive at this conclusion, but I do see common ground between the two of us. Kindred spirits.

We talk of this and that, village gossip while I finish my food. Then I drain my coffee and say, 'Okay, I must go, but please keep an open mind where Valentin is concerned. You might be pleasantly surprised.' I kiss her on both cheeks and leave her looking a little puzzled.

On the way back to my *gîte* I toss around the idea of speaking to Valentin on her behalf. I've never been a matchmaker, but this does feel right. Before I go home I'd love to see a relationship blossoming between them. Two lovely lonely people, just waiting for someone to bring them together. And that would be me. If I can't have my own happy ever after, then I'll make bloody sure other people can. If it doesn't work, then at least I tried. The prospect of getting a counselling job back home is so comforting. I'm glad I decided on that rather than teaching – it feels so right in my gut. Soon the Anyas of the world will have an ally, a point of reference, a helping hand. This is a worthy future to aspire to – who needs bloody Nathan Walker?

As I step through the door my mobile jangles in my pocket. It's either Mum or Immi. They're the only two people that have my new number. I pull it out and see an unknown number … my heart's thumping, my mouth's dry. Do I answer? Could it be that one of Ransom's lot found me somehow … through Immi? Have they harmed her? Instinct swipes my finger across the screen and I hold the phone to my ear with trembling fingers.

'Hello … who's this?'

'Bryony … it's Nathan.'

Chapter Thirty-Seven

Nathan. It's Nathan. Nathan? How the hell did he get my number? Mum or Immi? And why? Why now? A twisted lump of grief, anger and pain that I thought I'd buried explodes, fires words out of my throat in fury. 'Fuck off! I'm hanging up.'

'No, please don't!'

'Oh, that's ironic! That's what I said to you not that long ago, remember?'

'Yes, I do, but please listen. I didn't mean what I said back then—'

'Oh yes you did. You blocked my number, Nathan. Blocked me from your fucking life!'

'Please! This is very important!'

'Is it? Is it really? Well go tell it to someone who gives a f—'

'Ransom's dead, Bryony.'

The lump of grief and anger morphs into shock. I lean against the wall and take a breath. 'How?'

'Hanged himself.'

There's an image of Ransom hanging in his cell, bloated and blackened face, tongue protruding. I rub my eyes, push it away. 'When?'

'Yesterday.'

'Oh my God, does Immi know?' Why am I asking him? I don't know how he even knows about Ransom.

'I don't know. She … I think she's out of the country.'

By the tone of his voice he knows damned well that she is. 'Who told you about Ransom?'

'I don't want to explain it all over the phone. Can we meet soon?'

'No,' I say, suddenly worried that this is all a lie. Ransom's not dead and he's just fishing – trying to find out where I am. He could be back working for Ransom for all I know. Unlikely, but how can I trust him again?

'Please, Bryony. Come back to England. We …'

So he knows I'm abroad? Thanks, Mum or Immi! 'Who told you where I was and gave you my number?'

'It was your mum. I explained that it was really important I got in touch, didn't say why though. She was reluctant at first, because you told her we'd broken up but not why … and that you never wanted to see me again.' There's a pause. 'But she said she trusted me and that she thought we should try and patch things up.'

'Oh please! Mum's heart is in the right place, but she has no bloody clue what she's talking about! She has no idea who you really are for a start, or what you came down to Cornwall for in the first place. Can you imagine what she'd think of you if she did?'

Nathan breathes a heavy sigh down the line. 'Yes. But once we explain it all to her like we did with Immi—'

'It's not happening. Not in a million years.'

'Look, I don't blame you if you don't want to come back to me. But please, Bryony. Just come and hear what I have to say in person. Let me explain properly. I had to do what I did to protect you. We can meet on the beach at Fistral, where you saved my life, and I can try to make you see that breaking things off with you and … doing what I've done since … might have helped to save yours.'

What was that supposed to mean? Part of me wants to meet him, find out what the hell he's been up to for the past eight months, what he means by protecting me. The most part of me is wary, suspicious and worried that he's lying. Tell it like it is. 'How the hell can I trust you, Nathan? You might be working for Ransom for all I know and he's no more dead than you or I – you've lied to me in the past, or have you forgotten?'

'No, of course not. I don't blame you for being mistrustful. I don't expect anything else really, but I swear I'm telling the truth.

Don't you see, Bryony, with Ransom dead you don't have to hide anymore? Neither does Immi. Dawson's on remand awaiting trial, Jason too and a few more besides. They're all going down.'

This is all a bit too much to take in. I walk to the sofa, slump down onto it. 'I don't know, Nathan,' I say with a sigh. 'If you *are* lying I'll just be walking into your trap. How do I know that your mum isn't being held hostage again or someone else in your family, and you've decided that you have to finish what you started?'

Nathan clears his throat. 'You don't I guess. But if you remember how we were together, how much …' Another long sigh. 'Oh God, Bryony … How much I love you, then you wouldn't even consider such a thing.'

I don't say anything. I can't say anything. There are so many replies waiting on my tongue but none seem right. He loves me? Really? He never said that when we were together, but then nor did I. Confusion and anxiety chase each other round my head; if he loves me why did he leave? I run my fingers through my hair. He'll be surprised when he sees that it's past my shoulders now. Hang on … when he sees it? So I'm planning to meet him then? Part of me must be. The stupid gullible part.

I swallow hard. 'Look, I need to think, Nathan. Think very carefully … and do some investigating. If I decide to come I'll see you this Saturday afternoon at two o'clock on the beach. If I don't, then you'll have your answer.' I end the call before he can say anything else and then hold my breath, stare at my phone. He doesn't call back. Good.

In the next few hours I change my mind and back at least a dozen times. Before going home I'm going to get my second in command, DS Brendan Prosser, to do some digging for me. Brendan had told me that the day we went to the house on Westmorland Street together to arrest Ransom was one of the best in his career. He was sad to see me leave and said that if I ever needed anything to give him a call. I don't do that kind of thing, because I'm never sure if people mean it when they say that, but this time I have to call in the favour. It would be unsafe not to.

I must make sure he doesn't mention anything to Mark though. It was pretty clear after our last conversation that he wanted no more calls asking for his help.

The phone call to Brendan should be short and sweet. The digging bit will be largely redundant if Nathan is telling the truth. I wonder whether to have lunch before I call him or get right to it. No use in putting it off, but it's an important call … one that could be the beginning or the end of something. It's only one o'clock, but the bottle of amaretto on the shelf could be just the accompaniment to such a crucial call home. On the sofa I inhale the almond notes of the amber liquid and take a sip. Then I take another. Immediately I get a head rush and adrenalin is out of the traps and away. Putting the glass out of reach on the coffee table, I pick up the phone and dial Brendan's number.

'Great to hear from you! How's tricks?' Brendan says, a smile in his voice.

I can hear the bustle of the office in the background, the distant laughter of Maggie, the receptionist. Unexpectedly a wash of nostalgia runs through me and right now I wish I was back there amongst it all. 'Oh, not so bad, you know. I'm having a little time to decide what to do next … almost completed an online counselling course though, which I'm enjoying so much.'

'That's brilliant. I'm so happy that you're happy, Bryony.'

We talk of office gossip for a while and then I can't put things off any longer. There've been a few silences, mostly awkward, so I take the plunge. 'As well as ringing to see how everyone is … I was wondering if you could tell me about the delightful Kenny Ransom. I heard on the grapevine that he … he was dead.' I sit on the edge of the sofa, stretch my hand to the amaretto glass and hold my breath.

'Yep, he sure is, and I for one am not sorry in the least.'

The amaretto goes down in one and I flop back on the sofa cushions, blowing a sigh of relief down my nose. 'My God. Hanged himself, I was told?'

'Yeah … though there are a few rumours going round Wakefield that he had help from an old adversary. We're not buying that though, or at least a blind eye or two might have been turned. Good riddance to bad rubbish. And Dawson and some other choice characters will soon be residents of that jail, if all goes as it should.'

'Wow. You have been busy in my absence!'

'We have.' There's a pause. 'Don't you miss it, Bryony? You were a sad loss … a bloody good DI.'

A combination of his words, the realisation that Nathan was telling the truth and the downing of the drink draw a slew of emotion up from my depths. I sniff and swallow a lump in my throat. 'Oh, that's a nice thing to say, Bren. And yes, I do miss it, miss you lot … but not enough to come back. The day-to-day frustration of seeing shits like Ransom, Dawson and the rest ruining lives and getting away with it for the majority of the time got too much. I want to make a difference. See results of my actions more than once in a blue moon.'

'I get that. Still, the day we got that bastard was—'

'One of the best of your career,' I finish.

'*The* best, I'd say.'

'*The* best.' I sigh. 'Thanks, Bren. Promise I'll keep in touch.' And I will.

'See you, boss. Make sure you do.'

It's late afternoon and the weak winter sun is angling into my small backyard through the branches of a twisted olive tree. An idea to take up painting while I was here never materialised, but I have taken lots of photos of this place, the village and the breathtaking surrounding countryside. A promise to return here one day is as firm in my mind as the one I made to Brendan about keeping in touch. This place has been like a salve on an open wound. Healing, strengthening, restoring. I feel stronger, confident, and the need to control everything has lessened. Perhaps that got left behind with my old life.

I was wrong earlier about either or. The result of the phone call today means the beginning of something, but it's also the ending.

I can go home without the fear of being found, without having to look over my shoulder … to a new beginning. But I'll leave my life here. I have a few months' lease left on the *gîte*, but I can't see the point in going back to Cornwall on Saturday and then having to come back out here again to get my stuff. I might as well just go home for good. I can't wait to see Mum and Jen. I'm also very keen to find out just why Nathan did what he did. My head tells me that it won't be the same between us – we can't go back to how we were – but my heart wants to give him a chance to explain.

Deciding there's no time like the present I pull out my suitcase and holdall and start to pack. Tomorrow seems like a good day to close the door on the Loire. Valentin and Chantelle will be a bit surprised, and maybe a bit sad, but it's time. A smile curls my lips. I need to do a spot of matchmaking before I go too. There's also something else that I might have to do but really don't want to. Immi has been doing a similar thing to me for the same amount of time in Spain. We have only spoken a few times, but she seemed fine last time we spoke. She has a job behind the bar in an English pub in Barcelona and has made a few friends. At the heart of her I know she's raw though.

The old Immi has been crushed by the sins of her father, leaving her empty, withdrawn. Her chance of happiness with Jonathan was dashed before it even had a chance to grow. That's why we haven't spoken much, I think. She finds it hard to sustain the cheerful conversation, the jokey attitude, pretending she's still the person she used to be. I know exactly how she feels. It's exhausting. But now, I must phone her. I just hope she already knows about her father or I'm going to be the one that has to break it to her.

'Immi … how are you?' I sit on the bed, tuck the phone between my cheek and shoulder and try to fold a jumper.

'Oh, same old … keeping busy. You?' There's a babble of voices and clinking glasses in the background. I picture her wiping her forehead with a bar cloth and scurrying through a gaggle of customers.

Shit. She doesn't know. 'Oh I'm fine. So you've not had news from home?'

'No. I don't have contact with anyone from home. What kind of news?'

'Um …' I drop the jumper into the case and hug my knees to my chest.

'Is it about my shit of a father?'

I hear a door close behind her and then all I can hear is her breathing. 'Yeah. You might want to sit down.'

'If he's got out on appeal somehow, I swear I'll hunt the fucker down and kill him!'

Oh God. She's going to regret those words. 'No, he isn't out … he's …'

'For God's sake, Bryony, just tell me!'

'He's dead … killed himself.' I can't say I'm sorry, because I'm not, and she'd know I wasn't. I screw my face up, imagining her reaction all alone in some back room or store cupboard.

'How?' Her voice is hollow, monotone.

'He hanged himself.'

There's nothing on the line for such a long time apart from her breathing. Then there's a short sniff. 'Well, all I can say is the world will be a better place without him. I was going to cheer at first, say hurrah … but then I stopped myself because that would be crass. I'm not getting down on my belly to his level. I must say I'm not in the least bit sorry though.' Then there's a sigh and a giggle. 'But you know what? I'm so glad I can now finally go home. I'm so sick of this job I can't tell you!'

I tell her that I'm glad too, that I'm going home and that I'm meeting Nathan to find out what he has to say. She says I need my head examined but understands. She wishes she was coming to Newquay too as there's nothing left for her in Sheffield. I don't remind her that Jonathan is there. Immi knows that. Besides, now isn't the time to have a big conversation about plans for the future. Instead I say, 'If you're sure you have nothing to go back to Sheffield for, what's stopping you coming to Cornwall? I'm sure Mum would make up your old room.'

'Really! Oh, Bryony that would be fantastic! I'll work to the end of the week here and be with you after that. Oh, what a weight has been lifted from my shoulders.' Then her tone becomes more sombre. 'It's not normally what happens when you find out your father is dead, is it?'

'No. But then he wasn't a normal father, was he?'

'Far from it. I know your dad's no longer with us, Bryony, but at least he was a good man. He was someone you could look up to, follow in his footsteps. You'll always have wonderful memories of him. My memories, on the other hand ...' Immi's words turn into a sob.

'Hey, come on, love ... it won't be long before we can see each other face to face. We'll have a laugh and catch up properly. I've missed you, Immi.'

'I've missed you too.' She sniffs and then I hear someone calling her name and the babble of bar noise again. 'Right, must go. I'll keep you posted about when I'm coming to Cornwall. Bye.'

As bad news breaking goes, that was better than I'd expected. Of course I realised she wouldn't be distraught with grief, but people are unpredictable when faced with the unexpected. I remember that from past experience in my old job. Immi did sound more like herself at the end of the conversation, thank goodness. Perhaps we can put all this behind us in time and, in a few years, we will both be able to look back at this over a glass of wine and laugh ... or maybe not.

The sun has gone and evening shadows are creeping across the fields and over walls as I hurry down the winding lane to the bakery to catch Chantelle before she's off for the evening. Then I'll go and see Valentin to break some more unexpected, but much more pleasant news. My heart lends lightness to my feet and I run through the chill evening with excited butterflies in my chest. For the first time in a long time I'm looking to my future with optimism. It's about time things changed for the better and I have a feeling that at last my luck might be in.

Chapter Thirty-Eight

Windy beaches, shimmering white-topped breakers and sunshine. Heaven. Nathan decides that even though the place that has been his home for nearly nine months is stunningly beautiful, nothing can compare to the majesty of the scene in front of him. It wasn't until he got out of his car a little while ago and ran down the sand dune with the wind in his hair that he realised how much he'd missed the ocean, the salt in his lungs. Whatever happens, he knows he must make his home not too far away from a beach.

Looking at his watch every few minutes isn't going to make Bryony appear any quicker. And worrying that she's decided to stay in France instead won't help either. Nathan winds his hair around his fist and tucks it into his hoodie. Immediately a few strands find their way back out into the wind, bisecting his view of a young couple in wetsuits whooping down to the water's edge, bodyboards shoved under their arms. Unexpectedly, Nathan's blood runs cold. Are these kids experienced? The wind has whipped up a sizeable swell today … and what about rip currents? Low in the sky, the shimmering winter sun turns the water to mirror shards. Shielding his eyes against it, he sets off at a run to the shoreline.

It turns out that the youngsters are local and know everything there is to know about the ocean, but they thank him for his concern and then plunge headlong into the surf. Looking on, Nathan promises himself that he'll learn to surf properly one day, and learn about safety in the water. His cheeks flush as he remembers how foolish he'd been the day Bryony saved him. A quick look around. It's 2.20 and she's still not here. How long should he wait? Originally he'd thought an hour. Now he's here, he decides he'll wait until it gets dark. There's no way he's leaving until all hope is gone.

The nip in the air encourages a quick walk to the café to get a takeaway hot drink. No use making himself uncomfortable if he's in for a long wait. Once again a niggle of doubt whispers that she might not come at all, but he hides it under a broad smile and sets off back up the beach towards the car park and shops. A few moments later his heart misses a beat, because hurrying down the steep sand ahead is a figure dressed in black jeans and a red hooded jacket that moves like Bryony, is the same height, but … it can't be her. This woman is fuller in the hips, and the wind is making dark streamers of her long shiny hair. Closer now and his heartbeat quickens, her features are clearer … it is. It is her!

Nathan waves frantically but his hood blows down and once again he can't see because of his mass of wild hair. Bryony stops, shields her eyes and looks behind, as if she thinks he's waving at someone else. A laugh breaks free and is snatched away on the wind as he realises she doesn't recognise him either. Not surprising, especially with his beard. He powers forward and when he's a few metres away he sees her mouth drop open and then curl into a huge smile. Then the smile disappears and Nathan can tell that she doesn't want him to see she's pleased to see him.

'Bryony, so good to see you,' he pants, opening up his arms as he closes the gap between them.

'Hi, Nathan,' she says in a monotone, folding her arms and planting her feet apart in the sand.

He lets his arms fall to his sides. Serves him right for getting ahead of himself. 'You look lovely.' Nathan points at her hair blowing around her face. 'Hair suits you too.'

'Thanks. Seems you went for a similar style.' Bryony allows him a tiny smile.

'Yeah. Helps with my Viking disguise.' He grins and then there's an awkward moment in which they both clear their throats and look around the beach. 'So, shall we go to the café for our chat?'

She nods. 'Might as well. It will be warmer in there.'

From the counter, Nathan waves at Bryony sitting at a corner table against the big picture window overlooking the expanse of Fistral. He gets her attention and gestures at the cake stand but she shakes her head, so Nathan carries the two coffees over and then goes back for his chocolate éclair.

'Sure you don't want a cake?' Nathan asks and unzips his hoodie.

Bryony's gaze skims his chest, flits to his eyes and away. 'No thanks. Just let's get down to this explanation I've waited so long to hear.'

'Okay.' Nathan sits down and, unsure where to begin, takes a big bite from his éclair … and then wishes he hadn't as he notices ill-disguised mirth in Bryony's eyes before she turns to look out of the window. He knows why, and hurriedly scrubs a napkin at his chin and nose. The damned pastry had exploded its cream all over the bloody place. Then he reaches for his coffee cup a bit too quickly and it clatters, splashing a good mouthful or two onto the saucer and table. Bryony glances round and then looks away, her hand over her mouth. Shit. He needs to get his act together.

A few moments later Bryony has obviously got her amusement under control and raises an eyebrow at him while she takes a drink. She looks so beautiful, all he wants to do is take her in his arms, but of course he can't.

She places the cup carefully back onto its saucer and says, 'Just tell me straight, Nathan. No point in being nervous – you won't shock me, whatever you have to say.'

He takes a deep breath. Nods. 'Right. Well, after I got shot, I was in hospital for a week. I had plenty of time to think … mainly about you. There was no way you'd be safe if we were still together. Ransom hated me more than you; he wouldn't have stopped until he found me, and you too, obviously, if you were with me. He hated Immi more than you too. So I figured that with me out of the picture, you would be relatively protected, while Immi and I were public enemies number one and two.' Nathan attempts a smaller bite of his éclair while she holds his gaze intently in hers. Her expression is unreadable.

Bryony's mouth turns up at one side and she looks up to the left. 'Okay, I can see the logic in that to an extent. But after the shooting we could have left the country together, just as I did on my own. Ransom has his useful contacts, but he's not Interpol. There was no way he'd have found us tucked away in a little French village.' She looks back at him, though her gaze is softer.

'Even so, if we were apart you would be safer. You can't deny that. They'd be searching for two of us, not one. And as I said numerous times before, you saved my life and I wanted to go a small way to repay that – even if it killed me to do it. Being without you was …' He sighs and takes a drink. No point in getting emotional, he has a way to go yet. Nathan daren't look at Bryony though. Let's just get the words out. To the table he says, 'When I was in hospital I had a visit from two local police officers and with their help I decided to become an informer in return for new ID, a place to live, a job and a legit CV. It was down to me that the arrests I told you about were made.'

'Bloody hell, Nathan! I know I said I wouldn't be shocked, but this is something else.' Bryony's tone is encouraging and Nathan looks up from the table. Approval is shining in her eyes and there's a ghost of a smile playing at the edges of her lips.

'It's been a pretty shocking nine months, that's for sure.' He smiles at her and she gives him a genuine smile back.

'So where were you living? What job did you do?' She leans forward, her elbows on the table, warm hazel eyes searching his face. He tells her and she laughs. 'You do look like a Viking with that hair and beard. But Adam Jackson … there's no way that name suits you.'

'I couldn't get used to it, I must admit. Trouble is, if I want to use the CV, birth certificate and stuff to make a life on the straight and narrow, and I do of course, I'll have to keep it.'

'Yeah, guess you will. Unless you change it by deed poll …' Bryony mutters to the table, runs her finger around the rim of her cup, obviously lost in thought. She looks up at him, head on one side. 'So will you go back to Scotland to live now, or …?'

Nathan furrows his brow and leans back in his seat. Is this her way of subtly hinting that there's nothing for him here? Does she wish him far away? 'Um … no. I was hoping to stay near the sea if I could. Thankfully now Ransom's gone I won't have to worry about hiding away. I won't go back to Sheffield – too many bad memories, and there's nothing for me there now. Mum, as you know, is in Devon, so's my sister and my brothers as well. I can always visit.'

Bryony mirrors his pose and folds her arms. 'I see … right.' She looks out of the window at the sea for a moment and then back to him. 'A little odd that Ransom decided to top himself out of the blue like that, wasn't it?' She's doing her intense stare thing again, and he can imagine that many a criminal must have squirmed under it in the past.

He shrugs. 'Perhaps he just realised that he had a fourteen-year stretch or so in front of him and no daughter. Must have seemed a bit hopeless.' Nathan's glad his beard covers some of his face; he can feel the heat rising under his skin. He wishes that she'd stop staring so hard.

'You know more than you're letting on.' Bryony's statement leaves him no wriggle room. He could blatantly lie to her, but then he couldn't know absolutely what happened to Ransom. Not a hundred per cent.

'Well, there is a rumour that one of his old enemies caught up with him and made it look like suicide … but there's no proof and no fail-safe way of finding out. I think the coppers just turned a blind eye to gossip and that was it.'

She narrows her eyes. 'Hmm. That's more or less what an old colleague told me when I phoned to check that Ransom was dead.'

Nathan tries not to show surprise. She obviously hadn't trusted him enough to come back to England without checking – but then would he have in her shoes? He says, 'Well there you are then. I suppose we'll never know.'

'Ah, but you *do* know … you know more than you're letting on, don't you?'

Nathan shakes his head and shrugs. 'Not sure what you're getting at.'

'I think you do … but let's leave it for now. I think I fancy one of those éclairs after all.' To his shame she flicks a bit of cream from his beard and laughs.

When Nathan gets back to the table with more coffee and the éclair, he's pleased to find her more relaxed and open. They chat about France and Scotland and how weird their lives have been over the last few months, and it feels comfortable, normal … until Bryony looks at her watch. 'Right. I'd best get to the supermarket and back to Mum's. She's insisting on doing a big meal with champagne tomorrow to give me a proper welcome. Jen, Graham and Immi will be there too; I said I didn't want any fuss, but you know Mum.' She pushes her chair back and picks up her jacket.

Her words feel like a punch to his gut. Is that all? Is she just going to leave it like that? With an effort he assumes a calm voice. 'I do. How did she take it when you told her everything?'

Bryony frowns. 'I haven't told her anything yet.' She shrugs on the jacket. 'I thought I'd tell her in dribs and drabs. She'd freak out if I said I'd been in danger and had to leave the bloody country. She was overjoyed when I told her I was coming to stay the other day. I need a while to gather my thoughts.'

Nathan nods slowly and stands too. 'Will you tell her about me … about us?'

Bryony turns her mouth down at the corners. 'I don't know … suppose not. I mean, there is no us anymore, so why bother?' Her eyes skip away from the disappointment he knows must be writ large on his face. 'Mind you, as I said, Immi's coming tomorrow. After a few drinks, she'll probably let it slip if I don't.'

'Yeah … I guess she will. How did she take the news of her dad?'

'Oh, you know. Mixed. Mostly relieved I think.' Bryony zips up her jacket and gives him a wistful smile. 'Thanks for explaining why you acted as you did, Nathan … it was kind of you to put me first, and thanks for helping us …' She rolls her eyes. '*Us*, she says. I can't get used to not being a copper … the police, I mean, to get those evil bastards.' She gives him a long look. 'Anyway, goodbye, Nate. Be happy.' She steps forward and gives him a peck on the cheek and turns for the door.

No. No, this can't happen, I won't let it. As she walks through the door he hurries to her side, puts his hand on her arm. 'Hey, we can't leave it like this …'

She shrugs him off and walks outside, tossing over her shoulder, 'We have to. I can't trust you anymore … you broke my heart and I won't let you do it a second time.'

Nathan keeps pace with her as she hurries to the car park. 'But I told you why. I did it to—'

'Protect me, yes, you said. But you should have trusted me enough to talk it through, given me a chance to have a say. I'm not some delicate little flower that needs protection, Nathan. I'm a grown woman. A strong woman.'

What the hell is he supposed to say to that? Doesn't she get that he did it all for her? Strong people get killed, no matter how strong they are. She points her keys at a red car and bleeps it open. *Do something, for fuck's sake, before she gets in and drives away!*

'Bryony, wait! We can't leave it like this … us like this.' Nathan takes her by the shoulders and spins her round to face him. Her hair's lifting on the wind and her mouth's parted as if she wants to say something but can't think of the words.

'I've told you … there is no us. Not anymore.' There are tears in her eyes and she tries to get in the car, but he won't release her.

'There is,' Nathan insists. 'There is because I love you, and … and you love me.' *God, let that be true.*

Bryony shakes her head and looks down, a tear drop on her lip. 'It won't work … we're too different.'

Encouraged that she hasn't said she doesn't love him, Nathan lifts her chin, makes her look into his eyes. 'We aren't that different, but anyway, *vive la différence*. Tell me you don't love me, Bryony, and I'll walk away.' His heart is thrashing in his chest; his whole future is dependent on her answer. If it's a yes, he's a rocket blasting through a November night sky, a trail of sparkles in his wake ... if it's a no, he's drowning in a rip current, sinking to the depths.

Bryony blinks back more tears and takes a deep breath. 'I must admit ... I do love you, Nathan, but I want a happy future. I can't be wondering if you're going to up and leave again at any given time, can I? Just go off in the middle of the night without a word because of some misguided old-fashioned chivalrous idea that you've got into your head. God knows what you might do. And if we had children—' She puts her hand over her mouth as if to stop her words.

'I promise you here and now that I will never, never ever leave you like that again. I thought I was doing it for the right reasons, but it seems I was wrong.' Bryony's eyes look deep into his, so tenderly, and he thinks he sees light at the end of his tunnel. 'But please ... please give me a chance to make it up to you. Please, I—'

Nathan's words are suddenly stopped by her mouth on his, her arms clasped tight around his back, her body pressed close to his. *Thank God.* His arms go round her and he kisses her deeply, while rockets blast all around him in a November night sky.

Chapter Thirty-Nine

Considering it's November, the sun still has some heat in it. I'm sitting on Mum's patio, coffee in hand, legs stretched out in front of me, my face tipped to the sky, and all is good with the world. I've been reassessing my views. Happy endings are for other people. People in films and novels … or so I used to think. Since Dad was killed, then all this trauma with Ransom, Nathan getting shot and then disappearing, the past relationships that never worked, I never really expected true happiness. The thing is, this morning when I woke and remembered that Nathan's back in my life, that we admitted our love for each other, I am beginning to allow a tiny flame of hope to burn in the most secret part of my heart.

I'm not dopey enough to think it will end in wedding bells, confetti, and pink fluffy hearts anytime soon, because I for one want to take it slowly. But in the future, who knows? Well, apart from the pink fluffy stuff. I am not a girly girl, whatever the hell that means. Sometimes it's as if feminism never bloody happened these days. If I ever have a daughter I will make sure I dress her in blue on principle. And 'man up'? What's that all about? To be strong you have to act like a man? Aren't women strong? Woman up, it should be. I'll ask Immi what she thinks when she arrives in a few minutes.

As if on cue, the doorbell rings and I jump up, run inside, but Mum's beaten me to it.

'Imogen, come in, come in!' Mum stands aside and ushers her in. 'My goodness, look at your tan!' She tips her head at me. 'Look at her tan, Bryony.'

'I'm looking! It's so good to see you, Immi!' I step forward and give her a huge hug, then hold her at arm's length. She looks the picture of health: blonde curls almost white, blue eyes in bold relief against the tan, and a multi-coloured dress under her heavy winter coat. 'You're like a bit of Spanish sunshine come to brighten up our winter.'

'And my God, look at you!' Immi grins and spins me round. 'Your hair is gorgeous like that and you've got curves!'

I laugh self-consciously and tug my blue cashmere jumper down a bit more over my leggings. 'That'll be the dumping of the stressy job and stuffing my face with full-fat cheese, wines and fresh bread in France for nine months for you.'

Mum folds her arms and gives me a pretend angry face. 'Which she's still to tell me anything much about, Immi. She's been a bit vague, to be honest – perhaps you can get her to spill the beans. That Jacob one rang the other day too to ask for her number. No mention of him yet, either.'

Immi gives me a pointed look but keeps her mouth shut. I pick up her bags and say to Mum, 'Give me a chance, Mum. I've not been back five minutes!' I incline my head to Immi. 'Right, let's get your bags up to your room and settle you in.'

As we hurry past Mum up the stairs, she calls after us, 'That's code for let's have a good gossip out of my mother's earshot! I'm not as green as I'm cabbage looking, ya know!'

Immi laughs and once we're in her room she flops in the chair and pulls her long brown boots off. 'Oh, it is so good to be back here!'

I pat her on the knee and sit on the bed. 'I felt exactly the same when I got back the other day. And it's so good to have you here too.'

'Right. Why haven't you told your mum about Nathan? She still thinks he's called Jacob for God's sake.'

'Get right down to it, why don't you?' I laugh. I've missed her honesty and her direct approach. She raises an eyebrow and folds her arms, giving me no wriggle room. 'Okay … truthfully there hasn't been a lot of time to tell her it all since I've been back. And when I was away I couldn't tell her over the phone. She'd have been worried sick if she knew Ransom was after me and how Nathan fitted into it all. And then if she knew he'd just abandoned me, that would have made it all worse.'

Immi nods. 'So did you meet him yesterday?' I sigh and tell her I did. 'And what was his excuse? How did you leave it?'

I tell her everything and as I do her face runs the gamut of expressions from surprise, amusement, incredulousness and finally to approval. 'So we're giving it a go … but slowly,' I finish.

'Yeah, right. I need to go and buy a wedding outfit tomorrow,' Immi says and chucks one of my old cuddly toys at my head.

I laugh and chuck it back. 'No way. We need time to get to know each other properly and come to terms with what's happened over this past crazy year.'

Immi nods and hugs the toy to her chest. 'Yes … me too. It's been a fucking rollercoaster of a ride.

'You're right there.' Poor Immi. No matter what she says, Ransom was still her dad and she must have some good memories of him when she was little, at least. I think a change of subject might help. 'Now you're back, will you get in touch with Jonathan?'

A definite shake of her head. 'No. There's no way he'd begin to understand my life. Okay, we had not too dissimilar backgrounds, and I mentioned bits about my dad. But can you imagine what he'd think if I told him the whole truth about my father – what he did – what I had to do to make sure the scum was put away? It's all too sordid.'

'He might surprise you. Don't forget, when he called me to ask if I knew where you were, he was really upset.'

'Yes, I know, but he doesn't deserve someone like me – someone with more flippin' baggage than a jumbo jet.' Immi gives me a little smile. 'Anyway, we were talking about you. You have to tell your mum about it all and you have to do it before this celebratory meal tonight. It will be murder for me trying to remember what she does and doesn't know. I take it lover boy is coming?'

'I haven't invited him … but I was thinking about it.'

'Oh, you must. He should be a part of the celebrations, 'cos if it hadn't been for him then Dawson and that great hulk of an ape that tried to kill me wouldn't have been arrested, would they?'

'Nope.' I don't mention that I'm a bit suspicious about Nathan having something to do with Ransom's suicide. No point in stirring the pot until I find out more. Even then, would I tell her? Probably not.

'Right then. So in a bit, I'll go out for a walk to the beach while you have a chat with your mum and invite Nathan. Then we can all have fun and move on from this bloody nightmare, yes?'

'Yes ... I hope so.'

'Me too. It's about time stuff went right for us.' Immi jumps up, gives me a hug and starts to unpack.

Nathan was over the moon to be invited and promised to be on his best behaviour with Mum if she was a bit grumpy with him. I'm predicting she will be at first, when she knows everything, but she always says, 'If my daughter likes someone, then they must be worth getting to know.' I'm up in my room wondering how to broach it all with her and as usual am gawping out the window at the garden and glimpses of ocean beyond for inspiration. Next door's cat is on Mum's patio table again washing its face. It catches sight of me and stops mid-lick. I wave to it, but it's unimpressed and carries on with its routine. No inspiration from the cat or the view is forthcoming, so I decide to just spit it out and hope for the best.

Mum's in the kitchen preparing tonight's feast. The smells wafting up the stairs to greet me as I come down make my mouth water, even though I've not long since had lunch. 'Ooh, what smells so good?' I ask, pulling a chair out at the kitchen table.

Mum turns round, puts a floury hand to her red cheeks and puffs a strand of hair from her forehead. 'All sorts,' she says with a smile. 'My special stuffing, apple and caramel sauce for the pavlova, a selection of canapés, take your pick.'

'Can I?' I say, half rising from my chair.

'Sit down, madam. You'll wait until later like everyone else.'

'I could make you a cuppa?' Mum says she'd love one and once again I wonder how to start – and if this would be a bad time as she's up to her eyes. 'Er … Mum, don't suppose you have time for a chat?' Oh God, that sounded a bit ominous.

Mum glances across at me, surprised. 'Yes, love. I've more or less finished my preparation now. Everything okay?'

'Yeah, just need to fill you in on a few things.' I have to shout over the noise of the kettle, which makes it sound worse.

Mum washes her hands and sits at the table, a worried frown on her forehead. I finish making the tea and sit opposite. 'Don't look so worried, Mum. It's mainly about Nathan … I mean Jacob … no.' I roll my eyes. 'I actually mean Nathan.' Her frown deepens. 'I've invited him over to the meal tonight – hope that's okay?'

She brightens. 'Of course. I've made enough for a regiment.' Then I smile, sip my tea and do the thousand-mile stare. Where to start? Mum eventually comes to my rescue. She folds her arms and fixes me with her no-nonsense look. 'Right, there's something bothering you, so out with it – I'm listening.'

Chapter Forty

Mum's tea is on the table untouched, cold. I've never seen her this shocked, apart from when she heard the news about Dad. She's listened without much comment apart from a few 'Oh my Gods' and 'What were you thinking?' for the last twenty minutes, and now she knows all of it. Well, almost all. There is one last thing.

'So you see, Mum, it's all worked out, or is working out for the best. Ransom can't touch us anymore now, either, because guess what?'

Mum massages her temples, closes her eyes, sighs. 'God only knows, Bryony. I'm so glad I was oblivious to this. If I'd known how much danger you've been in – that Nathan or whatever his bloody name is was shot and you were on the run – I'd have been in my grave.'

'Yes. That's why I kept it all from you ... and Ransom is.'

'Ransom is what?' she asks wearily.

'In his grave.'

Mum's eyes snap open and her hand hovers over her mouth, fingers trembling. 'He's dead?'

'Yep, thank God. The worthless piece of shit decided to do us all a favour and hang himself.' There's a note of triumph in my voice and there shouldn't be – he was a human being after all. But I couldn't care less to be honest.

Mum shakes her head in bewilderment and her eyes fill. 'Oh my God ... my God.' Her trembling hands cover her face and her shoulders begin to shake.

I jump up, put my arm over her shoulder and whisper in her ear. 'Hey, don't cry, Mum – it means I'm free now. Immi and Nate too, don't you see?'

She nods her head vigorously and tears splash onto the table. 'Yes, I know ... I know. It's a relief, I suppose. But what a hell you've been through, love. And this Nathan. Ransom sent him to kill you ... and someone else to kill Immi too? Are you sure?'

'Yes, I'm sure. How could someone do that to their own child?'

This brings fresh tears from Mum and I hand her some kitchen roll. She wipes her face and says, 'Bloody hell, Bryony. It's all too much to take in. What a complete and utter bastard he was.' She looks at me from staring red-rimmed eyes and I wish I'd stuck to the dribs and drabs idea of information telling.

'I'm sorry, Mum. I've upset your day, and you were so looking forward to making the lovely meal and everything. We could put it off until later in the week—'

She holds up a hand. 'We bloody well could not! I'm not having that bastard calling the shots from beyond the grave after everything else he's done.' Mum wipes her eyes some more, blows her nose and gives me a watery smile. 'We are having this meal and we're going to celebrate your homecoming and a hell of a lot more besides, now I know what's behind it!' She stands up and holds me tight. 'Thank God you're safe, love, because if anything had happened to you—'

'Nothing has and nothing will,' I say, giving her a squeeze. 'Now I'm off to make myself beautiful while you carry on beavering away.' I look at her, pull a face and say in a grudging tone, 'Unless you want any help?' Without giving her a chance to reply I rush to the door. 'Thought not, see ya later!'

She chuckles and throws after me, 'Well that's just typical, you cheeky monkey!'

It could have gone much worse between Mum and Nathan tonight. I think she's too relieved that everything is fine now, that I'm safe, to be too angry with him. He apologised and promised that he would never have actually taken my life, regardless of the fact that I saved his, and she accepted it. She was also glad to hear that his mum had suffered no ill effects from being kidnapped and was doing well now in her new home and happier than she had been for years.

Jen and Graham are the only ones around the table that have no clue about what's really happened. We had to come up with a story for why Nathan isn't called Jacob anymore, so told part of the truth. We said Ransom had let slip that he was after me, and that Nathan, who worked for a friend of his, had overheard and came to warn me. He used a fake name because he was worried I might have come across his name in my investigations. We mentioned that Ransom had turned on Immi too, but not to bring it up in conversation – it's too upsetting and this is a celebration.

Immi is the life and soul of the party and has us all in stitches for most of the time. I'm so glad she's on form, but I do worry that she's overcompensating by going over the top and drinking too much. I don't want her getting completely rat-arsed because I have a little surprise for her later. Thinking of which, I check the time … nearly 9.30. Great, best get the coffee on.

Mum joins me in the kitchen and pours the last of the champagne into her glass. She's been drinking far more than usual too. Understandable, I guess. 'Coffee?' I ask, waving the cafetière at her.

'You trying to say I need soldering up?' Mum laughs and trips over a chair leg.

I crack out laughing at that. 'You *will* need soldering if you don't stop tripping over the furniture.'

'I didn't say soldering … did I?' Mum hiccups.

I give her a withering look and put the kettle on. There's a message beeping on my phone. I give it a quick glance. 'Right. Immi's surprise will be here any minute. Go and make sure she's not dancing on the table with no knickers on!' Mum shrieks with laughter and totters into the dining room.

Once I've checked that everyone is sitting round the table with coffee, I sneak to the front door and run down the driveway to a parked car at the end. The window goes down and I give the driver the nod. Then I rush back inside and grab Immi's arm. 'Can I borrow you for a moment, Immi?'

'Not the washing up.' She looks up at me and holds up the sign of the cross with her forefingers. 'Anything but that!'

'No. Something far nicer.'

Puzzled, Immi stands up and follows me out into the hallway and I close the dining room door behind us. Then her hands come up to her mouth and she shrieks, 'Jonathan! Oh, my word!'

Jonathan gives her a huge smile and steps forward, arms outstretched. As she runs into them, tears of happiness rolling down her face, I retreat to the dining room and my thumbs up is greeted with whoops of joy. Everyone has been in the know about Jonathan except Immi. I breathe a sigh of relief and sit down, thankful that this gamble has paid off.

Nathan takes my hand and kisses the back of it. 'Well done, Bryony. Immi can have her happy ever after now too, hopefully.'

'Yeah, here's hoping.' I smile at him and allow the little flame of hope for my own happy ever after a bit more oxygen.

An hour later, I kiss Nathan goodnight with a promise to spend the day with him tomorrow and send him back to the hotel in a taxi. He's a bit disappointed that we aren't spending the night together but, as I remind him, we are taking it slowly. Having said that, I can imagine that most of tomorrow will be spent in bed. Immi and Jonathan have gone to his hotel to chat things over, and with a satisfied smile on my lips I wander into the kitchen to find Graham stacking the dishwasher. 'Oh, I thought Mum and Jen were doing that?'

Graham looks up. 'Yeah, they were, but your mum got a bit tearful – think she's had too much pop.' He grins. 'Anyway, she went to the bathroom so Jen went up to see how she was.'

'Ah. I'll go see how she's doing.' I climb the stairs worrying that she's upset again about what I told her, and hope she's not telling Jen all about it – we'd agreed to stick to the doctored version. As I clear the last stair, I hear a sob from Mum's room at the end of the corridor. Sounds like Mum. Then Jen's voice comes low and urgent, but I can't make out what she's saying. Instinct tells me whatever they're talking about isn't for my ears, but I tiptoe along the dark corridor anyway. I stand outside the door and a sliver of light comes through the crack.

'It's no good torturing yourself, Gilly. It's over and done and you need to just forget about it,' Jen says. 'You've had too much to drink and it will all seem better in the morning.'

'How can it?' Mum wails.

'Shhh. Keep it down.'

Mum lowers her voice, so I press my ear to the slight crack in the door. '… do that to his own daughter? I mean, what kind of fucking monster was he?'

Right. They're obviously taking about Immi. Poor Mum is such a caring person; it's all hit her hard. I'm about to leave when Jen says, 'Come on, G. You know exactly what a fucking monster he was from the off. I wouldn't be surprised at anything he ever did.'

'Not at first, Jen. At first he was charming, sweet. He certainly bloody charmed me, idiot that I was back then,' Mum says and blows her nose. A prickling sensation starts at the base of my spine and I wrap my arms around myself. I want to leave, but my feet root me to the spot.

'As I said, no use in going over it. She'll never know the truth, thank God. You're lucky he took it to his grave. Beats me why he never told her just to spite her.'

'Not his style. He'd have seen it as some kind of weakness to have a copper for a daughter. And he would have looked bad in front of Immi – cheating on her mum – wouldn't he? No. He'd rather see her dead. Oh, Jen, what would I have done if he'd had her killed? I couldn't have gone on …' There's a heavy sigh. 'But as you say – she'll never know now, thank the Lord.'

I can't breathe. There's a giddy feeling in my head and then my feet suddenly decide to move me, but into the room instead of away. My fist comes up and I smash the door back on its hinges. The two women jump up from the edge of the bed, mouths agape, shock and guilt splashed red across both faces. Then Mum's face drains of colour as she sees the look of absolute fury on mine. A moment later I hear myself say in a strange, high-pitched voice, 'It's too late … she already knows.'

Chapter Forty-One

Nathan turns out the bedside light and breathes a sigh of relief. Thank goodness Bryony is eventually asleep. He settles down under the duvet and closes his eyes, wanting to put his arms around her but worried that he'll wake her. When he'd left her mum's tonight he'd wished she was coming back to his hotel. The wish was granted, but he wishes now it hadn't been – not like this.

Bryony had arrived at his room at midnight, completely distraught, and it had been at least ten minutes before he could get out of her what was wrong. Nathan could hardly believe what she was saying and had to ask a number of times if she might have got it wrong. What a terrible, terrible shock to find that Ransom had been her biological father. It didn't bear thinking about. The fact that he had known made it even more horrific. That monster had been prepared to have both his daughters murdered. Nathan turns over in bed and tries to block his mind.

Ten minutes later he's still thinking about it. What a mess. Bryony and her mum having a huge fall out, Bryony getting her stuff and leaving, Immi oblivious at the hotel with Jonathan and tomorrow, or today actually – the clock tells him it's 2.30am – Bryony will have to tell her all about it. The only positive thing to come out of it all is that Bryony and Immi are half-sisters. Perhaps he should be there when Bryony breaks the news so he can keep trying to inject the positive, because there's going to be precious little of that.

One other positive thing, from a purely selfish point of view, is that Bryony came to him in her hour of need. She didn't go to a hotel, or to Immi, she came to him. Okay, so going to Immi wouldn't have been fair on her as she was having a moment of happiness with Jonathan, but still. It felt good that she needed him. With all his heart he hoped that they would make it. No more lies, secrets or half-truths, just honesty and straightforwardness. Nathan closes his eyes again. Half-truths. He'd have to tell Bryony the other half of something he'd kept back from her if he was to have a clean slate … especially now.

The hiss of the shower wakes him. It can't be 8.30? It only feels like five minutes since he closed his eyes. Sitting on the edge of the bed, Nathan stretches and yawns just as the shower stops and Bryony comes into the bedroom wrapped in a towel. Well, two, one is wrapped around her hair like a turban. Nathan never could figure out how to do that, but women seem to have the method woven into their DNA. He'd like to take one of the towels away and sit her on his lap, but given the circumstances he'd probably get short shrift.

'Morning, beautiful,' he says with a big smile.

'Morning.' Bryony's smile is small, fake and fleeting.

'How are you feeling?' Nathan wonders if his brain has activated yet. How does he expect she'll be feeling?

Bryony finds her underwear, quickly dries herself and starts to get dressed. Nathan tries not to look. 'Oh, you know. Pretty crap. Not sure if I'm going to mention anything to Immi until Jonathan has gone back. It's really not fair.'

'Hmm.'

'What's that mean?' She glances at him, takes the towel off her head and scrubs at her hair with it.

'I think she might want to know. She'll want to comfort you – you can comfort each other. And like I said last night, she's your sister … that's something good, isn't it?'

Bryony looks at him, head on one side. 'I suppose you could be right. After all, I hate things being kept from me.' She combs her hair through. 'Let's consider it over breakfast.'

As they're finishing breakfast in the hotel dining room, Bryony's phone rings. It's Immi. Seems like the decision to tell or not has been taken out of their hands. From what Nathan can glean, Bryony's mum has phoned Immi to see if Bryony is with her. She has told her they had a huge falling out but not what it was about. Bryony ends the call and gives a big sigh. 'She's on her way over here.'

'Do you want me to stay … help out?'

'No. I think it's best if I do this – she might feel a bit more vulnerable if you're here too.'

Nathan nods and drains his cup. Now might be the worst time to tell his half-truth. It might be the best … who knew? Just do it. 'There's one thing I need to get straight. From now on our relationship has to be completely honest and … well, no secrets.'

Bryony's face falls. She looks at him, wipes her mouth with her napkin. 'God, Nate. I'm not sure I can take any more revelations just now. How bad is it?'

'Not sure. What I mean is, I'm not sure how you'll take it given the fact that you know now that Ransom was—'

She holds her hands up. 'Don't say it. He wasn't, could never be … yes, biologically he was, but my dad …' Bryony swallows hard. 'My dad was the best dad in the world and always will be to me.'

'Yes, of course.' Nathan takes her hand across the table. 'The thing is, you know when you asked if I knew more about Ransom's death than I was letting on?' A nod. 'I do. Well, I think I do, but not for sure. As you know, Dawson did the dirty on Charlie Kreswell and he and Ransom are old enemies. Well, when I found out, it rang a bell. His brother Rob's in Wakefield, so I thought a few well-chosen words sent round the grapevine might—'

'You thought that once Rob knew his brother was fingered by Dawson, Ransom's man, he might kill him?' Bryony's eyes are round with disbelief.

'No. I didn't know for sure that he'd kill him – perhaps hurt him. Maybe put him out of action for a bit so we had more breathing space.' Even as he says this he knows he's kidding himself. 'And anyway, they're only rumours that Rob had a hand in the "suicide", no proof. The coppers aren't that fussed about investigating either.'

Bryony takes her hand back, shrugs, looks at the table. Nathan wishes she'd say something. 'I see,' she says in an offhand manner.

Not quite what he was hoping for. 'Look, love. If I'd known what I know now, I wouldn't have done it. I just had to be straight with you.'

Her eyes flick up to his, cold anger burning in them. 'How many times? He was not my father! I have no feelings for him apart from loathing and contempt. If what you said on the grapevine got him killed, then so what? If it didn't, so what? He's dead either way, and I for one am very pleased that he is.'

Nathan leans back in his chair. 'Ri-ght.' That went well.

Bryony's eyes soften and she gives him a little smile. 'Look. I'm glad you told me because yes, if we're to make a proper go of things there must be no secrets, and I suspected you knew more anyway. It's just, right now, all I really care about is talking to my sister and trying to make sense of what the fuck my mother was thinking when she ...' Her hands come up to her face. 'When she did what she did.'

Nathan takes her hands from her face and holds them. 'Of course you do. I'll wait for you in my room, and call me if you need me, okay?' He kisses her and stands up. As he does, Immi rushes into the dining room like a mini tornado.

'Oh my God, Bryony, what the hell has happened with you and your mum?' she says, and runs at Bryony who's half standing and nearly knocks her flying with the force of her hug. Nathan thinks they'll be fine and decides to make himself scarce.

The hotel dining room is half full and some diners have already been treated to a scene of me ripping Nate's head off. The thought of more prying eyes and eavesdroppers turns my stomach, so I suggest to Immi that we go for a walk on the beach to talk. Immi is very impatient to find out what's been going on and practically drags me out of the hotel and down the steps to Towan beach.

The morning is cold and drizzly, so we mostly have it to ourselves apart from a few dog walkers.

Once she's perched herself on a rock Immi says, 'Right, so tell me.'

I sit myself down and suddenly find that my mouth is dry; the words can't get past my tongue. 'Bloody hell, Immi … I don't know where to start.'

She raises her eyebrows. 'At the beginning, and just say it. Come on, we've been through too much for you to worry about what I'll think.'

I take her hand and blurt it all out. Then I take my hand back, dig out a tissue from my bag and wipe my tears and snotty nose. 'So that's why I left Mum's. I'm so sorry to have to break it all to you. It's bad enough that you know everything he did without knowing that he cheated on your mum … with mine.'

Immi jumps up and rants, paces, swears so loud that a dog walker turns and walks the other way from us. Then she cries and I hand her a tissue. 'What the actual fuck was your mother thinking?'

'She wasn't. Clearly. She said it all began when Dad first started out as a copper and was away from home doing some training or other for about four weeks. They were up shit creek with money, apparently, and finding it hard to pay the mortgage. Mum had a part-time job, but they were only scraping by. Ransom was charming to her, went round with some groceries when they moved in, that kind of thing. Anyway, one day he saw her crying in the garden. He nipped round to ask what was wrong and at first they just talked about her problems. After that, he'd drop money round in an envelope, said he didn't want paying back … but not to tell your mum.'

'Oh yes! I can just imagine. That is so typical of him – slimy, stinking shit of a man!' Imogen's up on her feet again, this time kicking lumps out of the sand. 'And then he gets her into bed?'

'Yeah. The affair went on for the time Dad was away. He came back at weekends, but that was it. Then Mum came to her senses and ended it, so your dad …' I stop, realising that technically he fathered both of us. 'So Ransom stopped the money he was giving her because he was furious that she didn't want him anymore. An ego thing, he had no feelings for her – told her that.'

Immi comes back to her rock and sits down looking out to sea. 'He had no feelings for anyone except himself, that's the truth.'

'Yeah, that much is obvious.' I slip my arm around her. 'And we can say that Mum fell under his spell, allowed herself to be swayed … but she was a grown woman too, not a child. I can't forgive her for betraying my poor dad. I mean, what kind of a woman allows her husband to think she's pregnant with his child, when all the time …' I trail off, fighting back emotion.

Immi looks at me, furrows her brows. 'Hang on, how does she know that he wasn't your dad? He came back at weekends, didn't he?'

'That's what I asked her. But she said they only slept together once or twice as he was so knackered and she was so guilty. I said that nevertheless, there was a chance. You know what she said?' Immi shakes her head, takes my hand. 'She said that I looked too much like Ransom. She was in no doubt.'

Immi gives a humourless bark. 'You look nothing like him. You have hazel eyes, he had blue-grey … he had a long narrow nose …' She falters and I see doubt creep into her eyes. Then she digs in her bag, pulls out her phone and scrolls through her photos. When she looks at me I see an ocean of unshed tears in her blue eyes. 'You have the same nose … me too. You also have his jawline.'

I don't want to look at the phone screen she's holding up, but I have to. Ransom and Immi sitting in a pub somewhere raising a glass to the camera, Ransom and Immi on a beach somewhere abroad waving, a close-up of Ransom across a dining table at Christmas wearing a paper hat at a jaunty angle. Hi nose, his jaw – very familiar – I look at them every day in the mirror.

I push the phone back to her and release a slow breath. In all other aspects I look like my mum, the shape of my eyes, my mouth, my forehead … but there's no denying who fathered me. Dad always said I had his eyes because mine are flecked with green like his were … but I know that's not true now. The photos say it all. Thinking of Dad brings a new rush of emotion and Immi puts her arm round me, hugs me close, and for the next few minutes we let the tears come.

Immi is the first to speak. 'We could always do a DNA test?'

I blow my nose and nudge her arm. 'We both know there's no need … but just to be a trillion per cent, yes we could.' She gives me a watery smile. 'And there is one positive thing to come out of all this.'

'Yes, we're half-sisters,' she says with a little laugh. 'Even when I was going berserk just now, kicking the sand and yelling, there was a small voice saying: but at least you and Bryony are sisters.'

'I always wanted a sister growing up.' I stand up and dust the sand from my jeans.

'Me too. We used to say that we wished we were sisters, remember?'

'I do. So now we have our wish granted.'

'Yep.' Immi glances up at me and she looks just like she did sometimes when we were kids. Vulnerable, young and unsure. She always dressed in her over-the-top personality to cover it but, from time to time, the threads came undone and allowed a glimpse of who she really was.

'Let's go and get a cream tea. It will work wonders for our mood.' I hold my hand out, she takes it, and we hurry down the windy beach arm in arm.

'Will you go and see your mum later, try and work stuff out?'

'No. No, we're done.'

Immi drags me to a stop. 'What – for good? You can't mean it. You know how manipulative our d … he was. Surely you can see how she fell into his trap?'

I shake my head and start walking again. 'I can, but as I said, she was a grown woman. I'll never forgive her. I have no wish to see her again.'

'Oh, but she loved your dad. That much was obvious, even as a kid I could see that.'

'Yes, but she betrayed him. Betrayed him in the worst way. He was the best father and husband that anyone could wish for and she …' My thoughts are too raw, too messed up. 'Look, let's leave this now. I can't deal with it.'

'Okay … but please think on it. Gilly made a mistake – a pretty bad one, granted – but she's paid for it alright.'

I give a noncommittal grunt and we walk up the steep steps to the town. Thinking on it is all I've done since last night and I'm sure there will be many more hours of it. I'm also sure that Mum's words and horror-struck face will come back to haunt me every few minutes. So will the image of the way she got on her knees, sobbing her heart out, begging me to stay as I chucked my bags in the car and drove away. I should never have driven, given what I'd had to drink, but I just had to get away as fast as I could. Being around her made my skin crawl.

In the café we both determinedly avoid all talk of Ransom and my mother. Instead, we discuss Jonathan and Nathan, what we plan to do in the near future, and try to plan our happy ever afters. Last night I thought I'd got mine. Funny what less than twenty-four hours can do. Immi and Jonathan stayed up for hours talking, apparently. She was so grateful that I'd stuck my oar in and let him know where she was. Immi told him everything and he was calm and sensible about it all. So she'd been worrying for nothing. They're going to make a go of it in Sheffield and then, if Immi has anything to do with it, they're going to move to Cornwall at some point. Her father's estate should give them more options even though she wants to give most of the money away, given how he came by it. There are many charities that would benefit – in that way out of the misery at least some good will come.

Regarding our future, I tell her that Nate and I haven't got that far yet because of all the shit that happened last night, and the fact that we're taking it slowly, but I'm hopeful that we'll stay here in Cornwall – not Newquay now for obvious reasons – and try to do the same.

'Okay, but if you're staying in Cornwall you'd better teach him how to bloody swim properly!' Immi says, chortling.

'Yeah, or I'll be saving his life every week!' I laugh too and despite everything, I feel the dark clouds begin to lift. It will take me a very long time to process it all, if I ever do. Perhaps I'll need counselling, perhaps not, but one thing is for certain: I will not let an accident of birth ruin the rest of my life. Too much has happened, and I owe it to my dad. I want to make him proud of me every day. He used to say that every day was a gift, life was precious and not to waste a moment. Dad had his cut short, so I am determined to make the most of mine.

Chapter Forty-Two

Anya takes off her jacket and sits on the bench. It's unseasonably warm for April in England. It's been three years since she was here, but it feels like yesterday, even though so much has happened since she was in the house on Westmorland Street. It took her many months to come to terms with what happened, but with the love of her family and friends she managed to regain her confidence and identity, just as she told the police officer, DI Masters, said she would. She had travelled her country, speaking about her ordeal, warning others. She had taken a counselling course too and helped some of those poor girls that had fallen victim.

Today she will meet her again, this DI, or ex-DI. It seems strange thinking of her as a civilian and call her Bryony. They have spoken on the phone and it seems that Anya's story has inspired her to change professions, to do a similar thing in the UK to what Anya herself is doing back home. Soon they will do a talk together at the college behind her and Bryony will take her on a speaking tour of some more places this week too.

Across the wide expanse of grass surrounding the college, a tall shapely woman is striding towards her, sunlight on her long flowing hair. As she gets closer, Anya gives a start. Is this the same woman? It is, but her whole demeanour is softer, more relaxed. Bryony Masters must have left the spiky official persona behind with her old job. Anya stands as Bryony closes the gap between them, hand outstretched. They shake hands and then unexpectedly Anya feels the urge to hug Bryony, and it's reciprocated.

'My goodness, you're looking well,' Bryony says, standing back and taking Anya in.

'You too. I didn't recognise you at first!'

'I'm not sure how to take that,' Bryony says, but then adds a chuckle. Anya can tell it's to make her feel at ease, not embarrassed.

'No, I meant that you look different. You seem relaxed and calm … more open, if that's the right word.'

'I am. Leaving the police and living in Padstow, Cornwall, will do that for you. The stress of my old job and the fact that I had to watch the bad guys winning most of the time just all became a bit exhausting.'

'Good. And you like your new job?'

'I adore it. It's wonderful living in a small village, but I get the best of both worlds when I'm up and down the country in schools, colleges, and community centres in the big cities.'

'I love mine too. My life is so different from what it was only a few years ago.' Anya swallows a lump in her throat. Seeing Bryony has put her right back to the day in that vile house when Ransom was arrested. 'I have a boyfriend now and a normal life. I never thought any man would want me after … but Piotr did. I was honest from the start and he has been so supportive.'

'That's wonderful, Anya. I have a fairly normal life now. I do some advisory crime support type work from time to time, which can be a bit upsetting, but I'm in a relationship too. Well, we got married a few months ago actually. Believe it or not, Nathan used to be on the other side of the law from me.'

'Really? How did you meet?'

'Um, not sure we should go down that route – it would take too long.' Bryony smiles, but Anya knows it's best not to ask more.

'And do you see your friend, the pretty blonde lady that encouraged me to be so brave? Imogen, I think you said her name was back then.'

'I do, when we can – she lives quite a way from me. She's married now too, to a doctor, but she has plans to move down to Cornwall next year. He has to get a post in a surgery though. It's not that easy.'

Anya smiles. 'So the only person that is miserable now is Ransom. That's how it should be.'

'Actually, he's dead. Hanged himself a few years back.'

Anya tries to hide a triumphant smile but can't. 'Sorry, but this makes me happy. It is no more than he deserves. I hope his conscience made him do it.'

Bryony tips her face to the sun and closes her eyes. 'It would be nice to think so, but I doubt it. I doubt it very much.' She opens her eyes and glances at her watch. 'Okay, I think we'd better go in.'

Anya feels butterflies in the pit of her stomach. It's one thing talking to people back home, but it's another talking to students in a college in the UK. 'I might go and buy some water from the shop first.' She points down the lane past the college.

'Okay. But please don't be nervous. I'll be with you and you will be absolutely fine. Promise. You're the reason I'm here today and in a minute we're going to go inside and make a difference. If one person takes it in, and perhaps talks to someone else about what he or she heard, another girl like you once were might be saved.'

Anya nods and swallows hard. 'Thanks, Bryony. I will be back soon.'

From the bench I watch Anya's confident gait and straight back as she hurries to the shop. She is so far removed from the broken girl I remember, and this makes my heart glad. Of all the happy endings, Anya deserves hers. My phone goes off in my bag and I scrabble for it. 'Nate? What's up?'

'Nothing. Why do you always think something's wrong when I ring you at work?'

'I don't know – habit, I guess.'

'I told you, bad news is a thing of the past with us.'

'True, we have been lucky lately, but I'm not as optimistic as you, it leads to disaster in the end.' I laugh but kind of mean it … well, a bit. The last time I allowed myself to believe things were all good was the night of my celebration dinner at Mum's.

'I was wondering if it might be a nice idea when you get back tomorrow to invite your mum round for dinner?' Nate clears his throat. He always clears his throat when he's nervous.

'Oh, I don't know, Nate. We only just got talking properly a few weeks ago when we went out for that drink … I don't want to rush into things.'

'Yeah, but, well … I kind of ran into her today in town and, well, she's so sorry and misses you.'

'You've asked her already, haven't you?'

'Um …'

'Nate! For heaven's sake.'

'But she's your mum and she loves you. We didn't invite her to the wedding, I went along with you on that, but this is dinner – just dinner.'

'Yes, but then she'll expect to just fall back into our lives and—'

'No she won't because we'll tell her, lay the cards out. Unless we want her back in our lives … it has been nearly two years after all.'

Has it? Blimey, yes … I suppose it has. Nate sounds so hopeful, so eager to make things right. And all of a sudden I realise that so am I. Life is too short and I'm all about making a difference, so why not start at home? 'Okay, you've twisted my arm. But you can sort out the food. I won't be back until late afternoon.'

'Of course. I'll do it between my tourist drop off and my surfing lesson.'

'Surfing lesson?'

'Yeah … with your mum.'

'Nate! I can't believe that you would …' But then there's a guffaw and he's gone.

Little sod, he takes the biscuit. I have to laugh though. He wouldn't have done any of that if he'd not known me inside out. Nate must have guessed it was time for me and Mum to patch things up, but that I didn't know how. I can't wait to get home tomorrow and put my arms around him, tell him I love him.

Anya's on her way back with water, a big smile on her face. I join her and together we walk up the steps to the college. 'Right. Time to make a difference,' I say as she opens the door.

'Time to make a difference.' She nods and walks through.

As I follow her inside, I say a silent thanks to Immi for what she did back then, and to Nathan, and all the others that gave evidence, and to my colleagues at the station. My dad too, because without him I would never have joined the police, tried to do the right thing. Just at this moment, it feels as if they are all walking right beside us.

The End

Acknowledgements

A huge thank you to my nephew and scriptwriter Steve Langridge, who gave me great advice on all things crime related, and has always been so supportive of my work. And as always, my family, friends and the incredible team at Bloodhound Books.

Lightning Source UK Ltd.
Milton Keynes UK
UKHW01f2046240618
324712UK00001B/53/P